RAGESONG
AWAKENING

J.R. SIMMONS

Jace,
keep the magic of
music alive!

J.R. Simmons

Published by:
Magic Unleashed Publishing.

MAGICUNLEASHED

Paperback Edition:

ISBN-10: 193999330X
ISBN-13: 978-1-939993-30-4

ACKNOWLEDGEMENTS

A special thanks to my lovely wife, Staci, for her infinite patience and understanding as I spent many late nights working on this. Thanks to my sisters (Skylee Neff, Shayla Miller and ShaNae Simmons) and my parents for their willingness to read, edit and help close all of the open plot points. Thanks to the Fermician Godfadda, Dave Pagano, who kept the story moving forward by constantly demanding more and helping to open my mind to the wonders of Fermicia. Thanks to Wendy Knight for her advice as I worked my way through the writing process. Thanks to Hillary Barton and Vickie Johnstone for their fast and excellent work in editing. Thanks to Brooke Gillette for her wonderful cover art and constant updates. Thanks to Kit Beach for bringing Fermicia alive with her beautiful map. Thanks to Mikey Brooks for his all of his guidance and expertise in helping me move Ragesong: Awakening to the next level.

And of course, thanks to all of my readers for taking a chance on Fermicia!

DEDICATION

Dedicated to my beautiful wife Staci Simmons. You are my inspiration and the reason I always strive to reach higher.

TABLE OF CONTENTS

PRONUNCIATION GUIDE

Brael: Brale
Brucheiden: Brew-k-hide-en
Fermicia: Fir-me-sea-uh
Foldona: Foal-doe-nah
Gijora: G-ee-hoar-ah
Joraus: Johr-ahs
Kardonin: Car-doe-ninn
Kithalo: Kee-thah-low
Liakut: Lay-coot
Noajim: No-ah-jeem
Rugal: Roo-gull
Scur: Skuhr
Skidippy: Skid-ipp-ee
Swyf: Swiff
Tareel: Tar-eel

CHAPTER 1:

SIEGE

K lyle stood at one of the windows to his throne room, looking out over the ruins of his once beautiful city. A dark cloud of smoke swirled over the rooftops and obscured the majority of the carnage below, for which he was grateful. A gentle breeze brushed his cheeks, carrying with it the smell of death and destruction, but Klyle did not turn from his silent mourning of his doomed kingdom. As the air stirred the smoke, he caught glimpses of red and silver on the street below. The haze quickly coalesced, but he'd seen the bodies sprawled in the mud, unmoving.

Klyle fixed his gaze on the partially obscured cloak of a man lying motionless. He recognized the distinctive emblem on his back, identifying the fallen soldier as one of his personal guards. Each guard was marked with that particular insignia, so that every enemy would know who they stood against in battle. Rare it was for a man to stand and face those markings on the field of combat, and for the few brave enough to do so, it was always fatal. Those cloaks identified the most feared and respected fighters in the territory, and, until today, they had never known defeat.

Klyle's jaw tightened as he noticed a unique symbol under the emblem. The mark identified the fallen soldier as Morab, first captain of his personal guard. Klyle remembered well the contained excitement of the young man when he had knelt at his feet to receive the prized cloak and swear his fealty. The youth had served well, and Klyle regretted that he would never have the chance to publicly honor the warrior for his sacrifice. His hands clenched into fists as he stared down at Morab's broken body and it was a small relief when the smoke returned, obscuring his view once more.

"Sire," rumbled a deep voice from behind him. "We are running out of time. They have reached the staircase and the guard will not hold."

Klyle did not turn immediately, but continued to gaze somberly at the destruction before him. "Why has it come to this?" he asked quietly, not expecting an answer. "What could have pushed him to so completely abandon reason? Was there something I failed to notice or anything that I could have done to prevent this?"

"Sire," urged a second voice, higher and softer than the first. "We must go now if we are to have any chance of success."

With one last mournful gaze out the window, Klyle turned and faced the pair standing before him. "You are correct, of course," he answered quietly. "We need to act quickly. The instructions I gave you, do you remember them?" When the two nodded, he continued, "Follow the jewel and it will light the way."

Klyle crossed to the strongbox behind his throne and with a practiced hand he deftly opened the complicated lock. Reaching in, he carefully pulled something out before securing the lid and resetting it. Returning to face the humanoid creatures, he eyed them speculatively. They were indeed a strange pair, with their translucent bodies giving the appearance of invisibility. Only a slight shift in the objects behind them made it possible to mark their general location. Changelings were rare, and even with all the horror surrounding him, Klyle couldn't help but feel fortunate to count them as friends and allies. Their natural form made them perfect for spying, and their other gifts… well, those might well be the only things that could save his shattered kingdom.

"Your best chance is to split up until you reach your destination," Klyle said gravely. Reaching over, he hung a small pouch on the neck of the smaller of the two Changelings.

"Swyf, you must take to the skies. Your abilities are such that you may well be the only one able to outmaneuver the archers that *he* has, undoubtedly, stationed in wait. Keep a wary eye at all times until you arrive at the portal. His minions are cunning and there is no telling what traps he may have prepared. Flee quickly from the immediate vicinity, and then hide during the day and fly only at night. Await Joraus for the space of two days, and if he arrives not, you must go on alone."

"Yes, my liege," she replied in a light, musical voice. "It has been an honor to serve you," she added with a quick nod. "May your end be wrapped in the embrace of *Ragesong*."

She placed one hand on Klyle and the other on the larger Changeling standing beside her before sprinting to the window, and without a backward glance, diving through it. A quick shimmer marked her change, and Klyle and Joraus watched a magnificent blue-winged falcon speed through the air. It darted to and fro, dodging flying arrows, until it disappeared into the smoke from the city below.

Klyle turned to Joraus and hung a second pouch around his neck. "I have saved the most onerous task for you, my old friend," he said with a sad smile. "I know well that you would much rather make the run on all fours, but it is far too dangerous to travel overland. Brael's archers are formidable and they now have a taste for blood. Swyf has a chance of avoiding them, but I fear you would not. Move quickly, but do not be careless. He will undoubtedly have Scurs on patrol. Where the river empties into the sea, follow the coastline until you reach the mountain stream. You know what to watch for. Be careful, I beg of you, my friend. It has truly been an honor…"

Grunting his understanding, Joraus reached out a translucent arm to clasp forearms with the king. A deep boom echoed behind them and they turned quickly to see the door to the throne room bow inward.

"Go!" ordered Klyle, pulling his arm away and unsheathing the sword on his back in one fluid motion. Joraus sprinted to the window as the king raised his mighty blade and turned towards the door. "Find them, Joraus!" Klyle called after him. "Everything depends on you now!"

Anger seethed through the dark warrior as he marched up the stairs, callously kicking bodies out of his way as he climbed. Klyle would be waiting at the top, either dead or alive, regardless of which he wanted to see the fallen king.

The sight of the large helmet tucked under the warrior's arm, combined with the huge war axe strapped to his back, was enough to make even the most battle-hardened fighter recoil in revulsion and fear. His massive form belied an agility that would make a cat jealous.

It had taken too long, he was sure of it. As careful and quiet as the invasion had been, it had not been enough. The attack had depended on stealth, with no room for error. He had always been a gambling man and liked to play the odds. Tasks that no ordinary tactician would dare attempt simply excited him. He was certain every angle had been covered, but he had not counted on his second-best archer failing to kill his target. The fool had better hope to die in battle, for if he lived…

Although the archer's arrow had hit the guard, the man had managed to stagger to the warning bell and sound a single alarm before a second arrow silenced him for good. That lone toll was all that had been needed. Klyle's guard had immediately assembled and wasted no time in setting up defensive stances at all the key strategic positions throughout the city. Although the king's men had fought in a way worthy of their reputation, the dark warrior had personally trained his own fighters on how to defeat them. Though the losses were many, the end goal had been reached, and the last of the king's personal guard lay dead.

Once he had cleared the staircase, the echoes coming from beyond the broken door infuriated him. *Klyle!* The king had become a constant thorn in his side from the day of his exile. The dark warrior strapped on his helmet as he closed the distance to the throne room and gripped the handle of his giant weapon. Striding through the broken doors, he saw that his Elites had Klyle backed into a corner. He paused to watch as the stubborn king continued to fight. Begrudgingly, the dark warrior was forced to concede that the fool was indeed skillful. The bodies of six of his best troops littered the polished floor, attesting to the ability of this worthy adversary.

Suddenly, the thought of his men finishing this fight was unbearable. The dark warrior whistled sharply, and the Elites immediately sheathed their weapons and retreated to a safe distance. Klyle looked up quickly and his eyes flashed in silent rage as they focused on him.

"Brael," he snarled, raising his sword and planting his feet.

The dark warrior grinned without answering, hefting his giant axe in both hands.

Klyle forced down the fury that surged through him at seeing Brael again. There had been a time when they had been the closest of friends; when Brael had fought at his side and they had been nearly invincible. Together they had unlocked many of the secrets of *Ragesong* and sworn to keep the ability in check, lest its abuse should send the kingdom reeling into chaos. Time after time they had stood as one, wrapped in their newly discovered power, turning what appeared to be hopeless defeat into triumph.

Too late, Klyle discovered the addictive nature of *Ragesong* and the danger of sinking too deeply into its seductive embrace. He found that Brael had been secretly experimenting with the ability and using it in ways they had both agreed should never be permitted. Klyle still had nightmares about the day he had found his friend in a remote village, surrounded by mutilated corpses, with an expression of inhuman pleasure on his face. Four of his personal guards had died trying to subdue the massive warrior. Klyle could still recall Brael's bestial howl of rage as he turned and fled into the surrounding forest. That had been the last time he'd seen his friend. For years they had searched, but found nothing.

Now, here he stood in Klyle's own throne room, his handsome features lined with cruelty and hatred. Klyle pushed away his weariness from the previous battle as he glared at his former friend. Taking a firm hold of himself, he slipped into *Ragesong* and waited for Brael to make the next move. The big man unexpectedly charged, closing the distance impossibly fast, swinging his axe with brutal force.

Through *Ragesong*, Klyle was able to parry the blow, deflecting the strike and pushing it harmlessly out of the way. One advantage he had always maintained over Brael was speed. While his opponent was big and favored powerful weapons, Klyle, so lean and fast, favored speed over brute strength. He had nearly always bested Brael, making quick counters to his powerful strikes.

This time, Brael swung his axe as though it were a child's toy. Even though Klyle was embraced in *Ragesong*, he was barely quick enough to block the big man's attacks. With a sinking feeling, he began to notice the difference in his former comrade's fighting style. The power he recognized from before was still there, but Brael's once lumbering strikes were now as quick as a snake's. Growing panic flickered at the edges of *Ragesong*. Looking into the huge warrior's face, Klyle perceived the same wicked grin that he'd witnessed when he'd come upon him in that village so many years ago.

Brael swung his axe in a quick series of strokes, which Klyle tried desperately to block, but the power of his opponent's final blow knocked his blade away. Hands stinging, he dropped to his knees in defeat and Brael began to laugh. Klyle looked up into the face of his former friend and waited for what was to come. The awful laughter rang through his ears, and unable to bear the expression of contempt any longer, he lowered his head, breaking eye contact. At least Swyf and Joraus had escaped. *At least there was still a chance.*

CHAPTER 2:

ESCAPE

Joraus hated swimming. It was so much slower and more exhausting than running. He loved the feel of the wind as it rushed through his fur and the view of the world as he sprinted through it. Yet, despite his personal feelings, he knew that Klyle was right about the dangers of traveling overland. So here he was in a muddy river, fighting for every mile. The slow, eddying current was doing little to help with the speed he would need if he were to reach the portal in time to meet Swyf.

The river twisted and turned as it worked its way out to the sea, and Joraus would have to follow its curves until he reached the coast. This forced him to cover nearly twice the distance as Swyf, who could fly straight across the land. The water was muddy and afforded little in the way of pleasant vistas to help pass the time as he worked his way, mile by tedious mile, toward the portal. He wished he could use the shape of one of the larger saltwater fish found in the sea, but the fresh water here forced him to take the form of the slower, more awkward trout.

Something disturbed the water in front of Joraus and he looked up to see the vague outline of a bird ascending from its steep dive, talons outstretched. He swore before remembering the form he had assumed. The small bubbles rising to the surface seemed so inadequate. He couldn't even curse effectively as a fish! There were absolutely no advantages. Glancing up again, Joraus could just make out Swyf's falcon form flying low over the water. She was playing. *At a time like this, she is playing? Doesn't she understand how serious it is that we complete the task Kyle had set us?*

Swyf should have been a long way ahead by now. It wasn't until he heard her warning shriek that he realized his mistake; something was wrong, and he slowed enough to peek behind him. Through the murky water he could make out the dark outline of the Scurs. Although he knew he could very well be in serious trouble, Joraus smiled inwardly. He was competitive by nature and loved any chance to prove himself. Scurs were bred for quick pursuits and once they were within range of their quarry, their capture rate was unsurpassed. His best chance of survival was to outpace them. While they were extremely fast, they wouldn't be able to keep up the pace for long.

Running a quick set of calculations in his head, Joraus slowed down just a bit. He had to judge his speed perfectly. If he went too slow the Scurs would catch him, but if he went too fast he would run out of energy first and the result would be the same. He remembered his first encounter with the ugly creatures, and how shocked he'd been when he saw how fast they could move. Although they were humanoid in shape, the Scurs moved through the water as though they had fins. Joraus glanced back again and saw they were equipped with short, trident-like tareels. *So Brael wants me alive, does he?*

The thought of being stunned by one of the short-ranged energy blasts energized Joraus with a burst of speed. Occasionally glancing backwards, he saw the Scurs steadily gaining on him, but he nodded to himself after verifying that the distance was acceptable.

As Joraus sped through the water, he avoided rocks, weeds, branches and anything else that would slow his progress. Every so often, he checked that the closing distance was still manageable. It wouldn't be too long before the Scurs would start to tire, and he watched closely for the signs. When he saw one of the creatures take a gasping breath, Joraus slowed his pace just a bit. Although he knew it was dangerous, he couldn't help it. Swyf was not the only one that liked to play.

He let the Scurs pull in close enough to see them clearly through the dirt-brown water. Soon their lanky bodies came into focus, their webbed feet a blur as they kicked through the water. The spikes protruding through their cheeks puffed in and out with their labored breathing. Their light-brown scales enabled the Scurs to blend in with the murky river water, so it was the yellow horns extending from the tops of their heads that Joraus used to mark them. *Funny how Brael seems to attract ugliness to his cause!*

Joraus waited until the Scurs raised their tareels before shooting ahead with a quick burst of speed. The creatures yelled in surprise and, already celebrating, Joraus almost missed the net dropping into the river directly in front of him. At the last second he noticed the thin material and he pulled up short, his nose inches from the mesh. Spinning around, he saw the leading Scur give an evil smile and motion to the others. They fanned out, cutting off any hope of retreat, and advanced on him slowly with their tareels raised.

Joraus frantically examined the net for any flaws or weaknesses, and started to panic when he found none. In desperation, he sped towards the riverbank, trying to keep as much distance between him and his would-be capturers as possible. He felt a wave of dizziness as one of the Scurs fired at him. Although out of range of an incapacitating blow, Joraus still felt the draining effects of the energy blast. With seconds to decide, he shot forwards. Swimming nearly parallel with the net, he angled his nose towards the surface of the river. Blasts of energy heated the water behind him as the Scurs fired and he could feel his energy ebbing away.

Breaking the surface of the icy river, Joraus leapt into the air, shimmering into the shape of a hawk. Immediately spying some soldiers at the river's edge, holding the net, he bore down on them. He clawed at the face of the first man standing on the bank, causing him to lose his balance and topple into the river. Joraus shimmered again and changed into a mountain lion, claiming the ground vacated by the soldier who was now flailing in the water. He attacked a second man, clawing at his legs. The other soldiers dropped the net in panic and scrambled backwards, but it was too late. Before they could unsheathe their swords, Joraus ripped into them, biting and clawing anything within reach.

When he saw another squad of soldiers running towards him with their swords flashing, he screamed at them angrily before spinning around and sprinting back to the river. Joraus re-entered the water quickly, shimmering back into a trout. He looked around frantically for the Scurs and noticed that they were tangled in the now free-floating net. This did not stop them from firing at him with their tareels. He felt blasts of energy heat the water around him as he sped away. Relief dampened the joy he normally would have felt as the furious, fist-shaking Scurs faded into the distance in the murky water.

Swyf soared through the air, watching closely for any sign of the traitor's minions. She felt afraid for Joraus. While he should be able to outrun the Scurs, it didn't stop her from worrying. Hopefully, he would be able to keep his ego in check, because he liked to take too many risks. Diving towards the ground, using the rush of the fall to clear her mind, Swyf let out an exhilarated cry as the wind rushed past her.

Nothing was better than flying in the form of a graceful bird. Whether it be the fast, darting flight of a falcon or the slow, easy grace of a hawk's glide, Swyf felt more at home in the air than she did on the ground. She felt a little bad for Joraus, knowing how he hated swimming, but mostly she was just glad that it was not her in the murky river. Spreading her wings to halt her descent, Swyf's eyes were drawn to movement below. She was glad not to have to deal with Scurs, but Brael had other allies at his disposal and she did not want to be caught unawares.

Suddenly, she caught the foul scent of carrion. Rugals, she thought darkly. Of course, it would have to be them. Brael must have sent flocks of them flying at various intervals in the event that she had escaped. If she was close enough to smell them, she knew they would be aware of her presence.

The Rugals' scraggly, black feathers were, in Swyf's opinion, a pretty accurate summation of them. The birds' longer-than-average necks gave them a gangly, awkward appearance and their large beaks seemed somehow misplaced when paired with their small, beady eyes. Their form was deceptive though, as their powerful wings, sharp beaks and talons made them a serious threat. Challenging one Rugal by itself could be problematic; taking on a flock was beyond foolhardy.

Rugals were smarter than almost any other bird, and their ability to link minds with their leader made them extremely dangerous. The only way for one of the birds to take her place at the front was to dominate the minds of the other females; only then was she recognized as the flock leader. From that point on, all major decisions were made by her.

The Rugals were very effective at working together to bring down their quarry, but they had a weakness. Once they were linked mentally with the lead bird, they were very dependent on her. If Swyf could somehow take her down, the flock would falter long enough to allow her to escape. She banked hard to the left and flapped her wings, desperately trying to gain more altitude. Swyf knew the birds would try to attack her flanks and she didn't want to give them easy access.

One of the ugly birds screeched in protest, clawing at the spot where Swyf had been only a moment before. Another shot up from below, its wings beating the air frantically as it rushed her. Swyf dodged the sharp beak and looped to the right. She needed to draw out the entire flock to determine which Rugal was in charge.

Without warning the air was full of the filthy birds and their stench was overwhelming. Swyf swooped and dodged their outstretched talons, judging their reactions as she outmaneuvered them. One bird seemed to be the aggressor, attacking more frequently than the rest. She had a patch of gray mixed in with her black feathers and she was missing a talon. Swyf studied her long enough to be sure of picking her out of the flock. To test her character, Swyf flew at her, but the bird quickly ducked behind two other Rugals.

Coward, thought Swyf in disgust as she dodged more attacks. It was going to be hard to draw out the Rugal without being torn up by the rest of the flock. She took a dive towards the earth, keeping an eye on the leader, waiting for her to gather her courage again.

As Swyf neared the ground, an arrow flew past, catching one of the Rugals, which dropped out of the sky. *Archers and Rugals? Brael isn't taking any chances.* Swyf spiraled out of her dive and shot back into the air, arrows whizzing all around her, some of them catching trailing Rugals. Looping back into position, Swyf waited for the lead bird to attack again. When it continued to hide within the flock, she had an idea. It was dangerous, but it might work. She just hoped that Joraus would never find out, after all the grief she'd given him about taking risks.

Swyf remained just ahead of the flock, willing the dominant female to attack. All at once, the bird with the missing talon streaked to the front. Swyf, making sure it was right behind her, dove again, aiming herself directly at one of the archers, who quickly nocked an arrow and fired in one smooth motion. Swyf darted towards it before abruptly adjusting the angle of her dive. The arrow, meant for her, passed inches over her head and caught the lead Rugal in the breast. The bird crumpled and fell from the sky, her body fluttering limply as she sank to the ground. The other Rugals screeched in pain and dismay, as their mental link was instantly severed and their pursuit faltered.

Swyf found herself in range of the archers whose arrows were flying. One clipped her wing, spinning her around in the air. She beat her wings frantically, trying to regain the lost altitude. Another arrow nicked her leg, opening a shallow cut, while another narrowly missing her head. A few more whizzed by, but she noticed that most of the arrows were falling short. Soon she had outdistanced the archers and, with a quick glance behind her, she saw that the flock of Rugals had scattered.

Swyf flew on until she was out of direct danger. Once she felt safe, she slowed down to see where she was. The flight had pushed her west of her goal, so she made the necessary adjustments. Then she focused on the damage to her leg. Blood dripped from the wound, but she would be fine until she found a place to wait until nightfall. She could take care of it then.

Joraus better have made it through those Scurs, Swyf thought grimly as she flew on, the excitement of the flight now diminished. *And he better not complain about the stupid swim.*

A day and a half later, Joraus climbed the final steps to the hidden portal, rubbing his arms to stop them twitching. Between the exhausting journey and the lingering effects of the tareel energy blasts, his arms and legs felt like rubber. He glanced around, searching for Swyf, but he could not see her. When he reached the top step, he put his hands on his hips and took a good look around.

Tall pillars fanned out in a giant half-circle, with the last columns tying seamlessly into the mountains behind. The pillars on the far side framed a small cave, the opening of which was overgrown with hanging moss. A small spring trickled out of the cave, through the center of the pillars, and cascaded down a carved waterfall by the steps. It was truly a magnificent place and Joraus felt the peace of it, even through his weariness.

Unexpectedly, Swyf leapt down from the nearest pillar. "It took you long enough!" she said, laughing, as she approached him.

Joraus glared at her. "It was a long swim," he said flatly in his rumbling bass tone. "And then there were the Scurs. Have a pleasant flight, did you?"

"It was beautiful," she answered haughtily. "The weather was perfect and there was a delightful tailwind. Right up until the Rugals anyway."

"Yes, yes," Joraus interrupted. "I'm sure you have yet another story about how your journey was much worse than mine."

Spinning around, Swyf flipped her hair dismissively at him as she started walking along the stream towards the cave. Joraus watched her for a second and noticed with a touch of concern that she was limping slightly. She hadn't said anything, however, so instead of commenting he hurried to catch up. Together, they pushed through the hanging moss and entered the cave.

Inside, sunlight shone down from countless tiny holes in the ceiling, showering the place with radiant beams. The walls, reflecting this light, blazed with thousands of gems and shafts of precious metals, the effect bedazzling the eye.

Joraus studied the floor and spotted the circle of incomprehensible markings that Klyle had told him about. Taking Swyf's hand, he led her into the center. "Are you ready?" he asked her quietly.

"This is the only way left open to us. Do I have any choice?"

Joraus flashed a quick smile. "Not any that I'd care to consider. I'm glad we are going together though."

Swyf squeezed his hand softly. "Me, too."

As one, they began to sing, their voices rising in perfect unison. The symbols on the floor began to glow and the light reflecting from the various gems on the walls began to grow and pulse. When their song ended, there was a brilliant flash and the cave was empty.

CHAPTER 3:

NEW WORLD

Popping his head out of a small, metallic cylinder, Joraus blinked his eyes. He heard Swyf grunt as she wiggled her way out of a similar opening. He watched as she balanced on the edges and dusted herself off, before looking around. The building they were in seemed to be fairly old, yet it was immaculately well maintained. When he saw Swyf taking in the stained-glass window paintings, he secretly enjoyed her delighted smile. Finally, she finished gawking and noticed his exposed head.

Joraus forced his hands up onto the metal rims as he tried to haul himself out, but it was a tight fit and for a minute he was stuck. Swyf skipped over, but instead of helping, she simply watched him struggle and began to laugh. He was obviously too big for the tiny opening he had come through.

Joraus looked up at her and glared. Her tinkling laugh lit the quiet room and echoed through the other pipes. Gritting his teeth, he wriggled himself up through the pipe until he could get the leverage needed to push down with his hands and force his body out. Once he had finally extricated himself, Joraus balanced on the rim of the pipe and studied the room.

They were inside a church, by the sight of it. Glancing down, he realized that his metal tube was attached to a musical instrument of some kind. Peering over at Swyf and then down at himself, he couldn't keep a reluctant grin from spreading across his face. Klyle had told them to expect the unexpected when traveling through the portal, but, well…

To be honest, they both looked ridiculous. Their bodies were bright blue, with transparent wings attached to their backs. Swyf still kept her thin, muscular figure, but his own statuesque physique had been replaced by a short, squat frame with a belly spilling out over his middle. Judging by the largeness of everything around them, Joraus began to realize how small they must now be. He barked a laugh before quickly bringing his hands to his mouth in horror. His deep, and what he considered very intimidating, voice had been replaced by a high-pitched, nasally squeak.

Swyf was bent over double, laughing so hard that it seemed she might fall off the pipe on which she was balanced. Joraus shook his head in resignation. She always had all the luck. Her rich laughter was the same as it had always been. Only her form had changed, and not much at that.

"Are you done yet?" he squeaked spitefully. "We still have things to do, you know."

"I-I'm sorry, but, but, you…" Unable to get her words out, Swyf started to giggle again.

Joraus sighed. Once she was wound up like this, it would take her a few minutes to calm down. He sat on the edge of the pipe and waited for his companion to regain her composure. In the meantime he loosened the knot on the pouch around his neck and reached inside, pulling out the contents. He examined a tiny vial of red liquid and a jewel with a faint, golden glimmer pulsing in the center.

Finally regaining her composure, Swyf sat down next to Joraus and loosened the knot of her own pouch. She pulled out a second vial and a similar jewel, only it was pulsing silver instead of gold. "Well, that is pretty, isn't it," she remarked, and with a flutter of her wings she lifted herself off the pipe.

"Yes, well, you remember what Klyle told us: 'Follow the jewel and it will light the way.'" Joraus carefully stashed the vial back in his pouch and tightened the knot. Wings flapping, he joined Swyf in the air. Scowling again at her grinning face, he grumbled, "Go ahead and say it. I know you won't be happy until you do."

"I am just amazed that those wings can lift you off of the ground at all," she responded lightly. Then she flew close and to his surprise she gave him a quick hug. "Be careful, Joraus," she whispered in his ear. "I will miss you awfully."

Swyf let go quickly and flitted a few feet away. Although she had turned away, Joraus was sure he saw her swipe a hand across her cheek. He cleared his throat, trying to push down similar emotions. Never had he been separated from Swyf for long. Once they parted, he was not sure when, or even if, he would see her again.

Swyf, who had regained some of her good humor, was clutching her jewel tightly as she glided over him. "Be well, my chubby friend, and don't get stuck on the way out!" she called as she flew through a cracked window. The only things she left behind were peals of tinkling laughter, echoing dimly through the organ pipes.

Joraus, clutching his own gem and muttering to himself about the complexities of females, followed her to the window.

To his dismay, he found that she was right; he could not fit through the tiny opening. Eyeing the huge window in front of him apprehensively, he put his shoulder against it and pushed hard. It swung wide open and he tumbled out clumsily.

"Hmm," he mused as he straightened himself in the warm evening air. "So, apparently, I am a lot stronger than I appear."

Joraus glanced around quickly until he spotted Swyf flying off in the darkening sky. He raised a hand in silent farewell just before she faded from sight. "Be well," he whispered. "I will miss you, too."

Joraus flew to the top of the church steeple and glided in a slow circle, studying the gem intently. When he was about three-quarters of the way around, the jewel pulsed with a soft, golden hue. Taking one last, regretful glance over his shoulder in the direction Swyf had flown, Joraus sped off, allowing the precious stone to lead him onward.

The first thing Joraus noticed was how very different things were from home. Metal carriages rushed up and down the roads without being hitched to animals of any kind. Huge, splendid buildings lay sprawled out below and none of the people walking around were visibly armed. *What kind of a world is this?*

After a few hours of flying, the pulsing light in the gem intensified and Joraus slowed his pace to focus on the dwellings. Up until now, he had been so enthralled by everything that he hadn't paid much attention to where he was flying. It seemed that he was in a humble district of town and the homes all showed signs of wear, compared to those he'd flown over earlier. Descending, Joraus watched the gem closely. He circled the houses and when he passed over one particularly old one, the golden light of the stone flickered rapidly.

Stuffing the jewel into his pouch so that the light wouldn't draw attention, he studied the building. Though it appeared old, the surrounding land was well cared for, as though an effort had been made to make someone feel welcome. Noticing there were no lights on inside, Joraus darted around, searching for a way to enter. A couple of windows were cracked wide enough to enable Swyf to fit, but he judged that in his current portly condition, he would not.

As he flew past the back door, a high-pitched yapping sound startled him. Slowing, Joraus saw a small dog with long hair gazing up at him. Intrigued, he dropped down for a closer view, but the animal bared its tiny teeth threateningly and continued to bark. A light flicked on over the doorway and Joraus scurried to find a bit of shadow to hide in.

The door opened and there stood a tousled-haired young man, his mouth open wide as he let out a big yawn. "Come on then, Nala," he said, yawning for a second time. The creature yipped happily before darting between the man's legs and into the house.

As the man turned to follow the small dog, Joraus flitted through the door behind him, just before it closed. He waited, hanging just inside, as the man shuffled down a narrow hallway and turned into a room at the end.

The inside of the house was as neat as the outside. Painted, wooden carvings were on display, and beautiful paintings of people hung from the walls. Joraus approached one picture, marveling at the amount of detail it contained. It was of the man who had opened the door and he was holding a lovely, smiling young lady in his arms.

There were several more paintings and other decorations, and Joraus spent a few minutes gliding this way and that to examine them. Once he'd satisfied his curiosity, he reached back into his pouch and pulled out the gem again. Cupping it tightly in his hands to keep the light from disturbing the other occupants in the house, he flew slowly down the hallway. As he passed one of the rooms the pulsing stopped and the jewel shone with a brilliant golden light.

Looking inside, Joraus saw a small chair with a footstool in one corner and a cradle in another. As the strength of the light in the already dazzling gem continued to intensify, he flew over the cradle to see a small, sleeping child. Joraus tucked the gem back into his pouch for the last time and pulled out the tiny vial of red liquid. He dropped down to study the small child in fascination. It appeared to be male, although it was still young enough that the distinction was difficult.

So this is the one, he thought to himself as he gazed into the tiny face. It was strange to think that this tiny, helpless baby was destined to one day liberate his homeland from the evil that Brael had forced upon it. He smiled warmly as the child stretched his arms over his head.

Joraus settled near the child's head and quietly pulled the stopper from the vial, quickly covering the opening with a thumb as the liquid instantly evaporated, leaving behind a swirling, red gas. Carefully, he tucked the stopper into the pouch and then effortlessly lifted the head of the baby with one arm. Holding the vial under the child's nose, Joraus waited for him to exhale before removing his thumb.

The baby breathed deeply, draining the gas from the vial. When it was all gone, Joraus gently laid the child's head back down and watched as a soft glow emanated from high up on his chest. Joraus gently pulled the baby's collar down and grinned to himself as he gazed upon the same strange markings that he'd seen on the floor of the portal chamber; the same markings that Klyle had told him to watch for – the symbols of *Ragesong*.

CHAPTER 4:

WAKE-UP CALL

Jake groaned and slapped his hand down on the nightstand next to his bed, searching for the snooze button. Just as he found it and silence was blissfully returned, Jake was jolted awake by the sensation of cold water on his face. "What the...?" he cried out, spluttering and swiping at the liquid.

Laughing, his father jumped on him, pinned him under the covers and started to tickle him.

"Dad," Jake whined, "c'mon, I'm thirteen now!"

"I wasn't aware there was an age limit on when a dad had to stop beating the snot out of his kid," replied his dad, chuckling. "So, is the big, strong thirteen-year-old ready for his first day of Junior High?"

"Stop it," Jake said, trying not to smile. "Get off!" Finally, unable to hold it in any longer, he started to laugh. "C'mon, Dad!"

After a few more seconds, Jake felt the pressure lift and he was finally able to struggle out from under the blankets.

"Don't expect an awesome wake-up call like that every day," his dad remarked, still amused. "But, you didn't answer my question, are you ready for school? Nervous?"

"You have to help me make my bed since you helped mess it up," Jake said, but his dad was already holding one side of the sheet and waiting for him. He took the other end and started to pull it up.

"Well?" his dad challenged as they straightened the sheet and started on the second blanket.

"I dunno. Guess so," Jake answered.

"You guess what? That you are ready or that you are nervous?"

"Geez, Dad, I don't know. Both, I guess. Can't you give me a second to wake up?"

"You've had a second! How come you're guessing so much? I didn't realize know-it-alls needed to guess."

Jake studied his father, and without warning he sprung across the bed and tried to tackle him. Laughing, his dad danced to the left and then caught his arm, throwing Jake on the bed to tickle him again.

"Okay, okay, you win!" Jake gasped as he fought to free his arms.

"Don't you forget it, boy," his dad said, chuckling. "You have a way to go before you can take me on!"

They went back to making the bed and when it was finished, Jake's dad went to the door and opened it, before adding, "I have breakfast cooking downstairs. Hurry up and get ready, so you can eat before it gets cold."

"All right, I'll be down in a minute." Jake grinned as the door closed. He loved this tradition. His father took the morning off every year on his first day of school to prepare him a hot breakfast and find some elaborate way of waking him up. He just wasn't sure if he was a fan of the cold water method.

Jake studied the clothes his mom had set out the night before; jeans and a collared shirt. He hated those shirts, but he had given up arguing with her about it. At least she didn't make him wear them very often and, besides, his awesome new shoes more than made up for it.

After dressing quickly, he headed for the bathroom to fix his hair. He considered going out with his hair spiked in all directions, but decided against it. His mom wasn't nearly as much of a morning person as his dad, and he didn't think it smart to push boundaries this early in the day. Instead, he went with the simple soft spike that he normally wore and after a few squirts of hairspray, he opened the door.

As he walked into the hall, Jake thought he caught a glimpse of something blue out of the corner of his eye, but when he turned his head to focus on it, there was nothing there. Weird, he thought, but the smells wafting in from the kitchen quickly outweighed his curiosity. When he walked in, his mom was sitting at the table in her pajamas, with tousled hair and a sleepy expression on her face as she held a cup in both hands. Nala, the family dog, was lounging under her chair, eyeing the table hopefully. His dad stood at the oven, whistling as he flipped pancakes and stirred scrambled eggs. When Jake saw the cheese grater in the sink, he grinned. Dad always made the best eggs.

As he sat down at the table next to his mother, she gave him a drowsy smile. "Good morning, honey. How did you sleep?"

"Better than you, by the look of it," Jake replied, grinning.

She scowled. "It's a little early for you to be such a smart aleck, isn't it?"

"Mom has been a peach this morning," his dad called out. "I've never met anyone more equipped to handle mornings than your mother."

She picked a grape out of the bowl in front of her and threw it at her husband, but it missed and hit the counter before falling to the floor. Nala darted out from under the chair, but Jake's dad picked it up first and popped it in his mouth. The dog barked at him, and he swatted at her playfully.

"That's gross, Dad!" Jake remarked.

"Ten-second rule," his father answered, grinning around his mouthful.

"That's just a myth, you know," his mom commented.

"Well, I'm still alive, so there must be some truth to it." He brought the pan with eggs over and tilted it towards his wife, but she just shook her head.

"Yes, please," Jake said as the pan moved his way.

"So, are you excited to ride the bus this morning, sweetheart?" his mom asked as Jake dumped ketchup on his eggs.

His dad smacked him playfully on the back of the head. "I can't believe you ruin my eggs like that," he complained, returning the pan to the stove. "Those are perfectly seasoned."

Jake laughed. "They are now," he said, digging in for his first bite. "Mmm, yeah, I'm excited," he said to his mom. "Korey's older brother told us we're the second stop from the beginning, so we get to choose our seats!"

"I remember when I had to ride the bus," his dad recalled as he brought some pancakes to the table. "I was the last stop. You are lucky. I always had to ask someone if I could sit by them. Of course, it was easy to find a seat. I mean, who could resist this face?"

Jake laughed and scooted his eggs over, so they wouldn't get ketchup on his pancakes. He continued to banter with his dad and answer his mom's sleepy questions as he ate. When he was done, he headed back to the bathroom to brush his teeth.

As he walked into the room, he saw it again, a streak of blue in his peripheral vision, but when he turned to see what it was, there was nothing there. While brushing his teeth, Jake squinted and watched the mirror, hoping he might notice it again, but the only thing he saw was his reflection. Giving up, he rinsed his mouth and toothbrush, and walked back into the kitchen. His mom was still seated at the table, but she seemed a little more awake than earlier.

"Your backpack is by the door."

He went over and gave her a hug. "Thanks, Mom."

"Good luck today, sweetheart. I can't wait to hear all about it," she said, hugging him back.

Jake stepped over to his dad, who was now sitting opposite his mom.

"Stay out of the bathrooms," his dad joked, winking. "I've heard what they do to seventh graders."

"Thanks for breakfast, Dad," Jake replied, wincing slightly as he was wrapped in a tight bear hug.

"Be careful, son, and have a great day," said his dad, standing up and following him to the front door. Nala darted between his legs and he almost fell over, trying not to step on her. "Do you want to take the darn dog with you?" he asked as he scooted her out of the way with his foot.

"Don't kick my dog," his wife called out from the table.

Jake opened his backpack to double-check that he had everything he needed. When he was sure, he zipped it up, slipped it on his back and walked out the door. His mom joined his dad in the doorway, and together they stood watching him.

Jake turned once, and gave them a brief wave before giving in to his excitement and breaking into a run for the bus stop.

Joraus grinned as he spotted Jake running up the street. *It's nearly time.* He watched as the boy met his friends at the bus stop, where they fist-bumped, high-fived and greeted one another in nervous anticipation of the school year ahead.

Twelve years earlier, Joraus had discovered that while animals could see him, humans could not. At first the loneliness had not been so bad, but after a while he missed having someone to talk to, so he made friends with Jake's dog, but that just wasn't the same as having an intelligent conversation. Then he tried exercising, hoping to at least drop the belly fat he'd gained on his way through the portal, but after six months and no change in his physique, Joraus reluctantly accepted that his portly figure was more or less permanent.

The greatest shock came when he attempted to change form. Out of boredom one night, he tried to change into a bird, thinking that a midnight flight might clear his mind. In the past, all he had to do was picture the form in his mind and will it, but that time nothing happened. He tried again, over and over, but to his utter disappointment it appeared that he was stuck.

Joraus felt more relief than he'd expected when Jake consciously looked in his direction in the bathroom. The acknowledgement gave him hope that this period of isolation might come to an end. He flew slowly after the youth, idly wondering if the same thing was happening to Swyf.

CHAPTER 5:

FIRST DAY OF SCHOOL

Jake hopped off the bus after his friend, Korey. Reaching into his pocket, he pulled out a piece of paper on which was written his locker number and combination, before gazing up at the large 'SJH' on the sign above the door with the image of a warthog. *Seriously, I can't believe our mascot is a pig.* No sooner had he thought it than a student dressed in a furry suit with a giant warthog head walked out, followed by a bunch of cheerleaders. *And there it is, in all its glory.*

Shaking his head, he walked past the group and through the front doors. He turned to Korey and asked, "Is it just me or does it feel like we just walked into a Halloween party?"

Laughing, Korey eyed the orange walls and black lockers. "At least those are cool colors. Imagine we ended up with yellow and pink or something? What I can't figure out is why we're the Warthogs? Why not Tigers? It doesn't make sense."

Korey was a head taller than Jake and his straw-colored hair hung down past his ears. He shook it out of his eyes and glanced up at the large clock hanging over the hallway in front of them.

"Well, I have to hurry. My locker is all the way on the other side of the school. See you at lunch, okay?" Korey held out his fist, which Jake bumped obligatorily before watching him hustle down the hall.

Jake turned back and studied the entrance way. The school felt a lot different now than it had on introduction night, when his parents had brought him in to meet his teachers and find his locker. Last time the place had been nearly empty, with just a few other families wandering the halls. Now they were packed with boisterous kids, yelling and playing, letting off the nervous excitement of the first day back at school.

He looked around, trying to gain his bearings. If he remembered correctly, he had to take a right past the front offices and cafeteria, and head to the end of that hallway. Then, after passing the auditorium, he'd find his locker near the band room. That was awfully convenient, and he had a sneaky suspicion that his mom might have called and requested it for him.

Once Jake reached his locker, he studied the paper in his hand. *16-27-32.* He had practiced the combination when he'd been here before, and he was pleased when he pulled up on the handle and the door opened on the first try. Jake swung it open and reached into his backpack. Pulling out his binder, he set it inside temporarily. The locker was nearly empty since he didn't have any textbooks yet. Jake reached back into his backpack and took out the only other item he'd brought with him, a black case with steel clasps. He moved to set it carefully in his locker, but it was wrenched from his hands.

"What have we here?" asked a voice from behind him.

Jake turned around and watched helplessly as an older, much larger boy stepped back, holding the dark case above his head.

"Too small to be a trumpet – maybe it's a clarinet?!"

A couple of other kids laughed, but most turned their heads and tried to act like nothing was happening.

"Please give it back," Jake said quietly, as he gazed unflinchingly into the face of the boy in front of him.

"I just wanna see," the bigger boy said, laughing as he started unloosening the clasps on the side of the case.

"Is there a problem here?" a melodic voice from behind the boy asked, causing him to spin around and nearly drop what he was holding.

Jake turned his attention to the face of a blond woman dressed in a black skirt and a green sweater. "N-no, Ms. G-gladwell," he stammered. "I was just, uh…"

"I wasn't aware that a trombone could fit in a case that small, Jamie Gunther," the woman remarked. "Are you sure you haven't picked up the wrong instrument case by mistake?"

The boy she had called Jamie blushed before quickly handing the case back to Jake. After uttering an incoherent apology, he hurried away. Jake checked the clasps on the case and when he found them secure, he tucked it under his arm as Ms. Gladwell approached. The woman was taller than him, but not by very much. She wore her hair down and it flipped up at her shoulders. Jake thought she had a kind, pretty face and it seemed as though she smiled often, although at the moment her expression was very serious indeed.

"Hello again, young man," she said, stopping in front of him. "I would ask that you please let me know if he does this to you again." Her mouth thinned. "I will not put up with bullying of any kind."

Ms. Gladwell studied the black case tucked under his arm. "Hmm, Jake, isn't it?" she added. "Well, I don't see many male flute players, so I am very excited to see what you are capable of." She winked at him and started toward the band room doors. "I'll see you in third period."

"Thanks, Ms. Gladwell," Jake called after her. "I'm excited to play in a real band!"

The pretty teacher smiled over her shoulder and waved as the door closed behind her. Turning, Jake set the flute case inside his locker and picked up his binder. Glancing at the schedule in the clear front pocket, he hurried off to find his first class.

Joraus watched as Jake threaded through the mass of students, feeling proud of the way he hadn't backed down from the older kid. It wasn't the first time that Jake had stood up for himself, and Joraus liked the way he handled confrontation. His thin frame and short stature belied a power and quickness that few of his age could rival. Joraus was confident that the boy could handle himself in a fight, but he admired the lengths that he took to avoid them. Jake had a cool head and cheerful disposition that seemed to draw out the best in those around him. Joraus supposed it didn't hurt that he was such a handsome kid.

He had watched over Jake long enough to notice things that still escaped the young boy. During the last couple of years of elementary school, girls had continuously peeked Jake's way when he walked by and Joraus had overheard them on more than one occasion giggling about how handsome he was. Jake was oblivious, wrapped up in video games, friends, sports and the other interests of kids his age, but his light brown hair, bright blue eyes and slightly mischievous smile were sure to get him into girl trouble in the not-too-distant future.

Joraus floated slowly through the hallway, eyeing all of the 'Welcome back' posters, and trying to decide if he liked the orange-and-black school colors or not. He turned a corner and was just about to follow Jake into what appeared to be a math class of some kind when he saw a small, bluish shape at the end of the corridor. It was only for a brief second, but it was enough to pique his curiosity. Jake was meant to see blue, not him.

Joraus trailed Jake into the classroom as the bell rang. The overhead speaker sprung to life with the female voice of an overenthusiastic student body president, welcoming everyone to school. He watched as the math teacher, a tall, thin middle-aged woman, walked between the rows of desks, passing out a piece of paper to each student. Joraus settled on a shelf at the back of the class, but the azure shape kept nagging at him. I have fifty minutes, he thought to himself as he eyed the hallway. *What could it hurt?*

Joraus took off again and floated out the door lazily. Once outside the classroom, he glided down the hall and turned the corner at the end. He looked around, but could not see anything out of the ordinary. There was a line of classrooms on either side of the hall in front of him, and he peered into the first and second of them, not surprised when all he saw were teachers introducing themselves to their students.

Puffing his cheeks, Joraus sighed; maybe he was just getting his hopes up because Jake had caught a glimpse of him earlier. That morning had been the first time in a long while that he'd allowed himself to think of Swyf, and he guessed that he must just be seeing things. Not expecting anything, Joraus moved

36

onto the third and fourth classrooms, and he saw more of the same.

It was when he reached the end of the hall and turned back that he saw her. In a classroom on the opposite side of the hall, she was hovering in the air over the desk of a small, red-headed girl. Joraus blinked in astonishment. Swyf! Smiling in delight, he nearly called out, before catching himself. These opportunities didn't come very often and he wanted to take full advantage.

With a wicked grin he dropped to the ground and slowly walked into the class. With his back against the wall, he sidestepped his way to the rear of the room, keeping his eyes on Swyf all the time. She was staring at the blackboard, her eyes already starting to glaze over as the teacher read out the class syllabus from a printout in his hand. The man was short, balding and a bit overweight, and he was reading in a hollow monotone, seemingly unaware that the kids were already fidgeting.

When Joraus reached the back, he observed the room. To his delight he saw a bit of mud stuck to the foot of one of the kids. Carefully making his way over to the offending shoe, he pulled off a big chunk of dirt and began to shape it into a ball. It formed quickly, and Joraus studied it in satisfaction. "Perfect," he whispered to himself as he rose silently into the air.

Swyf was still staring blankly forwards. Joraus, taking careful aim, pulled back his arm and let the mud ball fly. Confident of hitting his target, he darted behind one of the kids, peering out to watch her reaction. Joraus covered his mouth with both hands to keep from laughing out loud. The mud ball hit Swyf square in the back of the head, flipping her over in midair. The expression of surprised outrage on her face as she spun around made Joraus double up in a silent fit of laughter. He landed on the ground at the foot of the boy he was hiding behind and ducked behind his shoe.

Joraus' head brushed the top of the boy's pant leg as he peeked around to see Swyf's reaction. He watched as she reached a hand to the back of her head and pulled at the gunk stuck in her hair. Totally worth it, he thought to himself, as he made his way slowly towards the door, darting from one desk to another. Swyf had begun to circle the room, her eyes narrowed as she searched. Suddenly, Joraus made a beeline for the exit, but just as he was about to cross the threshold, something bowled him over. He rolled out into the hallway and ended up on his back with Swyf pinning him down.

"Joraus! Why you…" she gasped, but then, without warning, she bent down and kissed him full on the mouth, before sitting back up and punching him in the stomach – hard.

"Oof," Joraus groaned, feeling the wind knocked out of him.

Swyf slowly climbed off of him and dusted herself off primly, before continuing to pull the mud from her hair. Joraus clapped his hands around his belly and groaned as he slowly got to his feet, grunting, "It's good to see you, too!"

"That was for the mud ball, you oaf! Twelve years and that's the way you greet me?" Swyf exclaimed. "A mud ball, seriously?" She flung some of the sticky stuff from her fingers before reaching out to wipe her hand clean – on him. When she was done, she turned to glare at him.

"It was what I had to work with!" Joraus protested, nudging her in the ribs with his elbow. "It was a good throw though. Even you have to admit it was an awesome throw."

"I don't have to admit anything," she sniffed, disdainfully.

"What are you doing here?" he asked, ready to burst with a thousand questions. "Is that your charge in there, the girl with red hair?"

"Her name is Samantha," Swyf retorted. "And yes, that's her. She just moved here with her mother over the summer. There were some, err, difficulties at her previous home. So where is your charge? You haven't lost it, have you?"

Of course not," Joraus scowled. "He's around the corner. I was on my way into class with him when I thought I saw you, and I couldn't resist. Do you want to come see him?"

His high-pitched voice, which he hadn't used much in a long time, made him feel self-conscious. Seeing Swyf again reminded him of how much he wanted to return to his homeland and his old self. "I've missed you," he said, flying into the air. "Well, are you coming? I mean, unless you'd like to stay here. That teacher does sound absolutely fascinating."

Swyf stuck her tongue out at him, but motioned him onward all the same. He flew back to the classroom where he'd left Jake, and after checking over his shoulder to make sure she was with him, he led the way inside. As he did so, Jake's head spun around and he looked directly up at them. Joraus froze and held his breath, causing Swyf to run into the back of him. "What's the big idea?" she muttered, pushing off of him, but her friend didn't answer.

While all of the other kids were taking notes, Jake continued to stare directly at the Changelings. Joraus grinned at Swyf's quick intake of breath. For a long moment, the youth continued to gaze at them before slowly shaking his head and turning back to his notes.

"Did he see us?" Swyf whispered as she studied the boy.

"Almost," Joraus answered excitedly. "He has been catching glimpses of me all morning. I think it is nearly time."

"What is his name?" Swyf breathed, still gazing down at the boy intently.

Joraus watched as Jake ran a hand through his thick, light brown hair. He could understand Swyf's awe. The youth had a handsome face and it wasn't hard to picture the man he would grow into. His high cheekbones and pointed chin bespoke an innate nobility and honor. Joraus knew that Swyf was seeing the same thing that he saw every time he looked at the boy. It was as if they were staring at a thirteen-year-old Klyle.

"His name is Jake," Joraus answered quietly.

"He looks so much like him," Swyf said, finally wresting her eyes off the youth. "What instrument does he play?"

A memory flashed through Joraus' mind at her question. Not long before Brael's invasion, Klyle had taken the Changelings into his study. In the middle of his desk was a series of drawings on a piece of parchment, alongside a map. Klyle told them the map marked the location of a secret vault that held weapons of unimaginable power. While all of the arms were formidable, one surpassed them all. Klyle had explained that each weapon was tied to one of the drawings. The pictures had vaguely resembled musical instruments, but it wasn't until Joraus crossed through the portal that he was able to identify them individually.

Joraus grinned at Swyf as he thought about the one sketch that Klyle had circled. "Can't you guess? Look at him! Would anything else suit him?"

Her jaw dropped. "Truly? The flute?"

Joraus nodded. "So you remember. Yes, his mother played for a local orchestra and he has wanted to play the flute for as long as I can remember. When she was forced to quit, so she could find higher-paying work, she gave him her old practice flute. It truly is a marvelous instrument. He took to it right away. Gifted is the word his mother uses to describe him."

"This is wonderful," Swyf remarked as she turned her attention back to Jake.

Joraus held his peace for a long time as she continued to study the boy, but finally he said, "So tell me about Samantha."

For a long moment, Swyf did not answer, but finally she turned to him and he saw a shade of doubt cross her face.

"I don't quite know where to begin with Sam," she said slowly. When Joraus raised an eyebrow, she rushed on, "Don't get me wrong, she has the skills necessary, but..." She faltered, and he was surprised to see that she was close to breaking down.

"I don't know, Joraus. She seems so disinterested in everything around her lately. She is so gifted in so many ways. She's smart, pretty, and then, of course, there is her musical talent. But she has such a negative view of world right now. It is depressing to be around her." Swyf looked away and sighed. "I know that isn't fair to her. She has gone through a lot in the last year, but... she worries me, Joraus."

Joraus cautiously put an arm around Swyf. He knew this would either be comforting or dangerous, depending on her mood, but instead of pulling away, she just laid her head on his shoulder.

"What instrument was she drawn to?" he asked curiously.

Swyf smiled. "The saxophone. Her father listened to jazz music with her when she was younger and she would always smile when she heard a saxophone. It's one of the few good memories she has of him, and when everything else started to happen... well, I can't say that I was shocked when she was drawn to that particular instrument."

"The saxophone," Joraus repeated, giving Swyf a squeeze. "Well that should complement Jake nicely. Don't you think?"

"I suppose so," she sighed, but then she drew away from him. "Well, I better get back. I suppose I'll see you in third period."

Swyf leaned in and kissed him on the cheek. "It really is wonderful to see you again, Joraus. I can't believe we are this close to finally going home."

Joraus watched as she glided out the door, unsure of what to make of their reunion. She had seemed genuinely glad to see him, but he was never sure with her, confused by the kisses and the punch in the stomach. Sighing, he turned his attention back to Jake and watched as the boy packed his things away in preparation for the ringing of the bell.

How long would it be before Jake saw him fully? Would he be ready for what was coming?

The bell rang and Joraus slowly followed the youth out the door and to his next class. As Jake settled into a new desk and a new teacher passed out a new syllabus, Joraus hoped it wouldn't be too much longer.

CHAPTER 6:

BAND

The bell rang, and Jake hurriedly tucked the stack of papers given to him by the teacher into a folder marked 'English' inside his binder. It was finally time for band! He shuffled out of the classroom with the rest of the students and hustled towards his locker in excitement. This was what he had been waiting for.

Jake had been taking flute lessons from his mom for years, but this was the first time he was going to get to play with a group. He sidestepped a group of slow-moving girls and paused for a quick sip of water at the drinking fountain before turning the corner to the band room.

There were a few students lingering in the hall and he threaded his way through them to reach his locker. When he arrived, he spun the combination lock and grinned as he nailed it again on the first try. Reaching inside, he set his new English and math textbooks on the shelf. Jake pulled out his flute and balanced it on top of his binder.

Glancing at the back of his locker, he decided to ask his mom if he could get some magnets, so he could hang some pictures inside. The boring gray was almost begging to be covered by something. Jake had some awesome videogame pictures saved on the computer at home, which he could print out. Thinking about which ones he'd like to hang where, he closed his locker and walked through the open band-room doors.

Once inside, Jake caught sight of multiple rows of chairs placed in a semicircle with a music stand in front of each one. Where the semicircle opened there was a carpeted dais with a raised music stand and a tall stool facing the seats. Over the chairs he noticed pictures of instruments dangling from strings. Jake figured they marked where the students should sit. Clearly, Ms. Gladwell had made an effort to make the room feel as inviting as possible.

Large cutouts of all the different instruments were stapled to the walls. To the back of the classroom he saw a closet and a small, windowed room, with a big door closing it off from everything else. The door was propped open and he could see shelves of instruments sitting inside. A teacher's desk was pushed up against a side wall, and beyond that, windows opened out to a view of the school football field.

Just as Jake finished scanning the room, a short, red-haired girl pushed her way past him with a big case in one hand and a folder in the other. "Excuse me," he started to say, but stopped when she didn't turn around or even acknowledge the fact that she had bumped into him.

Shaking his head, Jake walked over to the set of chairs with picture of a flute hanging over them. There was already a group of girls sitting there, and he stopped in front of an empty seat between a girl with short blond hair and one with a long, black braid. "Mind if I sit here?" he asked them politely.

The blond girl giggled and looked away, but the girl with the braid lifted her nose a bit and replied, "This is the flute section."

"I know," he answered patiently. "May I sit down?"

"Only girls play the flute," she retorted. "You're a boy."

Jake sighed, "I know I am a boy, but I play the flute too. Can I sit down? Please?"

"May I," she corrected primly, "and no, I'm saving this seat for someone else."

"You can sit down here if you want," called out another girl sitting a couple of chairs down.

Jake exhaled in relief as he walked over to the seat offered. "Thanks," he said.

"Don't mention it," she answered sweetly. "I'm Jill. What's your name?"

"Jake," he replied, still a little miffed at the rudeness of the black-haired girl.

"Do you really want to play the flute, Jake?" Jill asked, looking at him with a smile.

"Yeah, my mom used to play, and ever since I heard her, I wanted to play too."

"That's neat," said the girl. "I just picked it because it was cute and that's what all the girls play."

Jake didn't know what to say to that, so he just smiled. He was rescued from further small talk when Ms. Gladwell entered the room. "Did everyone find a seat?" she asked, as she crossed the floor to the dais and sat down on the stool facing the chairs.

There were a few students who were not yet seated, so the teacher waited patiently for them to find their seats before continuing, "Welcome to beginning band. I am extremely excited to see so many new faces." She smiled as she studied the room. "This is certainly a big group and I am glad to meet you. Now, by a show of hands, how many of you have played your instrument before?"

When Jake raised his hand, he saw about fifteen other kids do the same. He noticed that the red-haired girl who had knocked into him earlier was sitting with her elbows on her knees, staring at the ground, but she had one hand slightly raised. The girl with the black braid had her hand up too.

"Excellent," Ms. Gladwell exclaimed. "That is wonderful. Now, I have a tradition that I like to do on the first day of school with beginning band. I'd like to give you all an opportunity to play something in front of the class. This is completely optional, and you are by no means required to play, but it is an opportunity for you to show everyone what you have been working on."

Jake's stomach flipped, excitedly. He had hoped something like this would happen, and he had even spoken to his mom about what he should play. As he had been worried that some of the boys might tease him for playing the flute, they had tried to pick a song that might stop any jokes before they began.

"Is there anyone who would like to play something?" Ms. Gladwell asked.

Jake watched seven hands, including his own, pop back into the air.

"Wow, that is more than I expected," she said as she counted the hands. "This will be great. Why don't we start at the back with the brass and then we will work our way up to the woodwinds. Each of you may take out your instruments."

While the volunteering kids took their instruments out of their cases, Ms. Gladwell passed around a syllabus. "We'll go over this really quickly at the end," she said, working her way quickly through the rows. "Now let's start with the trumpets."

Jake watched as an overweight kid shuffled up to the front of the room.

"Go ahead and stand up on the square," Ms. Gladwell said, hopping off her stool and taking it with her as she stepped down. "Do you need the music stand?"

The boy shook his head and stepped up onto the square to face the rest of the band, a scared expression on his face.

"Don't be afraid," Ms. Gladwell urged, taking a seat at the back of the room. "Go ahead. Play anything you'd like."

The boy lifted the trumpet to his mouth and started to blow. After an awful squawk, a half-hearted note quavered out. Jake listened as the boy tried to play 'Row, Row, Row Your Boat,' missing half of the notes. When he finished, Ms. Gladwell clapped enthusiastically.

"That was wonderful!" she exclaimed as the frightened kid hurried back to his seat, blushing.

The rest of the class joined in the clapping, and the boy gave them all a somewhat embarrassed smile. Jake sat and listened as the other kids played through other beginning songs, such as 'Hot Cross Buns' and the like. When it came to the flute section, the girl with the black braid stood up and played 'Mary had a Little Lamb.' She curtseyed when she finished and flashed a big, and what Jake considered to be a brown-nosing, smile at Ms. Gladwell.

Once the girl returned to her seat, Jake stood and walked up to the dais, clutching his flute. Facing the band, he tried to ignore the low sniggers. His mom had warned him that it would be like this, but it was still a little embarrassing. He heard quite a few of the boys whispering to their neighbors and he could imagine what they were saying. Hopefully, they would change their minds in a few minutes.

Lifting his flute to his lips, Jake blew into it, testing the pitch. When it sounded a little sharp, he pulled the head joint out a little and tried again. Once satisfied with the tuning, he glanced up and saw a speculative expression on Ms. Gladwell's face. He counted to himself and then started to play his song.

The boys who were smirking jerked their heads up straight. Hearing whispers of recognition as he played, Jake smiled inwardly. His mom had been right; the song had gotten their attention. He played through *The Legend of Zelda* theme song and when he finished everyone started to clap without even waiting for the teacher's lead. No one was smirking now and a lot of the boys were talking excitedly.

"All right, quiet down now," said Ms. Gladwell as she attempted to bring the class under control. "That was lovely, Jake, thank you. It brings back memories." Winking at him, she laughed. "Zelda is one of my favorites, although none of the sequels have held a candle to the original. Graphics aren't everything you know."

All the boys started whispering again. Their teacher played games? How cool was that!

"Yes, yes, I play video games! I am not that old," she continued. "When I was a girl, I played the original first. Now please sit down, Jake, as we still have one more student who would like to play, and then we need to talk about the syllabus before the bell rings."

As Jake stepped down to take his chair, he spotted an undisguised mixture of jealousy and anger on the face of the girl with the black braid. He felt a little bad as he had not meant to show her up, only to make sure the boys didn't make fun of him for playing the flute. As he started to take his instrument apart, the red-haired girl stood up in front of the class, holding an alto saxophone.

She was dressed in an old, rumpled T-shirt and her jeans had holes in them. Jake was pretty sure the rips were not there on purpose, like the ones you could buy in store. Her hair was pulled back into a casual ponytail, and while she was pretty, she looked as though she didn't smile very much. Even though it was only an alto, the saxophone looked huge clutched in the girl's tiny hands. It was old and there were some dents in it, but she handled it as though it were a prized possession. Holding it carefully in one arm, she tightened the neck strap, bringing the mouthpiece closer to her lips.

The girl did the same thing as Jake, and played a note and listened. He judged her a bit flat, and was a little surprised that she knew to pull out on the mouthpiece. She played the same note again before pushing in on it slightly. The third time she played, the girl seemed happy with the sound and glanced out at her audience one more time before raising the mouthpiece to her lips.

Wow! Jake's jaw dropped as he watched her fingers dance over the keys. There were no squawks when she played. The song sounded like an old jazz tune. He didn't know the name of it, but he was sure he'd heard it before. The old instrument gave off a beautiful tone, and the girl knew how to swing the notes and everything. Jake found he was disappointed when the song ended and she lowered the instrument.

While the room had broken into applause when Jake finished playing, now everyone just sat there staring at the red-headed girl. Finally, Ms. Gladwell cleared her throat. "Do you like Glenn Miller, Samantha?"

The girl nodded, but didn't say anything.

"That was beautiful," Ms. Gladwell said, starting to clap. "Thank you for sharing it with us. 'In the Mood' is one of my favorite songs."

The rest of the band belatedly took up the applause, but it died quickly. Samantha carefully walked back to her seat and sat down as Ms. Gladwell returned to the front of the class.

"Thank you very much for sharing your talents, boys and girls," she said. "I feel truly honored that you were willing to stand at the front on the first day of school and play for us. I know how scary that can be. Now, if you would please follow with me in the syllabus…"

Joraus stared open-mouthed at Samantha as Swyf smiled proudly. "That was amazing," he finally gasped. "Where did she learn to play like that?" He turned to his friend, still goggling. "Do you have any idea how formidable she is going to be when we get home?"

Swyf flitted over to him and gently tapped his chin, closing his open mouth. "You'll catch flies," she said, with laughter dancing in her musical voice. "Yes, I have heard her practicing, you know. She picked it up herself. Sam badgered her mom for years for a saxophone, and although she wanted a tenor, her mom found that alto sax in a pawn shop. She got it for Christmas a few years ago, and she started to play along to the radio."

Swyf paused and stopped smiling. "It isn't her musical skills that I'm worried about," she confided. "You saw the way she acted. She is so introverted that she struggles with even the most basic social skills."

Joraus studied the red-haired girl thoughtfully. "Still, I'd rather have her struggle with that than the other way around.

Jake is pretty easy going. It may take a while, but he'll lighten her up."

"Speaking of Jake," said Swyf, "he sounded pretty good himself. Does he spend a lot of time playing video games?"

"Not too much," Joraus answered. "His mom set some pretty strict rules a few years ago, and he is a pretty obedient kid. Of course, he's also found out what happens if he abuses his video game privileges. He can be a pretty ornery boy when his mom takes away the power cord, and all he can do is sit there and gaze longingly at a dark T.V. screen."

Swyf laughed. "What a good mom. Samantha doesn't see too much discipline at home. Her mom works two jobs and her grandma is always out with her bowling league or bingo friends."

They both quieted as Samantha unexpectedly glanced in their direction. Her eyes grew large and she quickly looked back down at the ground, shaking her head slowly.

Joraus grinned. "Well, I'm sure she'll have someone to talk to tonight. I think she just caught her first glimpse of us."

When the bell rang, Jake stood up to walk out with the rest of the class.

"I need to speak with Jake and Samantha for a moment," Ms. Gladwell called out over the rising volume of chatter. "Would the two of you please wait for me at my desk?"

Jake tried to avoid the curious glances of the other kids as he picked up his flute case and binder, and strode over to the teacher's desk. Samantha soon joined him and together they waited.

After a few seconds of uncomfortable silence, Jake said, "That was really good, Samantha. Have you been taking lessons for a long time?"

The girl looked down at the floor, but quietly replied, "I don't take lessons."

"Really," Jake asked, astonished. "How did you learn to play like that?"

Samantha blushed, but continued to stare at the ground as she responded, "Online tutorials, YouTube, and just practicing."

"Wow," was all Jake could think of to say.

Finally, Ms. Gladwell walked over, ending the awkward conversation. "Thank you for waiting," she said, sitting down behind her desk. "I don't want to waste time because I know you have other classes, but I want you both to rearrange your school schedules. I need you in my advanced band. It is seventh period, and on occasion we stay after school if I deem it necessary. I'm afraid beginning band would be wasted on the pair of you."

She picked up a pencil and tapped it lightly on the side of her neck. "Honestly, I don't have anyone in my advanced band that will be able to compete with you. I will talk to the front office, so they will know what to expect. Please tell your parents they can either come in to meet with me or just call."

Ms. Gladwell reached over and pulled a blank page of paper out of the printer sitting on one side of her desk. Folding it in half, she ripped it in two before scribbling something on each piece. "Here, give that to your parents and make sure they get it. I need them to call me, so we can get you moved in there as quickly as possible. Prepare another piece to use as an audition song or use the same pieces. I am going to be assigning chairs at the beginning of next week, so please come prepared with something and be ready to sight read. Do you have any questions?"

When they both shook their heads, Ms. Gladwell handed each of them a signed note, so they wouldn't get in trouble for being late to their next class. Walking them to the door, she studied the oversized case in the young girl's hand. "Samantha, you are welcome to store that here in the band room, so you don't have to carry it to all of your classes."

"It's okay," the girl replied as she started walking down the hall. "I've got it."

Ms. Gladwell gave a shrug and smiled at Jake before turning back into the band room. He couldn't help but smile to himself as he went back over to his locker and opened it again on the first try. What an awesome day it was turning out to be. If only he could figure out what that weird, bluish thing was that he kept seeing.

CHAPTER 7:

STRANGE HAPPENINGS

nnoyed, Jake hopped off the bus. He quickly gave the usual fist bumps and high fives to his friends before turning for home. The morning had started out great, and he couldn't wait to give his mom the note from Ms. Gladwell, but all afternoon he'd been seeing that blue streak, and not just in his peripheral vision. During his last class he was almost sure that someone had been whispering in his ear.

He started walking home, scratching at his chest. It had started itching after lunch and it had been bothering him all afternoon. Abruptly, the azure streak appeared in front of him again, but this time it seemed to have a vague outline to it. He screwed up his eyes, trying to make out the shape, but a car honked behind him, making him jump. The image shimmered and vanished. Jake sighed in disappointment and turned to the car.

It was his father, and he couldn't help grinning as he waved. His dad pulled a face at him and revved the engine. Jake grabbed the straps on his backpack and pulled them tight, so that he wouldn't damage his flute, and then took off, sprinting for home, racing the car down the street. He was able to keep up for a little bit, but towards the end his dad sped ahead. By the time Jake arrived at the end of the driveway, his dad was already leaning against the car. He let out a big, fake yawn.

Jake elbowed him in the ribs playfully. "You cheated! I saw you gun it at the end!" he accused.

"I don't know what you're talking about," his dad protested, wrapping his arm around Jake's neck and putting him into a headlock. "So how is the big Junior High man? Did you have a good first day? Are you king of the school yet?"

"C'mon Dad," Jake protested. "Ouch! Cut it out! No noogies!"

His dad laughed, but let him go. "Well, come on, I'm sure your mom is just dying to hear about your first day of band," he said, laughing. "You'd think that band was the only class you go to, talking to her. It's not, of course," he added, raising an eyebrow, "right?"

"I know, Dad," Jake replied, rolling his eyes as he followed him into the house.

When Jake entered the living room, his mom shouted out, "It's about time!" Then she peered over his shoulder at her husband. "Oh, it's you."

The older man frowned. "It's good to see you too, beautiful."

"I thought I was going to get Jake to myself first," she said, pouting. "Fine, you can listen, but sit over there. He's mine for a minute."

She waited for her husband to obediently take his seat. Ignoring him as he mimed zipping his lips, she turned to Jake with a big smile. "How did it go, sweetheart? Was it exciting?"

"I already asked him that," Jake's dad teased.

"Yes, but maybe he'll be able to answer now that he isn't in a headlock," she retorted.

His dad grinned. "Touché!"

Jake's mom looked back at him. "Well?"

Just because he knew it would irritate her, he shrugged and said, "I dunno. It was okay, I guess."

His mom threw her hands up in the air in mock surrender and cried, "Boys!"

Jake snuck a peek at his dad and got a wink in return. "Just kidding, Mom!" he said. "Calm down! Seriously though, it was all right, though a little boring. In most of the classes the teachers just read through the syllabuses and stuff." He paused, considering. "Is that the right word? Syllabuses? Maybe sullabusi? Anyway, they talked about all the class rules and what they were going to teach, and they handed out textbooks. My locker is crammed full."

"I don't care about textbooks! Did you get to play in band???"

"A little, she had us play 'Mary had a Little Lamb.'"

"Oh," his mom frowned, disappointment written all over her face. "Well, that's nice, I suppose."

"Take a joke, will you!" Jake remarked as his dad burst out laughing. "Yes, we got to play. She let anyone who wanted to stand up and play a piece."

"I swear I'm going to feed you nothing but vegetables for a week if you don't give me some answers," his mom threatened, before turning to stare at her husband. "Both of you!"

Jake grinned. "All right, all right, most of the kids who stood up played the beginners' music. There were only two of us who didn't. They loved my song." Jake smiled at the memory. "Wanna know the best part? When I finished the teacher told us that she plays video games too. It was awesome!"

"Well, that is wonderful, dear," his mom said, smiling. "I'm glad she was able to hear you play on the first day."

"There's more though," Jake continued. "There was this other girl there, and she played the alto saxophone, and she was awesome. She stood up and played some jazzy song. 'In the Mood,' I think the teacher called it. It was way cool. I talked to her for a minute afterwards and she said she didn't even have a music teacher. She just learned from the internet."

"That's nice, dear, but what else did the teacher say about you?" his mom asked, dismissing the reports of the other girl.

"Was she cute?" Jake's dad asked.

"Quiet, you," his wife snapped. "He's too young to think about cute girls! Now go on, Jake."

Jake blushed, but ignored his dad. "Well, after class the teacher made me and the other girl wait by her desk until all the other students went out."

"Yes?" his mom prompted when he paused.

"C'mon, Mom, it's been a long day, and I'm thirsty," Jake teased.

"Son, if you try to stall me one more time, you are going to scrub toilets every day for a week! And guess where you'll be getting your drinks from then?"

"Wow," Jake mumbled, glancing at his father again.

"Don't look at me this time, boy," his dad said, holding his hands out in front of him. "I don't want anything to do with scrubbing toilets. You answer your mother."

"Fine. The teacher wants us to join the advanced band. She said the beginning band would be a waste of time. She gave me this to give to you."

Jake grinned again as he fished around in his pocket and pulled out the hastily scrawled note. "She said she wanted you to call her, so she could work with you to rearrange our schedules. She..."

That was all Jake could get out before his mom leaped out of her seat and jumped in the air, swinging her arms and tucking her legs under her. "This is so great, Jake!" she yelled as she pulled him out of his own seat and into a giant bear hug. "Way to go, sweetie!"

"You're crushing me, Mom," Jake gasped as he tried to pull away, but he blushed in pleasure and couldn't stop grinning. *Man, do I have the best parents or what?*

Later, after his parents had wrung out every last detail about his school day, Jake finally made it to his room. Closing the door, he hung his backpack on the doorknob. Then, breathing a sigh of relief, he flopped down on the floor in front of his bed. Grateful that there was no homework, he switched on the T.V. and picked up his game controller, but as he lifted it the strange blue shape appeared, making him jump. It seemed blurry, as though he were seeing it through someone else's glasses. Something inside the distortion called out his name, but then it vanished.

"What is going on?" he muttered to himself, waving the controller in the air where the vague shape had been only moments before.

His chest started itching again, only this time it felt much worse. Dropping the controller, he dug at his skin with both hands. It felt like his collarbone was on fire and the more he scratched the worse it got.

All of a sudden, Jake noticed a glowing light between his hands. It was shining right through his shirt. He stopped scratching long enough to rip it off, before staring down in dismay. His chest was glowing! Jake jumped up and turned to the mirror. Sure enough, the area right below his collarbone was glowing with a brilliant, golden light. As he gaped at his body, the blue thing popped back into view, floating right next to his head, only now it wasn't a streak or a blurry shape. Instead it was a weird, fairylike creature that was staring into the mirror and grinning at him.

"Hey, Jake!" it squeaked in a high-pitched voice. "How's it going?"

Jake took one more horrified look at his glowing chest and then at the fairy thing before toppling backwards on his bed in a dead faint.

CHAPTER 8:
INTRODUCTIONS

Jake jerked awake, spluttering. Looking around wildly, he sat up. His face was dripping wet and he wiped the water from his eyes. Opening them, he saw the little blue fairy circling over his head, holding a small cup. He closed his eyes again and groaned.

"Well, it worked this morning when your dad did it," the thing squeaked at him as it flew closer to his face. "I thought it might be a little creepy if I tried tickling you though."

Jake stared at it, his mouth agape. Suddenly, the fairy laughed and threw the rest of the water into his face. "Are you awake yet?" it squeaked, before zooming out of swatting distance.

"Yes, enough with the water!" Jake growled, jumping to his feet. "What in the world are you?"

"I'd quiet down if I were you," the fairy admonished, placing a finger to its lips. "You are the only one that can see me. You don't want your mom and dad to burst in here, and think you've gone crazy, do you?"

Jake narrowed his eyes and opened his mouth to say something. Then, thinking better of it, he abruptly flopped on his bed again and glared at the creature.

"Well, that didn't take long," the fairy said, laughing again. "You always were a sensible boy." Tossing the empty cup onto the bed next to Jake, he continued, "Now, I imagine you have some questions. I promise to answer them, but only if you then promise to listen to me. Fair deal?"

Jake nodded slowly, still not quite believing what he was seeing.

The fairy crossed his legs and settled on the bed in front of him. "Well then, you first, fire away!"

"Umm," Jake started to say, but all coherent thought had fled his mind. "Okay, okay, uh."

"Regular poet, aren't you?" the creature teased. "Come on, spit it out."

All at once, the questions came rushing back and he fired them off quickly. "Who are you? What are you? And why do I have a blue fairy in my room?"

"First things first, I am most certainly not a blue fairy," said the strange being, indignantly. "I'm a Changeling. My name is Joraus."

"What's a Changeling?" Jake asked.

"Well, in your world, I guess it is a little blue fairy," Joraus grumped. "Back where I come from it's a creature of great nobility and worth. We can change into any animal we want, and we are excellent spies. Our friendship is sought out by kings!"

"Really?" said Jake dumbly. "So you could even turn into an elephant?"

Joraus laughed. "Well, I haven't really needed to turn into one of those before. But, yes, I suppose I could if the need arose."

Jake goggled at him. "So how come you picked to be little blue fairy then? I mean you could've been something awesome, like a tiger, a wolf or a cobra."

Joraus stopped laughing and sighed, "My abilities don't work in your world." He scowled at the expression of disappointment on Jake's face. "Believe me when I say that no one is more upset about this than I am! How would you like to fly around looking like an overweight fairy?"

"All right, keep your pants on. Sorry I called you a fairy," Jake soothed. "What do you mean by 'my world' and were you the blue thing I kept seeing all day?"

Joraus nodded. "I mean that I come from a different world. As for the 'blue thing' you saw, well, that depends on what part of the day you mean. Was there any time that you saw two blue things?"

Jake remembered his first class and nodded. "During first period."

"Very good," Joraus exclaimed. "I wondered if you had been able to see her too."

"Her, who…?"

"Her name is Swyf. I'll explain more about her later. Any more questions?"

Jake looked down at his chest, but no longer saw a golden light. He sat a little straighter so that he could see himself in the mirror. Beneath his collarbone were some strange, black markings, dipping down in a small arc, which followed the bone from one side to the other. He gazed at it for a second before turning back to Joraus.

"What are these markings?" he asked, lightly tracing the unfamiliar characters with his finger.

"That, Jake, is an excellent question and it is not easily answered. I will explain those in a moment as well. Is there anything else that you want to ask about me? Because once I start talking, I don't want to be interrupted."

"Go ahead." Jake sat back on the bed and motioned for the creature to go on.

"Well, like I said," Joraus began, "I am not from this world. I am from a land known as Fermicia. Before you ask me where it is," he said, holding up his hands, "let me tell you that I don't know. I came here through ways that even I don't quite understand."

The Changeling suddenly stood and began to pace on the bed in front of Jake. "Fermicia is a lot different from your land. We do not have cars, or many of the conveniences that you, humans, have come to rely on. Fermicia is wild and untamed. There are huge mountains and beautiful valleys, sweeping rivers and endless seas, huge forests and rolling plains." The tiny creature's voice caught. "I have seen nothing in this land that could even begin to compare to the beauty of it."

Joraus turned away abruptly, and Jake thought he saw the small creature swipe at his eyes.

"Anyway," the Changeling continued in high-pitched squeaks, "Fermicia is broken into different territories. The one I am from is known as Kardonin. Many years ago, it was like most of the others — split into rival tribes, each striving for domination. These tribes warred constantly over the smallest of infractions, making Kardonin one of the most dangerous places in the land. It was instant death to be caught by one of the tribes anywhere near their boundaries.

"One day, two children were born into the most dominant tribe. Their names were Klyle and Brael. They were almost the same age and it was only natural that they became friends. As was the custom in that tribe, they were placed into training as soon as they were old enough to swing a weapon. The two boys quickly outstripped the other warriors in both prowess and skill, and by the time they were young men they were known throughout the territory as fierce warriors.

"Where Brael was big and strong, Klyle was lean and agile. Brael fought with reckless abandon while Klyle was patient and exploited any weaknesses in his opponents. When they fought together, it is said that they were unstoppable. It was like..." Joraus faded off, lost in the moment.

Jake waited patiently, and after a minute Joraus shook his head. "Sorry, I've tried not to think about home for a long time now. Reliving the old stories is... a little difficult. So where was I?"

"Klyle and Brael," Jake prompted.

"Ah, yes," Joraus said, before sitting once again. "So, one day their tribe leaders decided it was time to expand the tribal borders, and they sent Klyle and Brael out to scout the surrounding land. The youths decided to explore the Mountains of Kah first, but as they entered the foothills, Brael caught sight of a huge deer. Now Brael was an avid hunter, and naturally took off after the animal, leaving Klyle with the option to either follow or be left behind.

"The deer led them through winding game trails, up and over many ridges, and far out of their territory. Klyle tried to talk sense into his friend, but Brael would have none of it. They tracked the deer for hours until the sun hung low in the sky. Finally, it led them to a small spring, flowing out of a forest of tall trees. Klyle was fascinated by the area and pressured Brael to stop, so that they could explore. Brael wanted to continue hunting the deer, and when neither man could convince the other, they agreed to separate and meet the next day.

"Brael continued after the deer while Klyle followed the winding spring through the forest. Eventually, it led him out the other side and to a large staircase, carved into the mountainside. Klyle followed the steps to the top where a semicircle of pillars framed a small cave. The opening of the cave was covered with hanging moss and the place seemed as though it hadn't been disturbed in centuries.

"Klyle walked through the pillars and pulled back the hanging vines. Inside was the most glorious sight you could imagine. The cave walls soared above him, and they sparkled with gems and precious metals. On the ground was a large circle of ancient markings."

Joraus stopped and glided up to the symbols on Jake's chest. He traced them with a small, blue finger. "These are some of the same markings."

Jake blew out a breath that he hadn't realized he was holding. "What do they mean?"

Joraus shook his head. "All I know is that they have something to do with *Ragesong.*"

"What's *Ragesong*?" Jake asked quizzically. "It sounds like a video game."

Joraus laughed in spite of himself. "Yes, I guess it would to you. I'll explain it more in a minute. I don't want to get ahead of myself.

"So anyway, Klyle ripped his tunic and, using a piece of charcoal he'd brought with him, he started to copy the symbols down on the cloth, sensing they were somehow important. When it grew too dark to see, Klyle built a small fire near the cave entrance and spent the remainder of the night copying. He finished late the following morning.

"When he was done, the man went back to the place where he had left Brael. Klyle was excited to show him what he'd found, but as soon as he saw the big man, he knew it would have to wait. Brael walked into sight with the huge deer slung over his back and wearing a proud smile. He immediately began telling Klyle how he had run the animal to exhaustion and strangled it with his bare hands."

"He really strangled a deer with his bare hands?" Jake asked with an expression of revulsion on his face. "That's gross! Why would he do that?"

"I am getting us a little off track here," Joraus mused. "I do like to tell stories. To answer your question about Brael though, it's just the way he is; strong and physical, and he always preferred to kill something up close rather than from far away."

"Brael doesn't sound like a very nice guy if that is the kind of stuff he does for fun," Jake commented.

"He isn't," Joraus agreed, "as you'll find out if you will just listen..."

"Sorry."

"It's okay. Anyway, to make a long story short, Klyle became obsessed with finding the meaning of those symbols. For years he labored at them, and eventually he was able to uncover bits and pieces. It led him to the discovery of a long-forgotten power, which Klyle described as 'flipping on a switch in his mind,' making the world around him slow and sluggish. He said it removed all thoughts of fear and made him feel invincible. He told us that as good as the power felt, there were dangers; it was addictive, and every time he embraced the power, it became harder to let it go. Klyle called the power

Ragesong and worried that it might prove disastrous in the wrong hands."

Joraus paused and sighed. "The only one he instructed as to its use was Brael. Klyle warned him over and over again about the inherent dangers, but..."

Jake was having a hard time believing all of this. The only things that kept him from dismissing the story entirely were the markings on his chest and the little blue creature sitting in front of him.

"With the power of *Ragesong*," Joraus continued, "Klyle and Brael were able to quickly subdue the rival tribes of Kardonin, and bring them together under one rule. The two friends formed a mighty territory, built formidable cities and helped the people to prosper. Klyle trained an honor guard to defend the territory and Brael worked with recruits to police the land. For years there was peace and prosperity, but Klyle was unaware that Brael had begun to experiment with *Ragesong*.

"Something horrible happened and Brael snapped. When Klyle tried to bring him in, Brael fled." Joraus shuddered a little. "Klyle, fearing what might happen when Brael came back, turned to the symbols he had not yet deciphered. Through months of study he was able to make out one passage that pointed to a hidden manual. Klyle left the territory for more than a year and when he returned he looked like a wild man. The only things he brought back were his sword and a very old book.

"Klyle immediately isolated himself and committed to the study of the book. It told of a land that birthed certain people with the ability to completely control *Ragesong*. It spoke of a potion, which, if mixed correctly and given to the right individual, would awaken the ability within them. It did specify, however, that these individuals would need to discover and cultivate the ability themselves. The book explained that they would nurture the gift in their own world and harness the power in Fermicia.

"The book told of gems, which could be used to seek out those individuals, and it gave instructions on how to enter their land. The book described a portal, hidden in the very cave that Klyle had discovered, and it instructed that if the proper song was sung, a way would be opened. As soon as Klyle understood, he left again to travel the land, hunting the gems and the ingredients necessary to make the potion. These items were rare and he only found enough to make two small doses. After mixing the concoction, he carefully divided it into two vials, pairing a jewel with each one, and he sealed them away in his throne room."

Joraus flitted back into the air and towards Jake's closet as he continued talking. "Not many years after that, Brael returned to the territory with an army and attacked. The battles were fierce, but Klyle's army managed to drive them back. It was too late when we realized that the attacks were only diversionary. Somehow Brael managed to sneak his finest troops through the territory and to the borders of Klyle's capital city. His invasion was swift and brutal, and Klyle had only enough time to send Swyf and I to the portal before the city fell."

Joraus rummaged around on the top shelf of the closet until he fished out a small, leather pouch.

"Hold out your hands," he instructed.

Jake cupped his hands and Joraus dumped the contents of the pouch into them. There was a small jewel and an empty vial.

"Twelve years ago that stone pulsed with a golden light after I came through the portal. It led me straight to your house. When I got close to you, the pulsing stopped and the jewel shone so brightly that I couldn't look directly into it. It led me to you. As you lay sleeping in your crib, I gave you the potion."

"Wow," gasped Jake, his mouth hanging open in awe. "So, you've been here for twelve years?"

Joraus smiled. "Really, that's your next question? Not why me, or you seriously gave an unknown substance to a baby? You're a weird kid, Jake."

He picked the jewel and vial out of Jake's hands, and carefully replaced them in the pouch, which he hung around the boy's neck. "We are desperate. I've waited twelve years for you to be able to see me, and I am terrified to think of what might have happened to my home in my absence. Fermicia needs you."

CHAPTER 9:
RETURN TO FERMICIA

"I ... but... what do you...?" Jake started dumbly, but he was cut off by a knock on his door.

"Jake, time's up," came the muffled voice of his mom. "Turn it off and wash up for dinner."

"All right, Mom!" Jake called out, still watching Joraus. "I'll be right there."

"Don't take forever to save your game this time or I'll take away game time tomorrow," his mom added, walking away.

Joraus laughed. "You know that eventually she is going to figure out that most games let you just save immediately from the start menu, don't you?"

"Shut up," Jake said, standing up and walking over to the TV. He picked up the discarded game controller, and put it away. "I didn't even get a chance to play," he muttered to himself as he pulled his shirt over his head.

"Oh, come on, listening to me was better than any game!" Joraus argued.

"Says you," Jake retorted, picking up a case. "I was going to pl–"

"All right," Joraus interrupted. "I'll grant that you have some good games, but at least you can understand what I am saying. No text to read here."

The boy laughed. "Yeah, but your voice is even more annoying than Navi."

Joraus scowled. "Nothing is more annoying than Navi."

Jake laughed and grabbed the door handle. "I'll be back after dinner, and you can tell me why in the world you think I can save Fermicia."

"I am not kidding about this, Jake. I don't understand why you were chosen, but..." Joraus stopped and waved him towards the door. "Well, hurry and eat, and then we can finish talking. There is a lot more you need to know."

Jake shrugged and opened the door, shaking his head slowly as he walked out of the room.

As soon as Jake closed the door, Joraus pushed open the window and flew outside. Nala began to bark at him playfully, but he ignored her and soared up into the air. It was time to coordinate things with Swyf. He zoomed through the neighborhood, following the directions she had given him during the third-period band class.

Although it was still early in the evening, Joraus felt a sense of urgency. Things were delicate right now with Jake and he wanted to be back by the time the boy finished dinner. With the shock of discovering the *Ragesong* marks on his chest, not to mention seeing a blue fairy, Jake would definitely require some reassurances.

Lucky that Samantha was in the same school, he thought, as he flew over the rooftops. That meant he wouldn't have to take Jake back on his own. It was comforting to know that Swyf would be returning with him as well. When he arrived at the designated street, Joraus slowed enough to study the scene. The buildings seemed even older than the one Jake lived in, and not nearly as well cared for.

About halfway down the street, he found the house he was seeking. The numbers on the curb had faded, but he was able to read enough to know that he was at the right place. Studying the dwelling, he noticed that it was in desperate need of repair. The bricks were faded and some were crumbling, giving the house a pockmarked appearance. Shingles were missing on the roof and the fence was falling apart. Weeds grew from the badly cracked cement and the flowerbeds, and the grass looked as though it hadn't been cut in weeks.

Joraus circled the house and peered through the dirty windows for any sign of Swyf. The inside of the home did not offer much improvement on the outside. Dirty dishes sat in the kitchen sink, and papers were spread out all over the counter and table. The living room was stuffed full of trophies, pictures of league teams and other bowling paraphernalia. The furniture was dated and worn, and one couch gave the impression of 'sit on me at your own risk.' Joraus had always taken Jake's home for granted, but now he realized how lucky he had been.

Circling to a side window, he finally spotted them. Samantha was standing in the middle of a sparse bedroom, her saxophone dangling loosely from her neck, as she stared at Swyf in awe. The Changeling was talking fast, and Joraus felt sure she was having the same conversation with the small girl as he'd just finished with Jake. He rapped on the window and both individuals turned abruptly at the sound. Swyf gave him an impatient glare while Samantha just gawked, stupidly.

He tapped again and with an exaggerated sigh, Swyf pushed the window open. "We are in the middle of something, Joraus!" she growled as he flew inside.

"There are two of you?" Samantha asked, incredulously.

Swyf eyed him irritably before turning back to the girl. "Yes, this is Joraus. He came with me through the portal."

"How far into the explanation are you?" Joraus asked quietly. "I need to get back, but there are a few things we need to discuss first."

"This is very inconvenient," grumbled Swyf, before turning to the girl. "Sam, do you mind if I talk to him real quick? It will only take a second."

"Um, sure, I guess," said Samantha as she continued to stare at the pair of them.

After the two Changelings had flown back out the window, Swyf turned to Joraus. "What?" she asked, rather rudely in his opinion.

"It's good to see you, too," he protested lightly, but when she only glared, he gave up. "Were you planning on us all going back to Fermicia together?"

"Of course," Swyf said icily.

"Well, did you stop to think how we were going to coordinate that?"

"Why does it matter? I just figured that if you got there first you'd wait for me, and I'd do the same for you."

"Did you not think of the possibility of there being a time difference between the two worlds?" Joraus asked.

Swyf paused. "What do you mean?"

"I mean, what if time flows differently in Fermicia than here? What would happen if you and Samantha were to arrive first, and Jake and I didn't appear for a day or a month, or even a year, or vice versa? We don't know if the time difference between the two worlds is the same."

Swyf raised an eyebrow. "Hmm, that really is a good question. I'm surprised it came from you." She raised an eyebrow. "So what made you think of it?"

Joraus scowled. "I can come up with good ideas all on my own, thank you very much!" But then he blushed. "Though in this case, it was part of a story in a video game that Jake played once. It got me thinking about it."

"All on your own, my foot," said Swyf, laughing sardonically. "Anyway, so what do you suggest?"

"You still have the gem?"

"Of course."

"Well, at least you've managed that. Okay, what time is it?" Joraus asked.

"Let me find out," Swyf said before flitting back to the window. "Sam, what time is it?"

"Five seventeen," came the girl's muffled voice from inside.

"Thank you," Swyf replied, before returning to Joraus. "That is a satellite clock. Does Jake have one of those in his room?"

"Yes."

"Good, that should sync us up then. What time does Jake go to bed?"

"His mom tucks him in around 8:15, but it could be as late as 8:30," said Joraus.

"Okay, then I say we should do it at 8:45 on the dot. Can you have him convinced by then?"

Joraus nodded. "It shouldn't be a problem. I'll see you tonight." He suddenly grinned. "Back in Fermicia."

Swyf nodded, but did not return the smile. "Don't get your hopes up. Who knows how long Brael will have had to wreak havoc."

"Wow, you are such a buzz kill," he groaned, his grin fading. "Anyway, I'll see you at 8:45 at the portal."

Joraus flew off back the way he had come, the cool air helping him to shake off the gloom from Swyf's last statement. No matter what she said, in a few hours he would be home. The excitement started to bubble up again as he thought about it, and for a second he could almost taste the sweet open air of Fermicia.

"Okay, I'm ready," Jake said, entering his room and closing the door behind him. He looked around, but the little blue creature was nowhere to be found. "Joraus?" he called out softly, but there was no answer. "This isn't funny, Joraus. C'mon!"

When there was still no reply, Jake walked over to the mirror and lifted up his shirt. The markings were still there, so he was pretty sure that he hadn't imagined the conversation with the Changeling. He was just about to go back out into the hall and hunt for him when he felt a breeze come into the room. It ruffled the pages of an open strategy guide on his desk. Jake studied the open window, pretty sure that it had been closed when he left for dinner. *Did Joraus open it? Where is he?*

Moodily, Jake turned to his backpack. It was a cool red-and-black one that his mom had picked up for him earlier that week. She had been right in thinking they were the type that Junior

High kids wore, but a small part of him missed the old video-game character backpacks that he used in elementary school.

With a discontented sigh, he unzipped the biggest pocket and pulled out his flute case. It all seemed so weird, he thought, as he set up his music stand and prepared to practice. Faraway lands, blood-thirsty tribes and evil kings; it sounded like a story from a book or a video game. Jake put his flute together and tuned it by ear.

He quickly flipped through his music book to the current piece assigned by his mom and raised his flute to his lips. It was a piece from Bach and he really liked it. Although the notes were not that difficult, it was the hardest song he'd played so far. After his first time through the song, Jake paused for a second to catch his breath, and then he heard a high squeak behind him.

"Hey! Listen!"

Spinning around, he saw Joraus floating in the air behind him, grinning. "Bring back old memories?" he asked.

Jake pulled a face. "You *are* more annoying than Navi."

Joraus laughed. "Did you miss me?"

"I thought I'd gone crazy for a little bit. I had to look at my chest just to make sure."

"Sorry about that. I had a quick errand to run. Go ahead and continue pract—"

"I don't hear a flute!" Jake's mother called from the hallway.

"All right, Mom! Just a second, it's a hard piece. Give me a chance to breathe."

"She's quite the slave driver," Joraus remarked, peering over Jake's shoulder at the music. "It doesn't seem too hard to me. You have played faster stuff than that."

"Yeah, but Mom has me working on vibrato," Jake replied. "It takes a lot of wind on these slower songs." He put the flute to his lips and played through the piece again. When he finished, Joraus nodded approvingly.

"I see what you mean. Ouch," Joraus said, wincing a little. "Pretty song though." He flew to the bed and touched down on it. "Finish up, so we can talk."

Jake played for another hour, and then sat down on the corner of his bed to clean out the flute before putting it away.

"I never get tired of hearing you play," Joraus commented. "You've improved a lot over the last couple of years."

"Thanks," Jake answered, gently threading a cloth through the mouthpiece of the flute. "Did you want to tell me more about Fermicia?"

"Actually, no," Joraus said, shaking his head. "I think I've told you enough about it for now. I will, however, tell you where I went. Remember the other Changeling I mentioned earlier? Swyf? Well, she is also working with one of your kind. Klyle's original idea was that at least one of us would be able to bring someone back to Fermicia. That was why he sent both of us."

Joraus clapped his hands excitedly. "I saw Swyf earlier today at your Halloween school and discovered that she has a charge also. We needed to coordinate things, so that we will arrive at Fermicia at the same time."

"Wait a second," Jake interrupted, holding up his cleaning rod and pointing it at the Changeling. "What do you mean, we? I haven't agreed to go anywhere. I don't know anything about Fermicia or *Ragesong*! What do you expect me to be able to do?"

Joraus paused and stared Jake right in the eye for a long second, before replying softly, "Why, I expect you to learn, Jake. I didn't flee my home, leaving my king to die, and spend twelve years here so that you could tell me that you aren't going. I like to play around as much as the next Changeling, but I am not playing at all when I say that you have no idea of what I've had to go through to find you. My homeland is under the oppression of a wicked, evil man and my king ordered me here – to find you. We can argue about it if necessary, but you *will* be going with me to Fermicia."

Joraus relaxed a little at the expression of confused panic on Jake's face. "Relax, Jake," he said softly. "I am fully aware of what I am asking. I understand that you feel overwhelmed and completely unprepared. I wouldn't send you there alone. As fate would have it, you will have another human companion, not to mention two Changelings. Here I may look like a silly, fat fairy, but in Fermicia there are not many who would willingly cross me. You will be well protected, Jake, do not worry."

"What about my mom and dad? What do I tell them?" Jake asked in a small voice.

Joraus put a hand on his in sympathy. "We will leave them a note. It is the best that we can do. They will worry dreadfully, but it is better than disappearing on them without a trace. But let's not dwell on that," he said, clearing his throat. "Instead, let us talk about *Ragesong* for a minute. Do you remember what I told you about cultivating it here in the human world, so that it could be unleashed in Fermicia?"

Jake nodded as he resumed packing up his flute.

"Well, I have thought long and hard about this, and it seems to me that your abilities in *Ragesong* will be tied to your musical skills in this world. For years I pondered that passage in the book, but when I saw how quickly you took to the flute, I began to have my suspicions. When I met the other human who will be accompanying us, it only confirmed my belief."

"Who is the other person going with us?"

"I don't want to ruin any surprises," Joraus replied with a wink.

Jake stood up and tucked the flute back into his backpack. "Okay, so when I get to Fermicia, I'll be able to use *Ragesong*?"

"I don't think that's exactly how it works," Joraus responded slowly, considering the question. "The power has been awakened within you. That much is clear by the fact that you can see me. But, I think you will have to discover the power within yourself once you reach Fermicia."

"Oh," said Jake, disappointed. "So is there anything else you can tell me about *Ragesong*?"

"Not a lot. I am not trying to be deliberately secretive, Jake. From what I understand, it reacts differently in each person. Klyle was able to use it to increase his agility and reflexes in battle. Brael, before he lost control, used it to increase his strength. I am not sure how it will affect you, but I do know that it has already influenced you at least once in your life."

"When?" asked Jake.

"Well, for starters, you weren't drawn to the flute simply because of your mother; that was the work of *Ragesong*. I believe it was to help to prepare you for when you enter Fermicia. Remember, you will be at a distinct disadvantage, Jake. You will be facing warriors who have trained their entire lives to fight. I believe that *Ragesong* guided you to the flute in order to help balance that out. I don't want to say any more as yet, but I think that when we get there, you may be pleasantly surprised."

"How are we going to get there?" Jake asked.

"Ah, an excellent question. Do you remember the jewel I showed you?"

"Yeah, you said it guided you to me."

"That's right," Joraus replied, beaming. "Klyle called it a marker. I don't know exactly why it is called that, but I do know how it will help us to get back to Fermicia. I have been waiting a long time to use it." He paused and glanced up at Jake's clock.

When he saw that it read 7:47, he grinned. "Enough talk! It is nearly time. Why don't you write that note for your parents and I'll gather a few things. No use in going completely unprepared."

While Jake ripped a piece of paper out of his binder, Joraus flitted in and out of the room, making a pile of objects on the bed. A watch, one of dad's lighters and Jake's pocket knife were among the things he set out.

"Do you realize that you could sell this stuff in Fermicia and live like a king?" Joraus said with disgust as he examined the various items.

Jake was not listening. He had taken out his pen and was scrawling a short message on the paper. *Mom and Dad, please don't worry too much. I have had to leave, and I'm not sure when I will be back. Don't call the police. They will not be able to find me. I will return as soon as I can. I love you both, Jake.*

"Perfect," Joraus remarked, reading over his shoulder. "Short and sweet. Tuck it back in your binder until your mom tucks you in. I would get some jeans and one of your sturdy, long-sleeve shirts."

He pointed to the objects on the bed. "Put those in your jean pockets and hide them in your closet, then go and get ready for bed. Make sure to act tired, so your parents will not suspect anything."

Jake nodded silently, his emotions warring inside of him. He felt sick about abandoning his parents with just a vague note and scared stiff about leaving home. But at the same time, he couldn't deny the excitement he felt about the adventure that was about to take place. Fermicia sounded awesome and way better than any video game.

As he showered, Jake thought about everything that Joraus had told him. Did he really have *Ragesong* inside of him, just waiting to come out? How was he supposed to 'discover it within himself?' And how did Joraus expect him to fight against someone as powerful as Brael?

Questions plagued him as he brushed his teeth and went out to bid goodnight to his parents. He hugged them tighter than usual, and when his dad asked him if anything was wrong, he nearly broke. It was only the sight of Joraus floating silently at the entrance to the living room that stiffened his resolve. Jake told his dad that he was just tired and that it had been a long day. His dad laughed and agreed with him. Then his mom rose from her chair and walked Jake back to his bedroom.

Leaning against the door frame as he climbed into bed, she said, "Congratulations, sweetheart. I am so excited for you. You'll do great in advanced band." Approaching, she pulled the sheet up around him and kissed him on the forehead. Flicking off the light, she whispered, "Good night, Jake, sleep well," before closing the door softly.

"8:35," Joraus said tensely, after verifying that Jake's mom had gone. "We have ten minutes. Hurry and change, but do it quietly."

Jake slipped his pajamas off in the dark, and felt around in his closet for the jeans and shirt. After dressing, he felt in the pockets to make sure everything was still there. Then he pulled the note for his parents out of his binder and kissed it gently before setting it down softly at the foot of his bed.

"Are you ready?" Joraus asked.

Jake heard the excitement in the Changeling's voice. "I guess, but I'm pretty nervous," he answered.

"Of course you are," Joraus sympathized. "Everything will be fine. Now step over here and hold out your hand."

Jake did as instructed. Joraus gently set the gem in the center of Jake's palm, before laying his own tiny hand over the top, so they were both touching the stone. They paused there together and watched as the clock flashed 8:45pm. Joraus immediately began to sing, his high-pitched voice echoing around the room. For a second nothing happened, but then Jake felt the jewel grow hot in his hand. A wave of dizziness rushed over him and he felt as though he might faint. Closing his eyes to keep from throwing up, he waited for his head to stop spinning. It didn't take long for the dizziness to pass and when it did, Jake opened his eyes slowly.

Blinking in amazement, he saw that his room was gone. In its place was a dark, musty cave. The air felt thick and oppressive, and the thin shafts of moonlight entering from holes in the ceiling did not provide much light. Looking down, Jake could faintly see symbols carved into the stone. He heard running water and determined the source was a small spring, running along one of the side walls.

"Joraus?" Jake asked, glancing around uncertainly. The little blue fairy was nowhere to be seen. "Joraus, where are you?"

"Quiet, Jake," whispered a disembodied voice beside him. "There is someone right outside the cave."

CHAPTER 10:

TROUBLE AT THE PORTAL

J ake spun around to face the entrance, his ears straining for any sound, but all he could hear was the running water of the spring. He was surprised to feel the cave wall at his back, unaware that he had moved at all, and his hand that had been holding the small jewel was now empty. "Where are you?" he whispered into the darkness as he clutched at the wall.

"Don't worry, Jake," the voice replied, still low. "I am here, and I won't let anything happen to you. I need you to stay quiet though until I decide how to handle this."

The voice spoke to him familiarly, but it didn't sound anything like the high-pitched squeak Jake had come to associate with Joraus. After a tense minute of near silence, it cursed softly. "I hadn't planned for this. Where is Swyf? I would feel a lot better going out there if she were here."

Unexpectedly, Jake saw the air shimmer from within the circle of markings and he thought he heard a soft, feminine voice singing. As he squinted into the dark a small figure materialized out of nowhere with its hand outstretched.

"Swyf and Samantha," the deep voice whispered urgently. "Don't say anything. There is someone or something outside the cave."

Samantha? Oh, the saxophone girl! That's who the other person was that Joraus had talked about. Jake watched as she looked around curiously, probably searching for Swyf. "We can't see them," he whispered as he motioned for the girl to join him.

Samantha hesitantly walked towards him without saying anything and together they waited, listening. Jake could hear the two phantom voices whispering from somewhere in front of him, but he couldn't understand much of the conversation.

After what sounded like a hurried argument, Jake heard the female voice say quietly, "Fine, we'll do it your way, but don't take too long."

"Jake and Sam," she said, sounding as though she were right in front of them, "Joraus is going to take care of whatever is outside this cave. I am going to stay in here with the two of you. I need you to stay very quiet until he returns. You may hear some things, but don't be afraid. I am here."

When they both nodded, the voice continued, "Be careful, Joraus, this isn't the time to take chances. Just take care of things out there and get back in here."

There was a long, flat silence before Jake saw a strange shimmer and heard a faint skittering as a small animal of some kind ran across the stone floor. The moss hanging at the front of the cave moved slightly and all he could hear was the soft flow of the spring. Jake looked over at Samantha and tried for a reassuring smile, but he was afraid that it came out a little sickly.

The sudden scream of a mountain lion from outside the cave made him jump.

"Easy, Jake," Swyf whispered soothingly. "It's Joraus. He is taking care of whatever is out there."

Jake closed his eyes as he heard more screams and he felt a small hand take his to offer comfort. At the moment he was too afraid to be ashamed and he gripped it tightly as the night came alive with the cries of cat and men. He shuddered as he heard one man begin to shout orders, only to cut off quickly with a bloodcurdling yell. Soon only moans of pain filled the darkness, before they too were abruptly silenced.

Jake waited for what seemed like hours in the dreadful quiet before the hanging moss parted once more. He saw the outline of a large mountain lion briefly in the moonlight before it shimmered and was gone.

"All's clear for now, Swyf," boomed a deep voice. Suddenly it began to laugh, a rich timbre echoing around the small cave. "That was most invigorating. Oh, how I have missed this place!"

"You are sure it's safe to go out now?" Swyf's feminine voice asked acidly. "I'm so glad you are amused, Joraus. Perhaps we could take some time to introduce ourselves to our visitors now." The way she said it, Jake was sure it wasn't really a question.

"Of course, come on out," Joraus answered agreeably. "It is quite safe. There is even a warm fire that has been recently vacated. We can make our introductions there."

"I trust that you have already cleaned up?" Swyf asked archly. "The children certainly don't need to witness the after-effects of your 'fun' this soon upon arriving."

"Well," Joraus hedged, "I had hoped that you'd..."

"Yes," Swyf answered flatly, "go on."

"Nothing. Give me a few minutes," he grumbled, apparently giving up.

Jake watched as the moss was swept aside impatiently.

"Are you both okay?" Swyf asked as they waited. "I know what kind of a shock it is to jump from one world to another like that." Jake could hear a kind smile in her lilting voice. "Though, to be fair, at least you two are still human and didn't turn into some kind of blue fairy."

"I'm all right," Jake answered hoarsely, all at once realizing that he was still clutching Samantha's hand. He dropped it quickly, giving her an embarrassed grin.

The small girl flashed a shy smile of her own before ducking her head to study the ground. The gesture reminded Jake of their earlier meeting in the band room. He gave her a puzzled look, but before he could say anything, Joraus returned.

"You can bring them out now, Swyf," he called from the doorway, still sounding a little sullen. "Unless you want to come out and inspect things first?"

"That won't be necessary, thank you," Swyf answered, choosing to ignore his sarcasm. "Let's go, you two. We can talk by the warmth of the fire."

Jake followed Samantha across the dark cave and out through the hanging moss. The bright moonlight stung his eyes, which had grown accustomed to the dark, and he reached up to rub them with his knuckles. "Wow," he mumbled as he took in the sight in front of him.

It was just as Joraus had described. Tall pillars fanned out on either side of the cave opening in front of a giant stairway, carved into the mountain itself. All of the posts glowed white in the moonlight, and Jake stood still for a moment, simply admiring their cold perfection. As his gaze swept across the pillars, one gave off a muted, golden aura. Examining it closer, it felt as though he were seeing it through a pair of glasses with different colored lenses; it flickered back and forth between white and gold.

86

Curious, Jake stepped forward, noticing as he did so that Samantha was also approaching one of the tall columns. When he reached it, he tentatively lifted an arm to run his hand over the cold, hard stone. As soon as Jake's fingers connected with the pillar, it gave off a shower of golden sparks. Instinctively, he attempted to withdraw his hand, but he found that it was stuck fast to the stone. The column flashed back to a glowing white and a sudden light of the same golden hue as he'd seen earlier that evening on his chest began to trace an outline of his hand on the pillar.

Jake watched, mesmerized, as the golden lines connected and characters scrawled in a flowing script began to emerge from the white stone. The markings appeared to be the same as those upon his chest and the floor of the cave. As he studied the writing more closely, one set of characters jumped out at him. Without knowing how or why, he was sure that he knew what they meant and he whispered the word softly, "*Ragesong*."

Immediately, the golden light began to move up Jake's arms, disappearing under his shirt sleeves, and then his whole body felt transfused with it. He felt a joy so exquisite that it was almost painful and he heard an echoing song in his ears that drowned out all other sound. Abruptly, he felt as though a door somewhere inside him had burst open and he sagged forward against the pillar.

Glancing around, Jake saw that Samantha had her hand outstretched upon another column. He gingerly pushed himself upright and watched as she crumpled against it in a similar fashion. Looking back at the column in front of him, Jake noticed that it was now the same as all of the others. He put his hand back on it experimentally and the symbols returned. When he pulled his hand away, they vanished again.

"Jake, Sam!" Swyf called out. "Are you coming?"

Turning away from the tall, stone column, Jake strode towards the point where the stairs descended towards a forest. As he walked, he noticed dark puddles here and there on the ground, and a few dark smears over the stones. Averting his eyes quickly, he saw that at the edge of the tree line there was a campfire, its orange flames pushing at the surrounding darkness. Samantha joined him and together they walked down the stone stairs.

"Did your pillar glow golden too?" Jake asked as they descended, trying not to think about the dark puddles or the horrible streaks.

"No," she answered, "mine was silver, the same color as..." Her last words faded away.

Jake looked at her. "Do you have markings on your body too?" he asked quietly.

Samantha nodded. "On my chest, right bellow my collarbone. They just appeared tonight.

"Mine itched like crazy all afternoon," Jake remarked.

"Mine too."

"Did anything show up on the column you touched?" he asked, changing the subject.

"Yeah, but it was just a bunch of gibberish. The only word I could read was *Ragesong*."

Jake nodded. "That's how it was with me, weird, huh?"

They stopped talking as they approached the fire.

"It took the two of you long enough," Joraus grumbled as they sat down on two of the stumps of wood surrounding the flames. "What were you doing up there, touching the columns like that?"

"Could you please tell me why you are invisible now?" Jake asked. "It's pretty weird hearing you talk and not being able to see you."

"This is our natural form, Jake," Swyf replied. "Joraus, come and stand by me."

"But," he started to counter, but she interrupted him. "It is more important that they trust us right now. It will help with matters later on. Okay, Sam, go and sit by Jake."

Sam stood up and walked over to where Jake was sitting, so that together they were facing the fire and the direction of the voice.

"Now, both of you look into the fire," Swyf instructed. I want you to watch very closely."

Jake gazed into the orange flames, which immediately distorted, as though he were seeing them through a thin piece of glass. As he stared, he was able to gradually see an outline of where the fire distorted slightly. All at once he could see the form of a woman, outlined by the fire. It was like one of those Magic Eye pictures, Jake thought as he stared at Swyf, seeing her true form for the first time.

"Wow," whispered Samantha in amazement. "How cool is that?"

"I always thought so," Swyf said. "All right, Joraus, now you."

Jake watched as Swyf stepped out of the firelight and disappeared. He found it was easier to spot Joraus. He was taller and thicker, and more heavily muscled.

"Man, I see what you mean," Jake said, laughing. "It had to be hard being a fat fairy for twelve years if you normally look like this."

Joraus grunted sourly, "You have no idea."

Swyf chuckled and returned to stand next to her friend. "It is easier to see us in the daytime, but it can still be difficult. We are going to show you what else we can do. I don't want you to be alarmed. We will start with something familiar and nonthreatening." She turned her head to eye Joraus in silent warning, before continuing.

"There is something you need to know," she continued. "When we change form, we are limited on how we can communicate; meaning that we will still be able to understand you, but you won't understand us. Depending on what we change into, we may be able to nod our heads, but that is about it. Does that make sense?"

When both Jake and Sam nodded, Swyf took a breath, and Jake saw a shimmer before a small owl hovered in the air in front of him.

"Swyf? Is that really you?" Samantha couldn't help but ask.

The owl bobbed its head and then soared off into the night. It flew over the trees before circling back in front of the fire and shimmering away. It took Jake a few seconds to make out Swyf's feminine form again. "That was awesome," he cried out. "You can turn into any animal? What about you, Joraus?"

Instead of answering, Joraus shimmered.

"A warthog, seriously?" Jake exclaimed. "Out of all the cool animals you could've turned into, you chose a warthog?"

Joraus snuffled loudly, lowered his tusks at Jake and pawed at the ground.

"Okay, okay, I'm sorry. Calm down," Jake said, holding both of his hands in the air, peaceably.

Joraus shimmered again and the warthog was gone. "That was in honor of your school," he said with a smirk.

"So," Samantha asked quietly, "which animals do you each prefer? Do you have a favorite?"

"Of course we do," Swyf answered. "And you should both get to know them now. I love to fly, and while I can turn into any bird that I want, I've found myself rather attached to the forms of either a falcon or a hawk, depending on the circumstance. They are both quick and agile, not to mention beautiful."

"What circumstances?" Sam wondered.

"Well, if I need outright speed, evasion or to battle in the air, then nothing beats a falcon. However, if I am scouting or tracking, the hawk's wings are more suited to gliding, so it is easier to keep things in sight."

"Bah," Joraus spat in disgust. "Flying is useful on occasion to clear one's head, but there is nothing better than the feel of the earth pounding under your paws. You already saw me in my preferred form tonight. I like the grace and power of the mountain lion. He shimmered again and in his place was a large cat. It looked at them and bared its fangs before rending the night with a wild scream.

"Joraus?" Jake asked uncertainly. The cry of the great cat had unnerved him and he scooted back on his wooden seat involuntarily. It was the same cry he'd heard while waiting in the darkness of the cave.

"It's still him, Jake," Swyf soothed. "Though we may change form, our minds are still our own. We want you to get used to this now, because there may be times when we will have to change quickly. You need never fear, however, for we will never turn on you. Trust us and we will protect you, with our lives if need be. Now, it has been quite some time since we were last able to assume these forms. I want to stretch my wings and I am sure Joraus would like to run. We've been trapped in those fairy bodies for too long. Why don't you each take a little time to introduce yourselves while we stretch out the kinks? Don't worry, we will stay close."

She shimmered into a falcon and let out a piercing cry, which Joraus answered. She flapped her wings and darted away from the fire as Joraus bunched his legs beneath him and sprung into a run. Jake watched them fade into the night before turning back to his last companion.

CHAPTER 11:
TENSION

J ake glanced at Samantha, but she was not looking at him. She was staring into the flames as the firelight glinted off her red hair. The way the girl sat hunched up on the log gave her the appearance of being even smaller than she really was.

Well," Jake began awkwardly, "I guess I can understand why they'd want to stretch out for a bit, but there's nothing quite like being left all alone in the mountains in a new world."

"Honestly," Samantha muttered, still gazing into the fire.

"So, I guess you know my name is Jake. You're Samantha, huh?"

"Sam," she said shortly. "Don't call me Samantha."

"Okay, then, um, Sam. So, uh, how come you chose the saxophone?" he floundered, not knowing what to say.

"Really?" She turned from the fire to stare incredulously at him. The light of the flames danced in her deep green eyes, unsettling him a little. "That's all you want to talk about?" the girl demanded. "Nothing seems more important to you right now than band?"

"I don't know!" Jake retorted hotly, before calming himself. "Look, I don't know what I'm expected to do here anymore than you do. But, like it or not, we are going to be traveling together, so unless you can think of a better way to break the ice…"

Sam just stared at him until he turned away.

"I'm going to find some more firewood," Jake said with resignation.

"Fine," Sam muttered, turning back to gaze into the fire.

Jake shook his head and walked away, searching for any twigs and branches that could be used to fuel the flames. *What was her problem?* Jake felt angry as he studied the ground. Back in the cave, it had been Sam who reached out to give a comforting hand, so he didn't understand why she was acting like such a jerk now.

Jake pulled a small LED light out of one of his pockets. Good thing Joraus packed this, he thought to himself as he scanned the darkness. He spotted a big branch not far away and walked over to it. *You'd think I was the one who dragged her here.* Jake reached down to pick up the end of the branch before angrily breaking limbs off of it. The snapping sound echoed through the trees and he looked up quickly, afraid that the noise might have alerted something. When all he saw was darkness, he turned back to the task in hand.

Soon Jake had two armfuls of wood. Holding the LED light in his mouth, he walked back to the fire and dumped his load beside it. He was about to go back into the forest when a hand caught his arm. Glancing over his shoulder, he saw Sam behind him.

"I'm sorry, Jake," she said, and he was more than a little surprised to hear that she meant it.

He turned around to study her. Jake was not tall, but he was still a few inches taller than she was. "Sam," he said quietly, "I don't have any idea what to do here. I'm completely lost. I only met Joraus today, and he pretty much forced me to come. He somehow expects me to master this *Ragesong* power and defeat some boss-level bad guy with it, but I don't even know what *Ragesong* is. I'm terrified. Then I get here, and Joraus goes out and tears up a whole group of people I don't even know. Real people! It makes me sick."

Jake reached down, picked up a thin branch and started drawing on the ground with it. "Before today, all I wanted to do was play my flute, and video games and stuff, but now I'm expected to save a whole kingdom?! I get that you don't know me. I don't really know you either, but you're the only other thing that's real in this place. I have a couple of invisible protectors that can turn into animals and I have you."

He tossed down the stick and studied what he'd drawn in the dirt. To his surprise, it was the symbols he'd seen on the pillar, which formed the word *Ragesong*. "Does that make any sense?" he whispered.

Sam looked into his face and apparently saw something there that she liked, because she softened a little. "I get it, Jake. I'm scared too."

"You hide it well enough," he muttered, making her smile.

"Yeah, well, I've had lots of practice. Anyway, do you think we could sit down and start that introduction thing over again?"

Jake nodded gratefully and moved to sit in front of the fire when he heard Swyf's shrill cry. She swooped in from the night before shimmering into nothingness. "Run!" she screamed, grabbing them each by the arm and pulling them into the darkness of the forest.

Jake stumbled along behind her, trying to pull his arm back, but her grip was like iron. They crashed through the brush, not following any trail. Jake saw Joraus in his mountain lion form darting through the trees in front of them. Suddenly, the big cat pulled up and screamed its bestial cry. Swyf stopped, letting go of her companion's arms, and Jake massaged the place where she had gripped him.

"We are surrounded," Swyf whispered to them urgently. "Joraus and I are going to open up a path through them. I want you to run as fast as you can. Don't stop until one of us meets up with you. Stay behind us until we attack and then run. We will join you as quickly as we can."

Swyf shimmered into the form of a great bear and roared. Joraus joined her, and together they charged into the darkness ahead. Jake and Sam ran after them, keeping some space between themselves and the dreadful creatures. Out of the night, a group of men shrouded in dark clothing ran at them wordlessly with their swords raised.

Swyf barreled into them, swinging her massive paws and growling viciously. Joraus protected her flanks, clawing and biting anyone who tried to attack her from the side. Screams of pain and agony mixed with the wild cries of the animals in a horrible cacophony of sound.

As soon as all of the warriors were engaged in fighting the ferocious beasts, Jake grabbed Sam's hand and charged forwards. He crashed through bushes and thickets, ignoring the stabbing pain of sharp sticks and thorns as he ran.

"Jake," Sam gasped after about ten minutes had passed, "I have to slow down or I'm going to throw up."

Jake nodded, breathing heavily. While he could run further, he understood her fatigue. They slowed to a trot and continued through the trees. A crashing in the brush behind them made Jake spin around to see one of the dark-clad warriors break through a thicket. He was covered in blood and while one arm hung uselessly at his side, the other held a curved sword. When he saw them, the man gave an evil grin and started forward.

Jake scanned the dark forest floor frantically and spotted a thick branch near his feet. He reached down and picked it up before brandishing it in front of him awkwardly.

"Go!" he yelled at Sam, shoving her behind him and setting his feet apart. "Just like a video game," he whispered as he waited, holding his makeshift weapon in front of him.

The warrior studied him appraisingly before advancing. The evil man barked a laugh before swinging his sword viciously. Jake lifted his branch in an attempt to block the strike, but the power of the man's blow knocked the log out of his trembling hands. In desperation he tried to grab at the man's sword hand, but collapsed as a heavy boot caught him in the ribs. Jake gasped, clutching at his side while looking with horror into cold, pitiless eyes.

The soldier raised his wicked, curved blade over his head, but before he was able to carry through with the killing blow, something hit him in the middle of his forehead. His eyes glazed over instantly and he crumpled, the weapon falling weakly from his grip. Jake rolled over to see Sam standing behind him, getting ready to throw something hidden in her hand. Her eyes seemed to flash silver as she slowly dropped the object and shook her head as though to clear it.

"Jake!" she screamed as though coming out of a trance. "Are you okay? Did he hurt you?" she asked, rushing over. Reaching down, she tried to pull him to his feet.

Jake winced and waved her off. "He kicked me in the ribs. I don't think he broke anything, but, man, that really hurt!" He gingerly got to his feet and rubbed his side. "We need to keep going. Swyf said not to stop until one of them caught up with us. Are you okay?"

"Something happened," Sam said in wonder, almost as if he was not there. "I picked up that rock, but I didn't know what to do with it. I was terrified. I mean, that guy was huge! Then everything slowed down around me and I wasn't afraid anymore. When I threw the rock, I knew I couldn't miss. I know it sounds impossible, but I could have thrown fifty more and each one would've landed right where I aimed."

Sam glanced down at the fallen soldier, who had blood running down his face from where the rock had struck him. "Jake," she added, horrified, "I can't throw that hard. I mean, I thought I might just distract him a little, you know? Give you a chance to roll away or something, but..." She looked at Jake quizzically, but he had no answers.

"It was *Ragesong*," Joraus's deep voice announced.

Jake and Sam both glanced up to see his faded outline approach.

"That is how it works," Joraus continued as he stopped in front of them and peered down at Jake. "I explained to you earlier, remember?"

"Yeah," Jake said slowly, "But..."

"We can talk about this more later," interjected Joraus. "Let's go. We need to get out of this mountain range."

"What about him?" Sam asked, pointing to the man a few steps away.

"He'll be taken care of. We need to escape this area before more soldiers find us."

Joraus took the lead and the children followed him to an old game trail. "Follow this and do not deviate from the path. I will be right back."

The Changeling became a mountain lion again and headed back the way they had come. When the big cat caught up with them a couple of minutes later, something dark stained his muzzle and Jake had to fight down the urge to be sick. He knew that the soldier had been 'taken care of.'

They followed the trampled grass until it ended at another small mountain spring. Joraus stopped and dipped his head toward the water, his tongue flicking in and out as he drank. The children went a little further upstream and knelt at the edge of the running water. Jake cupped his hands eagerly. In all the excitement, he hadn't realized how dry his throat was. The cold mountain water burned as it went down, but he eagerly reached for more.

He glanced over at Sam and saw that she hadn't even bothered to cup her hands; she had simply put her face into the water and was slurping noisily. Thinking what a brilliant idea it was, Jake followed her lead and drank until he felt he might burst. Finally, with a contented sigh, he stood and wiped his mouth. Sam looked up at him and grinned. She took one more drink before rinsing her face, after which she examined her reflection critically in the water.

"What's wrong?" Jake asked.

"I dunno," Sam replied. "I just wanted to see how bad I look, but what difference does it make?"

Jake didn't think she looked bad at all, but he heard a touch of the resentment he'd experienced when they had first talked by the fire, so he quickly changed the subject. "Are you excited to play in the advanced band?" he asked cautiously.

"Yeah, I guess so. I'd rather play in a jazz band, but they don't have any of those until high school."

Joraus interrupted with a low growl to get their attention, before motioning with his paw for them to follow him. They started down a new trail that followed the stream and when Jake saw that it was wide enough for two, he sped up to walk beside Sam.

"So, the song you played yesterday in band was pretty awesome. What did Ms. Gladwell call it, in the… something?"

"Mood," Sam answered. "It's called 'In the Mood.' An old song by a guy named Glenn Miller. It has been one of my favorites since the first time I heard it as a little girl. I had to practice for months to learn it. I taped it off the radio, and then just played it over and over again."

"That's pretty sweet, the way you learned to play. I can't imagine just learning from listening to the radio and YouTube."

"You could do it," she said, looking at him. "I heard you play. You were really good. What was that song? Ms. Gladwell and the class seemed to really like it."

Jake grinned. "Really? You didn't recognize the game?"

Sam frowned at him. "I didn't even know that it was a game until I heard Ms. Gladwell. It sounds boring."

"Boring? It's the best series ever!" Jake exclaimed, huffing out an exasperated breath. "Anyway, when I told my mom that I was worried about playing the flute in front of other guys, she suggested I learn a song that was cool enough to make them forget what instrument I was playing it on."

"Why do you care what other people think?" Sam asked, studying him out of the corner of her eye. "You are really good. It shouldn't matter what they think about you."

"Yeah, but, I…" Jake floundered before glancing at her. "I, uh, don't really know. I just didn't want people to laugh at me, I guess."

The sky started to lighten as the two of them talked, and their conversation helped to keep weariness at bay. Eventually, the stream took them out of the forest and Joraus led them to the start of yet another trail, which zigzagged down the mountainside. As they walked, Jake glanced up to see a hawk circling above them. With a relieved smile, he pointed out the majestic bird.

Sam looked up and nodded. "Must be nice," she said, "being able to change into an animal any time you want, not to mention being invisible."

"True enough," Jake answered, speculatively. "I bet it was hard for them to be in our world for so many years. Joraus said they couldn't change while they were there."

"Really? I didn't know that. Swyf never told me."

"Yeah, he said he tried to change one time, but it didn't work. I think he was a little upset about it. He kinda laid into me when I told him I wasn't sure about coming here. Put me through a major guilt trip."

"I was excited to come," Sam said softly. "Anything to get away from home for a bit." She seemed somber for a moment, but then brightened, adding, "This wasn't quite what I expected though. That pillar thing was definitely weird. Did yours have writing on it too? What color was it?"

"Gold and, yeah, there was a lot of stuff written on it. I couldn't understand any of it though. It all looked like gibberish, like you said. I could only read the one word. It said *Ragesong*, just like yours. The weirdest thing," he added, "was how it felt. I dunno, almost like something burst open inside of me."

"I felt that, too," Sam mused. "It made me feel really happy. Then all of a sudden something just opened up. It was pretty weird."

"What was it like?" Jake asked, thinking of the silver light that had flashed in Sam's eyes. "The *Ragesong* thing, I mean. I kept expecting something to happen as I stood there holding the branch in front of that guy. Like I would turn into a ninja or something, but all I felt was scared. That stuff always seems so easy in the movies. When that guy came at me with his sword I froze. It felt like I was barely able to move my arms." He shook his head ruefully. "Man, the way he knocked that branch out of my grip, my hands hurt almost as bad as my side."

As soon as he finished saying it, Jake wished he hadn't. Thinking about his side made it ache again, and he had to force himself not to grab at it in front of Sam. The girl was not looking at him, however. Instead she appeared to be studying the mountainside.

"It was really strange," she said, distractedly. "At first I felt scared, same as you. When I saw that man knock the stick out of your hand and kick you, I just reached down for whatever I could find. As soon as the rock was in my hand…" She paused, and walked in silence for a minute.

Jake did not press her, but waited patiently for her to continue.

"All the fear just went away," she continued. "The rock felt, I don't know, right somehow, like it fitted in my hand. As soon as I stood up, everything felt different. The night did not feel as dark and the man wasn't scary at all. It took forever for him to lift his sword over his head and when I wound back to throw the rock, I knew exactly where it would hit; kinda like there was a huge target right in the middle of his forehead." She gazed at

Jake intently. "I couldn't have missed. I picked up a second rock just in case, but I knew that I wouldn't need it."

"It was like your eyes flashed silver," Jake remarked, avoiding her gaze. "Right before you shook your head and snapped out of it, they flashed."

"Silver is the color of the rock Swyf gave me back at home," Sam said thoughtfully. "It is also the color of the marks on my chest, and what appeared on that pillar."

"That's cool," Jake said enthusiastically. "You should get a silver-colored saxophone!"

They both laughed and Jake realized that he wasn't afraid any more. The combination of talking to Sam and the rising sun had quieted his fears. Looking around, he was surprised to see that they were nearly out of the mountain. He stepped to the edge of the path and peered down through the trees. Two switchbacks below, he spied a huge meadow with tall, green grass and a lot of flowers.

"Wow," Sam sighed, gazing longingly over his shoulder and into the meadow below.

"You're such a girl," Jake said, pulling a face at her. "Maybe I could talk Joraus into turning into a goat. Then he could eat some of those flowers."

"Don't you dare!" Sam threatened, still gazing down at the beautiful scenery.

They followed Joraus down the rest of the mountain and out into the sun-drenched field. Jake looked up in the sky for Swyf, but he could not see her. He wasn't too alarmed by the fact, knowing that if there was trouble, she would warn them. Jake slowed to enjoy the walk, his feet grateful to be off the stony dirt path. The grass felt soft under his shoes and he was contemplating removing them altogether when a sparrow burst into sight, aiming straight for Joraus.

Right before it reached the Changeling, it shimmered, changing into a dark panther that plowed into the mountain lion, knocking him over. Jake and Sam gaped in surprise as they watched Joraus roll in the grass before regaining his feet. He rushed the panther, changing into a large ape just in time to wrap his huge arms around the black cat and pick it up in a bear hug. In turn the panther shimmered into a tiny, flying squirrel and bit the big ape on one of its meaty fingers. Joraus roared in pain and shook his hand, flinging the creature high into the air.

The squirrel spread its arms and legs to glide towards the ground. Joraus quickly changed into a bat and flew over the top of the animal, while shimmering again into a pig. The two Changelings plummeted towards the grass, the squirrel still on the underside. Just before they landed, Jake saw a faint shimmer underneath the fat pig. A kangaroo landed on its back and with a mighty heave of its feet, it sent Joraus sailing through the air with a surprised squeal.

Jake and Sam started to laugh as the pig passed over their heads before landing hard in the grass.

"Man!" Jake wheezed, slapping his knee. "Where is a 'if pigs could fly' line when you need it?"

Sam was clutching at her stomach as she chortled. When Jake heard her snort, it made him laugh even harder. With each of them feeding off the amusement of the other, it was some time before they regained their composure. When they finally stood up, wiping tears from their eyes, Joraus and Swyf were waiting in front of them. In the sunlight, Jake could see them easier. With the Changelings so close, he could even see the big smile on Swyf's face and Joraus' dark scowl.

"She cheated," he growled, glaring at Jake and Sam darkly.

"Don't pretend you didn't spend as much time with Google as I did! Just because they aren't in this world," she retorted.

"Bah, I don't want to hear it. I had you dead to rights. Who thinks of a stupid kangaroo?" Joraus complained. He turned on the children. "Are you two ready to go yet?"

When the question only made them start giggling again, he spun around and marched across the meadow, the shreds of his tattered dignity trailing behind him.

CHAPTER 12:
THE COVE

"Do we have any kind of plan?" Jake asked once Joraus had cooled off.

Their small group was now walking along a coastline. The path they were following hugged a steep overhang that cut off abruptly, reminding Jake unpleasantly of those cliff-jumping YouTube videos. He wasn't particularly afraid of heights, but after a quick glance over the edge, he was happy to keep his distance.

"Yes," the bigger Changeling called out from up ahead. "We are going to follow the coast for about fifteen more miles. There is a secluded cove there where we can make a shelter. Swyf and I need to finish explaining things, and then we should decide what to do next."

Jake studied the shape of the being in front of him. Even though the Fermician Joraus was tougher and more intimidating, he found himself missing the earlier version – the fat, blue fairy he'd first met. The old Joraus liked to joke around; this new one seemed a lot more serious. Jake figured it had something to do with the Changeling coming home. He supposed that he'd probably feel the same way if he had to stay away for twelve years. On the spot he decided it was time to bring back a little of the old Joraus.

"Hey, Joraus!" he called out. "My legs are tired. What are the chances of you turning into a horse, so I could ride for a while?"

The Changeling turned to stare at him incredulously, but when Jake grinned impudently, he gave a rueful smile and shook his head. "Don't push your luck, kid," he rumbled. "If I have to walk, so do you."

"Do you have any idea how cool you guys would be as video-game characters?" Jake asked, still trying to lighten the mood. When they had spoken the night before, it had sounded like Joraus was interested in video games. "Man, imagine the things you could do with a Changeling for a companion in any of my games? That would be awesome."

"That would be pretty cool," Joraus agreed with a wink. "Although, it would be even cooler if you played the Changeling, but that would make all your games too easy, and let's be honest, they are pretty simple already."

"What's that supposed to mean?" Jake asked, continuing to nettle him.

"C'mon, Jake, you know they hold your hand and baby you! Infinite lives, saving anywhere you want, and starting right back where you left off after you die? Give me a break. Now, take the games your dad used to play when you were small, they were challenging. When you died in those, you had to start all over again from the beginning."

Jake smiled inwardly as they continued to argue about video games. The Changeling was finally showing a little bit of the fun he had seen the previous night in his room. *Was it really just last night? It feels like ages ago.*

"Boys are so boring," Sam said, after listening to them argue for an hour or so. "Who cares about video games right now?"

Joraus and Jake both stopped talking, and gaped at her, disbelievingly.

"Seriously?" asked Jake.

"Have you even played one?" Joraus inquired.

Sam just gave them an imperious stare. Jake and Joraus were reduced to splutters as they gawked at her, dumbfounded.

"Look around, Jake," she continued, ignoring their goggling. "How could any video game compare to this? Life is so much better than a game!"

"You sound like my mom," Jake muttered with reproach.

"It's true, you do sound like his mom," Joraus agreed.

Jake was quiet for a minute, before admitting a bit begrudgingly, "Although I do have to admit that this place is pretty cool, Joraus."

"I guess," Joraus answered, somewhat less enthusiastically. "So was that last *Final Fantasy* game you played."

"When I stayed at Korey's? You were there?" Jake asked.

"I was always there, Jake," Joraus answered, grinning.

They continued on, mile after uneventful mile. Jake felt a blister forming on one of his toes and stopped briefly to remove his shoe. A small stone fell out and Jake regretted not taking the time to remove it when he'd first felt it there hours ago. It was late afternoon by the time Joraus led the group down through a fissure in the cliff, which emptied into a small, protected cove.

As tired as he was, Jake couldn't help but appreciate the beauty of the place. A small grove of trees grew in the shelter of the cliff and a freshwater spring filtered through them, winding its way out to sea. The beach was made of golden sand, sparkling in the setting sun, while surf lapped gently against the shore, and the cove seemed like a picture right out of a calendar.

"I'm starving," Sam announced abruptly. "Does anybody have anything to eat?"

"Let's get settled in first," Swyf said. "Then I will catch something."

"Well, one of us will," Joraus challenged.

She just gave him a condescending smile before motioning Sam to follow her towards the water.

Jake grinned at Joraus. "Do you guys always compete like this?"

"We're Changelings," he answered, looking at Jake as though that should explain everything.

"Joraus, the only things I know about Changelings are the bits you've told me," Jake reminded him.

"Ah, yes, that is true, I suppose. Well, we are pretty competitive by nature. I grew up with Swyf, and we've been trying to best each other ever since we were small."

"Are there lots of Changelings in Fermicia?" Jake asked, eager to learn more.

"Not anymore."

"What happened?"

When Joraus hesitated, Jake wondered if he had asked the wrong question. He followed the big Changeling as he walked towards the grove. After a time, Joraus spoke. "We were a very secretive and close-knit race. We had a small village in a territory much further south from here, called Brucheiden."

He stepped carefully through the trees as he explained. "There is an isolated forest there, and we lived deep within its protecting graces. Each Changeling is born with a different degree of mastery over their gift and the majority of them have to be very cautious when they change into an animal.

"For most of us, when we take the form of a creature, those thoughts and instincts start to override our own. The more aggressive the animal, the more quickly our minds can be overridden by its brute instincts. It was not unheard of for a Changeling to disappear from the village forever. Not long after such disappearances, we would receive reports of strange beasts in the forest attacking animals or lone travelers.

"We would do nothing to those who lost their minds to the transformations unless they attacked a village directly. They were our family, after all, even if what had made them so was now gone. Their aggression also helped to make people fear the forest, and that gave us an extra level of security and protection."

Joraus stopped before a fallen tree and began to strip off the bark, motioning for Jake to help him. He continued, "When Swyf and I were born, we were considered to be freaks among our kind. For some reason, when we changed, no matter what we changed into, our minds were not affected. We always had full control over our thoughts. We were shunned by other children our age, and our parents only provided the basic necessities for living. At first we avoided each other, convinced by our kin that there was indeed something wrong with us. But, eventually, when we realized that no matter what we did, we would be rejected by other Changelings, we became friends.

"Our kind competed in every task. Cooking, hunting, running, it was all a contest. Whenever Swyf or I would try to challenge anyone, however, we were refused or chased off. It was Swyf who came up with the game you saw us playing earlier. We would sneak off into the surrounding woods and try to think up different ways to best each other, without causing serious damage. At first it was just a fun diversion, but eventually we came to see how much it helped us to increase our gift."

Standing up, Joraus picked up the pile of bark he'd stripped from the dead tree and turned to exit the grove. "For you to understand completely, I should probably explain how my gift works," he added. "When I want to change into an animal, I form the image of what I want to be in my mind, and then I force myself into it."

"That doesn't sound too hard," Jake remarked, following him back onto the beach.

Joraus shook his head. "Not just the way the animal appears on the outside, Jake. I have to form everything in my mind, from the inside out; the heart, lungs, muscles, bones, brain, everything. Missing something out could be anywhere from uncomfortable to deadly. Take my mountain lion shape, for example. If I changed and forgot my claws, it would be very difficult to run and hunt, but I could still breathe and think. But imagine if I forgot the heart or didn't picture the brain correctly? See what I mean?"

"Yeah, I guess so," Jake answered slowly. "But how did you figure out all these different animals if you have to know all of that stuff?"

"Books and experimentation," Joraus replied. "My village had tons of books and scrolls outlining the anatomy of different creatures. I studied them endlessly with Swyf. Our contests in the woods forced our minds to think fast and overcome the inherent risk of forgetting something. Eventually, it just became second nature."

"So that was what Swyf was doing in the meadow, playing a game?" Jake asked.

"She was always fond of games. I can't believe I let her win as a kangaroo," Joraus muttered. "I thought I had her."

"Why in the world did you choose a pig?"

"I was trying to embarrass her. Pretty dumb on my part." He burst out laughing. "I bet I did look pretty ridiculous, flying through the air like that."

"Still one of the coolest fights I've ever seen though," Jake said, enviously. "An ape wrestling a panther? Man, you can't make that stuff up. So why do you always pick such normal animals? I mean, I haven't seen you pick any weird Fermicia-like animals yet."

Joraus smiled. "Because the animals that seem normal to you are rare and exotic here, in Fermicia — those were the animals that Swyf and I were drawn to."

They continued to talk as Joraus led Jake back into the grove, and instructed him to hunt for dead branches and sticks. It was strange for him to glance up to where Joraus should be, only to see a bundle of sticks floating in midair. It still took him a couple of seconds to focus on the Changeling's outline, though the moment he saw it, he could instantly see the full form. Jake shook his head and returned to stick gathering. *I wonder how much weirder things are going to get around here?*

When Joraus was satisfied with the piles of branches on the sand, he showed Jake how to separate the bark into stringy pieces, so that it could be used as kindling to start a fire. They leaned a bunch of smaller twigs against each other, like a teepee, over the bark. When Joraus was content, Jake pulled out his dad's lighter and flicked at it until a small flame rose from the tip. He held it against the bark and it began to smoke.

Jake angled his head away, and watched as the small flame transferred to the thin, stringy wood and began to grow. The kindling crackled as it burned and Jake looked on in pride as the fire grew, spreading to the bigger twigs surrounding it.

When they were certain that the fire would stay lit, they strolled over to the beach where Sam sat, gazing out over the endless waves. The late sunset glinted dully off of something sitting next to her, marking Swyf's location. They stopped talking as the guys approached and Jake noticed two fat fish lying on the sand in front of them.

"How did you catch those?" he asked.

"With my bare hands," Sam answered with a mocking smile.

"Really?!" he gasped.

"No! Geez, Jake, Swyf caught them." She laughed at his sudden scowl and pointed back over her shoulder. "You started a nice fire."

"Thanks," he answered dryly.

A slow breeze stirred Sam's hair, and Jake snuck a closer peek at her while she studied the sea. He didn't know where her earlier comments about not looking good stemmed from, but sitting there in the fading sunlight she was extremely pretty. Jake was a little surprised at his thoughts. He had never really thought about girls like this before, but he couldn't deny that this one was lovely. Her delicate facial features fitted her heart-shaped face perfectly and her deep green eyes shone with intelligence. As if she could feel his eyes on her, Sam turned her head to look at Jake. He blushed and hurriedly glanced away. "I'm gonna go clean up," he said, feeling embarrassed.

"I'm not stopping you," she answered playfully. "Hey, Joraus, Swyf said you were going to clean the fish."

"She said what?" Joraus demanded.

"I said that girls shouldn't have to clean fish," Swyf replied with a smile. "We caught them, so you clean them up. C'mon Sam, let's go warm up by the fire." They rose and started walking toward the winking flames of the campfire.

"So now you're a girl?" Joraus called after their retreating forms, but he was only answered by the fading sound of laughter.

"Swyf has picked up some bad habits," he grumbled to Jake. "She spent too long in your world. Here, hand me your pocket knife."

Jake reached into his jeans and pulled out the knife he'd received for his birthday the previous year, and flipped it to Joraus.

"Last time I checked, you were a boy too," the Changeling said. "At least that's what I gathered when I saw you watching Sam."

"I was not!" Jake exclaimed, mortified that he'd been caught.

Joraus laughed. "Don't worry Jake, she's a cutie. Your secret is safe with me. Besides, I've got my eye on the other one, so who am I to say anything? Now get over here and watch me gut the first, and then you can do the second."

"Really?" Jake asked, still embarrassed. "You like Swyf?"

"Are you kidding? She is attractive, funny, smart and strong. What else could I possibly want? Not to mention she's the only one of my species left," Joraus added as he bent over the larger of the two fish.

"I'd leave that last one off when you tell her," said Jake as he watched his companion neatly slice through the thick scales.

"I'm not ready to say anything yet," Joraus replied. "Before yesterday, I hadn't seen her for twelve years. Changelings are not quite as bold as humans in this particular area. I need to take some time to get to know her again first."

When Joraus finished, he pulled out the guts of the fish and flung them back into the sea. He handed Jake the knife and walked him through the process. When they were done, they walked to the edge of the water. Jake was just going to rinse his face, but he suddenly felt himself being lifted off his feet and thrown bodily into the cold sea. He came up spluttering, but Joraus was nowhere to be seen.

Jake went to put his feet down and was surprised when they didn't touch anything. *It must be a pretty steep drop-off.* He scanned the beach, but could not find the outline of the Changeling anywhere. Spinning around to look at the sea, he found himself staring into the gaping mouth of a huge shark. He scrambled backwards, shouting in terror as the large teeth chomped together, right in the spot where he'd been seconds before. The shark shimmered away and Jake saw water running off Joraus's transparent body.

"Not cool, man, you scared the crap out of me!" Jake yelled angrily over the Changeling's deep, rumbling laugh.

"That's for laughing at me earlier when I was a pig!" Joraus wheezed. "By Brael's teeth, Jake, you should've seen your face!"

"This isn't over," Jake threatened as he side-stroked to a place that he could touch. Climbing out of the sea, and still ignoring Joraus's deep laughter, he stalked back to the campfire. With water streaming off him, he fell onto the sand.

CHAPTER 13:

THE SKIDIPPY PLAIN

Jake rubbed his swollen stomach and tried to reposition himself on the sand. He'd eaten too much food way too quickly and his stomach was protesting. He had always had a problem with eating too fast, especially when he was hungry, and this was usually the result. Sam sat across from him, finishing her meal.

While he had attacked the cooked fish with his hands, Sam had borrowed his knife and used it to slice hers into more manageable bites. When she finally finished eating, she walked over to the stream and cleaned the knife, her face and her hands in the cool water. When she was done, she handed him the knife and Jake tucked it back in his pocket.

"Thanks," she said simply as she returned to her seat in the sand.

"Don't mention it."

Joraus cleared his throat. "Well, I guess now is the time that we decide where we go from here."

"Wait," Jake interrupted, "I thought you said you'd explain *Ragesong* some more. I have questions."

"Well, I…" Joraus began, but both Jake and Sam started grilling him at the same time.

"How come I didn't feel it?"

"How long does it last?"

"What happens if I can't do it?"

"Can I turn it on whenever I want?"

"What was the deal with the pillars?"

"What do the colors mean?"

"Okay, okay!" Joraus yelled, stemming the flood of questions. "Look, to be honest, ah, well, hmm."

Swyf laughed. "What Joraus is so eloquently trying to say is that we don't know. Actually, we understand very little of how *Ragesong* works. After what happened with Brael, Klyle kept the secrets of *Ragesong* to himself. He didn't share them with anyone, not even us. He told us enough that we would be able to give you a brief description, but no more than that. Klyle said it was too dangerous to tell you too much before you were ready. That was what led to Brael's downfall." She studied the other Changeling inquiringly. "How did he word it, Joraus?"

"Knowledge without understanding."

"Yes, that's right. Klyle basically meant that if you learn too much of a thing too quickly, then it can either limit your understanding or cause you to overreach. He wanted you to know the basics of what *Ragesong* could offer, but then figure out for yourself what more you could do with it. Does that make sense?" asked Swyf.

"Yeah," Jake said slowly, "I guess so. Kinda like if you were playing an open-world game and someone told you exactly what to do. You'd miss half of the game because you didn't experiment and figure it out yourself."

"Nice analogy, Jake," Joraus started to congratulate him.

Sam interrupted. "Seriously, are you going to bring everything back to video games? Didn't you ever do anything else? Geez, Jake, you are such a geek."

"I was just trying to make sure I understood," Jake said, defensively.

"Anyway," Swyf continued, as Sam opened her mouth to say something else. "What we really need to do is figure out where to go from here. By now Brael is certain to know that we have come through the portal, and we need to move quickly if we want to avoid capture. The traitor has many different kinds of minions at his disposal and right now we are very vulnerable. Joraus and I offer a bit of protection, but even with us you are both in great danger."

She looked over at Joraus speculatively. "What we really need to do is arm them and, if at all possible, give them time to train. That would also give us a chance to scout around and see if we can't learn a little about how things are now."

"Not bad," Joraus mused. "We don't even know how long we've been gone. We were in the human world for twelve years, but there is no telling how much time has passed here." He turned to study Jake and Sam. "Not long after Klyle returned from his journey to find the potion ingredients and the stones, he told us about a hidden vault. If we cross the eastern end of the Skidippy, it should not take us more than two days to get there."

"What's in the vault?" Sam asked at the same time as Jake said, "What's the Skidippy?"

"It is a weapon vault," Joraus answered. He walked over to pick up a stick from the pile he and Jake had made before scratching something in the sand. "Let me give you a quick Fermician geography lesson. The Kardonin territory lies in the northeastern part of Fermicia. The territory has many towns and cities, but Klyle's castle is located here," he said, stabbing a point on the makeshift map, "in the city of Foldona. That's where he ruled until Brael invaded. We are here," he added, pointing to a spot to the northeast of Foldona. The portal we came through was on the eastern side of the Mountains of Kah."

He made another mark in the sand. "The weapon vault is located here. It lies at the edge of the Skidippy plain and the Gijora Forest. The Skidippy is a large plain that makes up the central part of the territory. It is not far from here, actually. The road we need to take is occasionally patrolled, but I think I can get us there without too much trouble."

Joraus looked up proudly from his drawing to catch Jake mid-yawn. Sam was rubbing her eyes sleepily. He sighed before continuing, "Tomorrow is going to mark a long journey. It is too dangerous to stop for extended periods on the Skidippy, even for seasoned warriors. We are going to have to walk from tomorrow through the next day. That means all of tomorrow night. We will take short breaks, but that is about all we'll be able to afford. It is imperative that you get a good night's sleep. Swyf and I will split the watch tonight, but from thereon we will each take a fourth."

He peered over at Swyf. "Do you want first or second?"

"First," she said without missing a beat.

Joraus nodded. "All right, let's go to sleep. Swyf will keep the fire going." He threw a couple of the biggest branches on before nestling down into the sand.

Jake had not really thought about this part of adventuring. He glared distastefully at the ground. Was he just supposed to lie down and sleep? He glanced at Sam, who gave him a 'when in Rome' shrug before lying down next to Joraus. Jake watched her incredulously. *It isn't that easy!* He wanted to brush his teeth and get the taste of fish out of his mouth, and he wanted a blanket and a pillow to lie on. *What I really want is my bed!* In every game he had played, there had always been an inn or something where you could sleep at night.

Jake sulked as he lowered himself to the sand. Even though it had been a warm day, the chill of night was settling in. At least the sand was still warm and they had a fire. Maybe he could talk Joraus into finding him a cool cloak, like the ones talked about in books, which he could use as a pillow or to wrap around himself to stem the cold night air. That would be a little better.

The back of his shirt felt a little damp from his unplanned swim earlier on. Jake wished he'd thought to take it off and hold it in front of the fire to dry. He gave himself a little shake, trying to dispel the negative thoughts seeping in. It was funny how fast that could happen when he started to dwell on the bad things. Glancing over at Sam and Joraus, he saw that they were already asleep. He watched them for a second before closing his own eyes.

He listened to the sound of the waves and was just nodding off when he felt a familiar pressure. At first he tried to ignore it, but finally he sat up. Stupid water noises, he thought furiously, as he jumped to his feet and darted into the grove.

The next morning, Joraus woke the group early. Jake sat up and stretched deeply, before wincing in agony. It felt as though someone had jabbed him all over with hot needles.

Joraus laughed. "Are you a little sore, Jake? Stand up and walk around. Work the stiffness out and you'll start to feel better."

Jake gingerly stood. Hoping that Joraus knew what he was talking about, he started to walk around slowly, shaking out his arms. Sure enough, the sharp pain quickly settled into the dull ache that followed a hard workout. The only exception was his side, where Brael's soldier had kicked him. He fingered it carefully, but even that light touch was enough to send pain shooting through. Lifting up his shirt, he saw the beginnings of a large purple bruise. Well, at least it looks cool, he thought as he traced the edges.

Joraus led the way out of the cove and they followed the coastline until about midday before turning inland. After Jake had loosened up and the aches faded, he began to enjoy the walk immensely. The rocky coastal area gradually gave way to a lush, green plain and the broken trail eventually opened into a wider dirt road.

"This is the Skidippy," Joraus announced, pointing to the wide open grasslands in front of them. "Most of the more dangerous creatures keep away from the main road, or at least that is how it was when Klyle ruled. He used to have soldiers patrol the road to keep it safe for travelers and merchants." He glanced down at Jake and Sam. "We need to hurry through the Skidippy as quickly as possible. You are very vulnerable out in the open like this and the sooner we can get off of this plain, the better."

Joraus set a brisk pace, but Jake was so transfixed by the sights of the Skidippy, that he didn't even notice. Animals roamed the plain and while some seemed familiar, others were very strange indeed. At first Joraus tried to hush the children's inquiries, worried that the noise might draw unwanted attention, but with so many new sights, they couldn't keep quiet for more than a couple of minutes.

"Don't worry so much, Joraus," Swyf chided. "Remember how new and different the human world was when we arrived? I wish there had been someone to tell me about cars, buses and electricity, and other things back then. This is the first real look they have gotten of Fermicia that hasn't been tainted by fear or exhaustion."

"Well, can we at least agree to keep our voices down a little?" Joraus said petulantly. "There are other dangers besides Brael's forces, you know."

Swyf grinned, and patiently began to answer the unending stream of questions regarding the plant and animal life of the Skidippy. She told Jake and Sam about the healing properties found in petals of the deep purple Micora Rose and the juice of the ugly brown Talupis Root. Then she showed them the secret of the Tsory Grass and how you could extract copious amounts of sweet-tasting liquid by sucking on it as you walked. Swyf also pointed out the mild Wraxus Deer with their huge antlers and golden fur, and warned about the fierce Skidippy Lions when they saw a pack in the distance.

Every so often either Changeling would change into a small bird of some variety and scout ahead. It wasn't until evening that Joraus returned and announced that a patrol was coming. Jake felt a twinge of fear as the Changelings hustled them off the road and into the deep grasses of the plain. When they were well away from the road, Joraus instructed Sam and Jake to lie low.

"Keep your heads down and don't move until I say," he warned. "With any luck it is a standard patrol and they won't stray from the road."

Jake watched as Joraus whispered something to Swyf before they both shimmered into two of the Wraxus Deer he'd seen earlier. The two creatures positioned themselves between the children and the road. Jake peeked over at Sam, who nodded at him once before returning her attention to the path in front of them.

For a couple of tense minutes, all Jake could hear was the rush of an evening breeze through the grass, but eventually the heavy booted footsteps of soldiers began to reach his ears. He glanced up through the grass and way out in the distance some tiny soldiers materialized. Jake watched as the warriors grew bigger as they approached. They were dressed in dark clothing and each wore a curved sword, belted to his side, along with a cloak. He recognized them as the same type of soldiers who had chased them at the portal.

As they walked by, Jake noticed that the men appeared scruffy and dirty. Most of them had scraggly beards and smudged faces. They did not march together and their conversations were full of loud, raucous laughter and lewd gestures. The men didn't even look in their direction and Jake began to relax a little. He heard snippets of sentences as they passed.

"Execute the whole squad. That's what I heard."

"Don't know how they expected to capture Changelings in the dark."

"Could be anywhere in the territory by now."

"I heard there were two kids with them when they came out of the portal."

The words faded in and out as Jake tried to make sense of what was being said. It frightened him when he heard they were searching for two kids. One of the men stopped and motioned to a neighboring soldier. "Watch this," he said, chuckling as he unslung the bow from his back and drew an arrow.

He took aim at the deer that was Joraus, but the Changeling was too quick and skipped out of the way of the speeding dart. The soldier's friend laughed. "Hah! You couldn't hit a castle wall from twenty paces."

The man cursed before nocking a second arrow and pulling back the string. A third soldier stepped up behind the shooter and slapped him on the back of the head, causing him to jerk the bow upwards in surprise. Loosened, the arrow sailed high into the air and out of sight, far from its intended target.

"Why did you do that?" he demanded, angrily spinning around to face this friend. When he saw who had smacked him, he jerked to attention, the bow dropping to his side. "C-C-Captain," he stammered. "I—"

"Put that away, soldier," his superior barked. "What were you going to do with that deer after shooting it? Were you going to carry it on your back for the rest of the day?"

"N-No sir, I was just—"

"I don't want to hear your worthless excuses! Get moving and don't let me catch you out of line again!"

"Yes, sir," replied the soldier as he watched the captain turn and stalk off down the road. "Thanks for the warning," he complained to his friend, as he replaced the bow on his back. The other man just laughed and together they continued on with the rest of the patrol.

Jake heard a soft rustling behind him as the soldiers continued their undisciplined march. Very carefully, so as not to alert anyone on the road, he turned his head, only to see a Skidippy lion crouched about twenty-five feet behind him in the grass. Under normal circumstances, Jake would have found the sleek black coat, glowing red eyes and twitching, forked tail of the lion fascinating, but right now it was studying him as though he would make an excellent evening snack.

"Joraus," Jake whispered urgently.

Both deer pulled their heads out of the grass to stare at him. Then they saw the lion. Jake could almost hear the wheels in the Changelings' heads churning. The lion was an immediate threat, but if Joraus changed into something that stood any chance of fighting it, he would attract the attention of the soldiers.

Swyf did not wait, but spun around and leapt over Jake and Sam's hiding place. She ran right at the startled beast before cutting across the field right in front of it. The lion, goaded by the deer, exploded into action. Joraus didn't waste any more time, but sprinted after them. Jake watched the strange chase in terrified amazement. The last of the soldiers also noticed and they pointed excitedly.

Swyf sped through the grass, but the lion was right on her heels. She tried to dart sideways in an attempt to create some room between herself and the big cat, but the beast's agility was surprising. It quickly closed the distance and Jake held his breath when it leaped at her. The lion's outstretched paws would have ripped into her sides had Joraus not lowered his antlers and slammed into the side of it.

The force of the blow sent the lion crashing through the grass, and Jake could hear the soldiers hooting and hollering. The cat quickly regained its feet and turned its glowing eyes on its opponent. It roared in anger and sprinted towards Joraus, but he danced out of the way and tore through the grass, straight into the group of gawking soldiers. The men yelled as the deer crashed through them, the lion not far behind.

While the soldiers were sprinting away from the huge cat, Joraus shimmered and disappeared. The lion skidded to a stop on the road where the soldiers had been moments before, its head darting to the left and right as it searched the plains for its prey. The men recovered and taking advantage of the distracted beast, they quickly encircled it with swords raised. Seeing the new threat, the lion roared once and leapt at one of them.

Jake shuddered as the man's scream rang out over the plains. Once outside the ring of swords, the lion sped off in the opposite direction and Jake breathed a sigh of relief, glad that the clumsy men had not butchered the fierce animal. A squeak near his face made Jake look down and he saw a small field mouse squatting in front of him.

"Joraus?" he whispered tentatively.

When the mouse gave a single nod, Jake sighed with relief and settled himself in the grass to wait. Not long after, Swyf returned, still in the form of a deer. She took up her position between the road and their hiding place as she dipped her head serenely into the grass as though nothing had happened. The soldiers continued to talk excitedly about the lion and Jake heard many boasts of what would have happened if it had attacked them. They kicked at the soldier who had been mauled until he staggered to his feet, clutching a bleeding arm.

The patrol continued on their way, but Swyf waited until long after the men were out of sight before trotting out onto the road. She checked both ways and then returned to the group before shimmering back into herself.

"Okay, let's go," she said, motioning for everyone to stand up and follow her. "That was quite invigorating," she added with a laugh.

Joraus grunted sourly. "Klyle would never have let the soldiers get away with such unruliness. Things have definitely changed since I was last here."

"That was pretty awesome, Swyf, the way you just charged the lion like that," Jake breathed.

She gave him a winning smile. "Good thing that soldier was such a bad shot, huh, Joraus?" she said, mockingly.

Snorting, Joraus stepped back onto the road. "We still have a long way to travel," he said, turning to peer over his shoulder. "We will need to walk all night if we are to arrive at the vault tomorrow. Are you two up for that?"

The children nodded and the group set out again.

The night was filled with wonder for Jake and Sam. After the sun went down, more animals began to stir, some coming right up to the road to study the travelers with curiosity. Many of the flowers gave off their own light at nighttime, and their different colors made the Skidippy seem as though it were glowing. The moon rose high over the plain and soon the sky was dotted with millions of winking stars. Jake watched in fascination as flying insects landed on the glimmering flowers and flitted away glowing with the same shade of light. Joraus was right about not being able to describe the beauty of the place. Jake had never seen anything to compare to the wonder laid out before him.

"I told you so," said Sam, nudging him smugly as he stared out at the plain.

"Told me what?" he answered, only half listening.

"Real life is better than video games!"

"It feels like I *am* in a video game," he said, still looking around. "This is so cool!"

Jake studied Sam discreetly as they walked. The girl had a contented smile on her face as she gazed at all the beauty surrounding them. She had somehow managed to pull her shoulder-length hair behind her head, using a band of grass to tie it in place. He was constantly amazed at how she seemed so at home in this strange land. While he had felt like a fish out of water since their arrival, Sam acted as though she'd lived here her entire life. Jake wished he could handle things as well. Suddenly, he wanted to know more about her, and he debated inwardly about whether to ask her about her past. In the end, curiosity won out over any caution.

"Hey, Sam, can I ask you a question?" Jake asked carefully.

"Hmm?" she responded distractedly, still focused on the plain. "Oh, yeah, go ahead."

"How come you moved right before Junior High? Didn't you want to go with your friends from elementary?"

When she did not answer immediately, Jake was afraid that he might have overstepped. "I didn't mean to pry," he said quickly. "It's just that I don't know much about you."

"It's all right," she replied quietly. "It's just that I haven't really talked about it with anybody, even my mom. She wanted me to get counseling, but I told her I was fine. It was easier to just push it down and bury it."

"You don't have to tell me about it if you don't want to."

Sam tucked her hands into the pockets of her jeans. "It's okay, really." She took a deep breath. "When I was younger, my dad lost his job. At first, he tried to search for another, but when he couldn't find one he started spending time with some bad people."

The girl stopped for a second and kicked at a stone in the road. "I don't know what he was doing, but when he came home he was usually pretty upset. He would mumble things as he stalked around the house. For a while, Mom ignored it. She just kept saying he would snap out of it as soon as he found another job, but…"

Jake noticed her swiping her cheeks. It made him feel bad that he'd brought the subject up. "Look, you really don't–" he started to say, but Sam didn't seem to hear.

"One night he came home really late," she continued quietly. "I was already in bed, but I heard the front door slam. He was raging, but I couldn't understand him. I heard my mom run in and try to quiet him. She told him I was sleeping, but he… he hit her. Knocked her down and started yelling at her. I snuck out of my room and went to see what was happening, and I saw my mom on the ground crying. He was kicking her and screaming. I didn't know what to do. I just stood there, staring as he kept beating her. Then he said something about more money and went back outside. He didn't even see me.

"As soon as I heard the car, I ran over to my mom, but she just lay there, curled up on the floor. I called 911 and they came to the house. Everyone told me that I'd done the right thing, but…" Sam sighed and shook her head. "They took my dad to jail, but one of his friends posted bail. As soon as Mom found out, we packed up and moved in with my grandma. Mom had to take two jobs and things have gotten a little tense at home."

She looked at Jake and gave him an awkward smile. "I guess that's why I was so glad to come here. Even though certain parts have been scary, at least it isn't home."

When he didn't say anything, Sam sighed, "Jake, I didn't mean to throw all this on you. Like I said, I haven't told anyone about it and when I started talking, it kinda just came out."

Jake shook his head. "I'm sorry Sam. I'm not quite sure what to say. I can't believe you had to see all that. I can't imagine anything more awful. I–"

"What about you?" Sam interrupted.

"What about me?" he asked, confused.

"What about you and your family? I told you about me, but all I know about you is that you play a girl's instrument and that you're a video-game nerd."

"It is not a girl's instrument," Jake began hotly, but stopped when he saw her smile.

Grinning sheepishly, he told her about his mom and dad, his dog Nala, and what his home was like. He felt a little self-conscious about how normal his life was after listening to Sam's story, but she didn't act bitter or resentful. It was fun talking about home, and when Jake finally looked around he noticed that it seemed to be getting lighter. They had chatted all night and it was interesting to him how time flew by whenever he was talking to her.

CHAPTER 14:

THE VAULT

By the next morning, the joys of adventuring had faded to a dim memory. Instead of seeing the wonder of the Skidippy, Jake simply saw endless grass. He couldn't feel his legs anymore and his eyes were starting to droop. Before arriving in Fermicia, he had hardly ever pulled an all-nighter. The only exceptions were the times Jake had slept over at Korey's and stayed up all night playing games, watching movies or talking. Now he'd done it twice in three days. In a daze, he continued to automatically place one foot in front of the other.

The weary travelers had to stop for two more patrols, and each time Jake found it harder to rise from the soft grass when Joraus gave the all-clear. Sam looked as tired as he felt, and he tried to talk with her so that they would both stay awake, but in the end their conversations inevitably led to indecipherable mutterings and glazed eyes.

By late afternoon, trees materialized in the distance. At first Jake could not tell whether he was seeing things or not, but as they continued along the road the trunks grew larger. They walked for another hour before coming to a small stream that passed under the road. Jake immediately stepped off to the side where water was gathering in a small pool, cupped his hands and drank. The cool liquid felt wonderful to his parched throat. He quickly drank his fill and splashed some water on his sweaty face. It had the desired effect and helped to wake him up. Afterwards he tried to rise, but his legs refused to cooperate and he began to topple forward. Swyf caught him and helped him to his feet.

"We are almost there, Jake," Joraus said, sympathetically. "We'll follow this stream for about a mile and it will lead us to the top of a hill. What we are searching for is at the base of that hill."

Jake nodded and shook out his legs. When everyone had gotten a drink, Joraus led them away. Fifteen minutes later, Jake was standing next to Sam at the top of a large hill. Looking down to the bottom, he could see that the grass was gradually replaced by tall trees.

"Finally," Jake breathed to Sam. "I was getting so sick of all that grass!" Turning to Joraus, he asked, "What exactly are we looking for? Is there a door in the hill or something?"

"There's a hatch. It should open to an underground stairway." Joraus pointed to the foot of the hill. "It will be down there somewhere, but Klyle wasn't very specific."

Joraus started to walk downwards. After taking one last glance over his shoulder at the endless, rolling grasses of the Skidippy plain, Jake followed. He saw that the hill was not too steep and that the grass went all the way to the bottom. Studying the nearly transparent back of the Changeling, he grinned wickedly. He'd been wondering how he could get even for the shark attack and this seemed like a good opportunity.

Jake lined himself up and then ran at Joraus, jumping on his back as soon as he was in range. The Changeling gave a grunt of surprise as he was thrown forward, head first. Laughing, Jake did not even try to stop himself as they both rolled head over heels to the bottom of the hill.

"What was that for?" Joraus demanded angrily when they finally stopped.

"What do you mean what was that for?" Jake chortled, still sprawled out on the grass. "What do you think it was for, Sharkman!"

"You could have broken my neck," Joraus grumbled as he slowly stood up.

"Suck it up. At least *you* could've turned into something that could handle the fall better."

They both looked up when they heard Swyf and Sam laughing.

"You truly are a creature of grace," Swyf mocked.

Joraus scowled at her. "I notice that you didn't have a monkey jump on your back halfway down the hill."

Sam came over and held her small hand out to Jake. "Why did you call him Sharkman?"

Jake blushed; he hadn't meant for her to hear that part. "Um, nothing really, just a little prank that Joraus played on me back at the cove."

Sam raised an eyebrow. "Oh, so what did he do?"

He gave her a pained look. "If you really have to know, he threw me into the sea and then turned into a big shark. It scared me… a little."

Sam giggled. "Ah, so this was you getting even?"

"Yep, I just wish I could've seen his face." He called over to Joraus, "Hey, Sir Change-a-Lot, are we even now?"

Joraus gave Jake a flat stare before turning his back. "Spread out so we can find this hatch. The sooner we get inside, the sooner we can rest."

Jake combed the grass, but he didn't find anything out of the ordinary.

"I found something," Sam called about ten minutes later. "It feels like a handle, but I can't get a grip on it."

Curiously, Jake followed Joraus over to where the girl was crouched. Joraus reached down through the grass and felt a cold, metal ring. "Very good, Sam," he complimented. "Swyf, it's over here!"

Joraus pried the ring loose from the earth and brushed it to dislodge the attached dirt. Jake studied it as the Changeling held it loosely in his hands. The ring was separated into five sections, each piece composed of different symbols, and they all spun independently. It reminded Jake of a numbered padlock; the kind where you spun the dials at the bottom until you entered a combination. In this case, however, the separate parts of the ring appeared to form the sequence.

Joraus worked the dials until they could all spin freely. He tried various combination sets, but nothing seemed to happen. In frustration he pulled on the ring, his neck muscles bulging from the effort, but the hatch did not budge so much as an inch. "Well, that's just great," he huffed, dropping the object and stepping back with a scowl.

Jake stepped forward and carefully picked up the ring. He spun the first dial, not expecting anything, and was surprised when he recognized one of the symbols. It was the first part of the word he had seen on the pillar; the one that meant *Ragesong*. Curious, he spun the second dial, and sure enough he found the second part. Quickly, he spun the remainder until the entire word was spelled out.

The ring grew warm in his hand and he quickly motioned for Joraus. "Something is happening," he cried out.

With a curious glance at Jake, Joraus gripped the ring in both hands and, setting his muscular legs, he yanked sharply upward. Jake grinned as the hatch easily separated from the earth this time, causing Joraus to nearly topple over backwards. Jake stepped forward to look into the opening and saw a fine, wooden staircase twisting into the darkness and out of sight. He peered down apprehensively and reached into his pocket for his light.

With an approving nod to Jake as she passed, Swyf started down the steps. He followed, shining his light into the shadows of the stairwell. It didn't show very much, but it was better than being stuck in complete darkness. Sam trailed Jake, holding on to the back of his shirt as she descended. When they had gone down far enough, Joraus carefully lowered the hatch as he descended. Jake braced himself for the pitch black as the last of the sunlight disappeared, but, instead, torches flickered to life along the staircase, inviting them deeper into the hidden vault.

"Fascinating," Joraus whispered. "This is not at all what I expected. Put your light away, Jake, so you can save the batteries. You won't need it here."

Swyf led the rest of the way down to a large, wooden door bearing carved symbols. She pushed it, but it wouldn't budge. "What now, Joraus? It won't open."

Joraus pressed against the door experimentally. "To be honest, I don't know. Klyle did not tell me about any of this."

Jake examined the door and recognized the symbols for *Ragesong*. "Hey," he said, pointing them out to Sam. "Look familiar?"

"As a matter of fact…" Sam reached out and traced the symbols lightly with her fingertip. The door flashed silver and opened on its own accord.

"What did you do?" Joraus asked, flabbergasted.

"Those are the only symbols that I understand on there," she replied. "They say *Ragesong*."

"Klyle and his secrets," Swyf huffed. "How did you know what they meant?"

"I don't know," Sam admitted. "They were the same symbols as the ones on the pillar, back at the portal. Jake said he saw the same thing."

"This is the second time I've heard you mention those pillars," Joraus said. "Did something happen? I saw each of you approach one and put your hand on it, but nothing happened."

Jake was surprised. "You didn't see the lights?"

Joraus frowned. "What lights?"

"Hers was silver and mine was gold. It was the same color as the symbols on my neck and the light in the jewel you showed me. Didn't you see the door flash silver when Sam touched it?"

Joraus shook his head. "She touched it and it opened. That's all I saw." He looked at her, inquiringly. "Do you think you could do it again? I'd like to try a little experiment." When Sam nodded, he reached out and closed the door. "Okay, try again. See if you can open it."

The girl traced the letters once more and Jake saw the door flash silver again before opening.

"Did you see the light again?" Joraus asked.

"I saw it," said Jake.

"Me, too," Sam echoed.

"What about you, Swyf?"

"No, I just saw the door open," she answered.

"Okay, once more," said Joraus. "This time you try to open it, Jake."

After the entrance closed, Jake reached out and traced the symbols with his finger, and this time the door flashed a rich gold before opening.

"What color did it turn, Sam?" Joraus asked as he reached out and touched the wooden surface.

"Gold."

Joraus looked at Jake. "Same for you?"

When he nodded, the Changeling turned to Swyf. "You?"

"No colors, just an open door," she replied. "Are you about done?"

"Don't you think this is at all interesting?" Joraus asked, studying the door. "I wonder why we can't see it."

"Does it matter?" Swyf asked, pushing the door the rest of the way open and stepping through. "I mean, we knew that *Ragesong* was going to be different with... wow!" She stopped and stared at the sight in front of her.

Wow is right, Jake thought, as he gazed into the room. Racks of weapons lined the rear walls and even more lay scattered on numerous wooden tables. Other tables held clothing and assorted equipment. All of it was laid out so neatly that Jake could not help but feel that he was expected. On one side of the room he saw some straw sleeping mats, and in the center there was a big circle marked on the ground.

"Klyle couldn't have prepared all of this," Joraus growled as he looked around. "What is going on?"

"Who cares?" exclaimed Jake. "Check out all this awesome stuff!"

He hurried over to the tables, gawking at all the polished steel. The weapons looked as cool as anything he had ever seen in a video game. There were swords, knives, axes, spears, maces, hammers, claws, bows, crossbows, blow guns, staves and weapons he couldn't even put a name to. Some of them were well used while others appeared to be brand new. He saw hilts covered in jewels and gold, or simply wrapped in leather. A number of weapons were etched with symbols and some glowed faintly in the flickering torchlight.

Jake, his exhaustion forgotten in his excitement, was immediately drawn to the monstrous, two-handed weapons. He reached down and grabbed the handle of a giant battle axe, but it would not move. Gripping it tightly with both hands, he pulled, but it was as if the thing were glued to the table.

Joraus came to stand beside him. "I learned an expression while I was in your world. Ever hear how curiosity killed the cat? Don't touch anything else until we've had a chance to look around, okay? We don't know what might happen if you touch the wrong thing. Some of these weapons are extremely dangerous. I recognize a handful from Klyle's descriptions and they aren't something you want to mess around with carelessly."

Jake let go of the axe as though it might bite him. "Spoilsport," he muttered under his breath.

To keep himself out of trouble, he joined the girls as they walked slowly around the room. Swyf stopped at a table filled with water skins, satchels and other things that would come in handy for a journey. Glancing down, Sam spied a piece of folded parchment sitting in the middle, and she reached down and picked it up. The front of it read 'Wielders of *Ragesong.*'

"That's Klyle's writing," said Swyf, peering over her shoulder. Sam started to hand it to her, but the Changeling shook her head. "It is addressed to you and Jake. You should read it."

"How come we can read it?" Jake began to ask, but Sam hushed him and slowly unfolded the letter. She read it out loud.

Friends,

If this parchment has reached your hands, then you have already arrived in Fermicia. I extend my welcome to you and my gratitude for accepting the request of aid.

"Request?" grumbled Jake. "It didn't feel much like a request to me."

Joraus swatted him on the back of the head. "Hush," he hissed before motioning for Sam to continue.

I know not whether I shall be alive when this falls into your hands, but you will be well cared for in the company of these Changelings. Listen to them and follow their counsel. They were my most trusted advisors and most loyal friends.

Stock yourself with whatever you feel you may need from this room. The clothing and provisions are yours to do with as you will. The weaponry on the back wall is safe, but be wary of the weapons on the tables, for I know not what they are capable of. I can feel the power emanating from them even as I write this.

Jake looked guiltily over at Joraus before focusing again on what Sam was reading.

All I can tell you is to let Ragesong guide you in your selection.

Swyf and/or Joraus, it is difficult for me to give you advice as I am writing to you from the past. I am unsure of what fate awaits our kingdom, but if you are here now, I fear the worst. The more I learn of Ragesong, the more it terrifies me what Brael will be truly capable of. Do not make the mistake of underestimating him.

As for what to do next, my friends, I can only give the most general of advice. First, educate your charges. Tell them what you have learned of Brael and his minions. Teach them of Fermicia, the territories and the cities. Explain to them the dangers of what lies in front of them and keep them safe.

Second, seek out those sympathetic to our cause. Depending on when you read this, you may have to discover these allies for yourself. Fortunately, it should be well within the capabilities of either of you. Find or make friends to build up your strength. You will require as much help as possible to take on the might of Brael.

I am sorry to thrust this responsibility upon you, my friends. I wish it could be otherwise, but if you have cause to visit this vault then I have done what I could and the future of Fermicia is now in your hands.

Hail and farewell,

Klyle.

When Sam finished reading, Jake glanced at the Changelings. Joraus was studying the floor and Swyf was wiping her cheeks.

"Klyle… I can't imagine how hard that must have been for him to write," Swyf said, her voice breaking.

Sam nudged Jake, and together they walked to the back of the room to give the Changelings a chance to compose themselves.

"What do you think Klyle meant when he said 'Let *Ragesong* guide you in your selection?'" Sam asked as they walked between the tables of weapons.

"I dunno. You are more experienced with *Ragesong* then I am. I haven't even felt it yet," Jake answered. "So which ones do you like best?"

"None of them," she said, scrunching up her face. "I don't really want to hurt anybody."

"Me neither, but it's better than nothing. I mean," he added, giving her a sly smile, "there might not always be rocks."

"Yeah, yeah…" Sam stopped in front of a section that held ranged weapons. "I guess if I had to choose, I'd pick something like this. At least then I wouldn't have to be so close."

"Really? I'd go for one of those big swords," said Jake, "they are awesome!" He lowered his arm and blew out a breath. "But who knows if I'll even be able to lift one. I tried to pick up one of those big axes and it was like it was glued to the table."

140

"Come back over here, you two," Swyf called out. "I think I might have an idea."

When they rejoined the Changelings, Joraus asked, "First of all, did either of you two feel anything while you were over there?"

When the children shook their heads, Swyf looked at Sam. "You've already experienced *Ragesong*, so this might be easier for you." She led the girl over to the first row of weapons. "Try to empty your mind of everything. When you feel ready, just start walking around and see if *Ragesong* triggers anything.

"All right," Sam replied.

Swyf rejoined Jake and Joraus, and together they watched.

"Do you really think—" Jake started to say, but a quick, cutting glare from the Changelings silenced him.

They waited quietly, and after about five minutes Sam started walking around. She moved slowly up one row and down another. Jake focused on her as she studied the weapons, but she did not touch anything. Finally, she reached a set of fine bows. She slowed down as she wandered beside them, and then suddenly stopped and held out her hand over one. It had long, curved, white arms that were lovingly shaped by an obviously skilled artisan. The grip gave off a rich, silver gleam, which complemented the white limbs and gave the bow a majestic appearance.

Sam reached down tentatively to grip the handle of the bow and lifted it from the table. Jake saw the familiar flash of silver as her hand connected with the grip, and he felt a twinge of jealousy at how quickly she had felt *Ragesong*. The girl held the weapon out in front of her and gazed at it in wonder.

"Well done, Samantha," said Joraus quietly as the girl slowly made her way back to the group. When she rejoined them, he had her bring the bow close so that he could inspect it. "As I thought," he said, pointing to an engraving at the bottom of the bow. "Look at this, Sam."

She looked closely at the small marking and gasped, "No way!"

Joraus smiled down at her. "Some of the most powerful weapons of ages past were engraved with these pictures. Until I entered your world, I always wondered what the images were. They were so exotic and foreign, but now things are beginning to make more sense."

As he spoke, Jake peered down at the engraving and saw a small alto saxophone painstakingly carved into the wood. "That is so cool," he exclaimed. "Is it my turn to choose one yet?"

Jake studied the weapons excitedly, already picturing himself wielding a giant, two-handed hammer against the dark-clad soldiers of Brael.

Joraus nodded and walked Jake over to where the tables started. "Let's try the same thing that Sam did. Wait here until your mind clears and then walk slowly along the rows of weapons."

Jake stood still, trying to clear his head, but nothing seemed to happen. Finally, deciding that he had waited long enough, he moved between the tables. *C'mon, turn on the* Ragesong *thing!* When he reached the end of the last row, he threw a disappointed look at Sam and the Changelings.

"Come here for a minute," Swyf called out.

Jake trudged back. "I didn't feel anything," he said, disheartened.

"We've had an idea." Swyf held up a long piece of cloth. "Turn around and close your eyes."

When she was done tying the blindfold in place, Joraus took Jake by the arm and led him to the center of the room. "This time I want you to hum to yourself," he instructed. "I don't care what it is; it can be your favorite classical piece or your favorite video-game song. What we want is for the tune to override your thinking. We know that *Ragesong* is somehow tied to your musical ability, so let the music fill you and try again."

After Joraus let go of his hand and stepped away, Jake wondered what song would help him to forget what was going on around him, and he finally settled on the old Bach piece he had been practicing at home. At first he felt stupid, standing alone and blindfolded in the middle of the room, humming to himself, and for the first couple of minutes nothing happened. But soon his worry and embarrassment drained away, leaving just him and the music. Jake was not aware that he had moved until he felt something solid in his hand. He pulled down the blindfold, fully expecting to see a magnificent, rune-etched weapon.

Instead, his jaw dropped as he stared at the item gripped in his fist. "Aw, c'mon, really?"

In his hands was a plain-looking long sword with a stained, metal blade and a worn hilt. It had lain by itself on a table, and when Jake had studied the weapons earlier, he hadn't even given it a passing glance. He turned to Joraus and Swyf. "Can I try again? I think my *Ragesong* is broken."

Joraus grinned. "Think so, do you? Do you have any idea what you are holding in your hands?"

Jake scowled at the sword. "Yeah, it looks like something that got put on the table by mistake." He pointed at one of the racks on the wall. "I'll put it over there and try again. I thought I felt something, but–"

"Jake," said Swyf gently, "nothing in this room can hold a candle to that blade. I saw it resting on the table earlier, but I didn't dare to say anything. I found myself hoping, especially after I found out what instrument you played."

Joraus stepped towards Jake, still smiling broadly. "Don't base everything on appearances, Jake. Brael would give half the kingdom to own a weapon as fine as that. The fact that *Ragesong* led you to it is…"

"…very exciting," finished Swyf softly.

Joraus pointed to the hilt. "Look at the pommel," he encouraged.

Jake rested the tip of the sword on the ground and studied the metallic ball over the hilt. There, etched at the very top, glowing a faint golden color in the flickering torchlight, was a flute.

CHAPTER 15:

TRAINING

Jake fought to keep his aching arm up as Joraus rushed forward with his blades whistling through the air. He raised his sword in defense and met the attack. All three metal surfaces clashed together briefly, but he spun to the left and allowed Joraus' forward momentum to push him off-balance. Jake extended his blade in the spin, and the sword whipped around in a lightning quick arc, stopping inches from the Changeling's exposed back.

"Excellent, Jake," Joraus panted, lowering his twin blades and stepping cautiously away from the powerful weapon.

"Can we please take a break for a minute?" Jake begged. "My shoulders are throbbing. Sam can shoot for a little while, and then we can go at it again."

Joraus nodded, and together they sheathed their weapons and stepped over to the table where Swyf and Sam sat watching.

"He's gotten rather good, hasn't he?" Swyf commented, offhandedly.

Joraus scowled at Jake. "I had to train for years to grasp concepts that he appears to pick up instantly. He is quick and agile, just like Klyle. He still has a long way to go, but what he has learned already is astounding. Are you positive that you still haven't felt any traces of *Ragesong*?"

Jake gave a disappointed shake of his head as he sank wearily into a vacant chair. Ever since the moment he first held the sword, he had not been able to touch the power he'd briefly experienced. Though he had tried many different things, nothing seemed to work. After watching how quickly he learned, the Changelings speculated that perhaps *Ragesong* was present, even if Jake could not feel it.

For the last couple of weeks, Jake and Sam had spent every waking moment preparing. When they were not training with their new weapons, they were in deep conversation with the Changelings about Brael or Fermicia.

Joraus gave a more detailed account of Brael's history, and a comprehensive analysis of the warriors and creatures that served the evil king. He pointed out the strengths and weaknesses of each foe, and where they were likely to be encountered. While Jake worried about all of these different enemies, it was when Joraus explained the Elites that he felt real fear.

"The only thing more terrifying than facing an Elite in battle is coming face to face with Brael himself," Joraus explained. "They are fast, incredibly powerful, and have the stamina to fight for hours without tiring. During their training, Brael removed nearly every shred of humanity from them, until only the overpowering need to fulfill his will was left. They are fanatical to his cause and would gladly die to accomplish his smallest whim."

Pretty soon Jake was seeing the shadows of huge warriors in his dreams, and more than once he woke up in a cold sweat.

Whenever it happened, Sam was there, sitting beside him, ready to talk to him about home, music or anything else that would calm him until he was able to go back to sleep.

This girl stuff was still new territory for Jake. Up until now, he hadn't had much use for them, so it was surprising to find how easily he could talk to Sam. Before, he'd always felt awkward and shy around girls, but for some reason it was different with her.

This was not to say that everything was easy between them. Although the vault was big, it was still a single, closed-in room. When Joraus and Swyf went off on their scouting missions or to find food, the walls seemed to close in. Jake and Sam were both young, willful teenagers, and at times the Changelings would return to a shouting match or to find them on opposite sides of the room in a huffy silence. The fights never lasted long, and after their initial anger cooled, the children were quick to apologize.

While Joraus taught them about Brael and his minions, Swyf instructed them on the other inhabitants of Fermicia. Jake was amazed at the diversity of the land. He was keen to visit the Valley of the Shadow Wisps, and the traders of Yoliesk sounded equally interesting. But, as fascinating as the lessons were, the sheer volume of information quickly overwhelmed him. After a while his brain began to feel like a wrung-out sponge.

Whenever he was thoroughly boggled, Jake would pick up his sword and head for the training circle. It did not matter if he was sparring with Joraus or practicing forms on his own, but when the sword was in Jake's hand, his mind cleared instantly. Once his initial disappointment with the weapon passed, he discovered some of its more discernible powers.

The first thing Jake noticed was that the sword felt weightless. At first this had been a little disappointing. Like every young boy, he wanted to feel the weight of the steel in his hand. During his first lesson with Joraus, however, his opinion quickly changed. It was amazing how tired he could get, even with a weightless blade.

Jake discovered the second noticeable peculiarity of the sword quite by accident. The first time Joraus attacked him, he retreated, fearful of blocking the Changeling's attack. When Joraus questioned this, Jake realized that the fear stemmed from his first night in Fermicia, when the soldier had knocked the branch from his grip. His hands had stung for hours afterwards, and the phantom pain returned as soon as Joraus raised his weapons against him.

Naturally, Joraus had been very worried about this. After all, what good was an immensely powerful sword in the hands of a fighter who was afraid to wield it? Joraus retrieved a wooden dummy from a corner of the vault and wheeled it over, so that Jake could practice on it. After only a couple of swings, Jake realized that he could barely feel when he struck the thing. Though the wooden man spun and rocked, Jake felt nothing in his arms and only a slight vibration in his hands. The sword seemed to absorb the impact.

When he pointed this out to Joraus, the Changeling instructed him to hold out his sword and brace himself. He swung at it, softly at first, but then with increasing power each time. On the last hit, Joraus struck at Jake's blade with as much force as he could, but his arms didn't so much as tremble. Jake was still unconvinced, right up until the moment when Joraus stalked over to the practice dummy, and with the same powerful strike he sent the head spinning across the floor.

From that moment on, Jake's confidence grew exponentially. As he became more daring and confident with his weapon, he noticed another of the sword's abilities. Due to the blade's apparent weightlessness, Jake had struggled to determine how hard he was hitting. It was not until Joraus stopped in the middle of a sparring match and dropped his swords to shake his stinging hands that Jake realized how hard he was attacking. While he waited for Joraus to recover, he took some practice swings at the dummy and was astounded to see large chunks of wood fall away with each blow. Jake knew that he, alone, lacked the toughness to do that kind of damage; the sword was somehow amplifying the power of his attacks to compensate for his current lack of strength.

Jake was sure the weapon housed other secrets, but the Changelings could not, or more likely in his view, would not tell him more. They seemed to think it worked the same way as *Ragesong*, and the only way for him to fully tap into the sword's abilities was to figure it out for himself. But, for Jake, trying to be patient with his blade was just as difficult as being patient with *Ragesong*.

Sam's bow turned out to be nearly as wondrous. When she had first brought it over for the Changelings to inspect, Joraus had expressed a worry that the weapon had been sitting there, strung, for too long. He feared that either the bowstring or arms might have been weakened by the prolonged pressure of the string. Upon examination, however, the bow looked to have been newly made. The limbs were full of spring and vibrancy, and the string felt as though it had never seen a full draw.

Joraus set up a makeshift shooting range by placing one of the practice dummies against the wall opposite the sleeping mats. He showed Sam which way to stand and how to grip the bow. While she waited, he retrieved a quiver he found hanging along the back wall of the vault. He had just begun to fill it from a barrel full of arrows when Swyf began to laugh.

"Don't bother, Joraus!" she called out.

"What do you mean, don't–" he said, turning just as a bolt of light streaked across the room and slammed into the dummy. "How did you do that?" he gasped, gaping at the silver arrow protruding from its wooden chest. The half-full quiver of arrows dangled from his shoulder, threatening to spill all over the floor as he stared at the small girl.

Sam shrugged. "I pulled back on the string and it just appeared. I don't know what else to tell you. I held it there, and then all at once I got the same feeling as I did when I threw a rock at that soldier. Before I released the string, I knew where the arrow was going to land."

"Have you ever been trained with a bow?" Joraus demanded, setting the quiver down on top of the barrel of arrows.

"Joraus, I've never even held a bow before. I mean, I've seen people shoot them in movies and video g–" she trailed off with a guilty look, before trying to say something else, but Jake immediately interrupted her.

"So you *have* played them!" he yelled, incredulously. "You said you hadn't! You even called them stupid."

Sam sniffed. "I never said I hadn't played them. I only said that I couldn't believe you were trying to compare Fermicia to them. Honestly, Jake, what kid hasn't played video games? I didn't grow up under a rock, you know."

"You knew," Jake accused Swyf loudly. "You knew she'd played them the whole time."

"What does it matter?" Swyf asked with a laugh. "So she has played video games, what does it matter?"

Jake narrowed his eyes. "You said you didn't recognize the song I played in band," he accused Sam. "You can't not have recognized that song if you played video games."

"So maybe I lied a little," she replied with a shrug. "I've been online, Jake. I've seen how goo-goo eyed boys go when they hear that a girl plays games, and I've made the mistake of telling guys I play them before. Then that's all they want to talk about, all the time."

"So what games do you play?" Jake started to grill her. "What system do you have? What–"

"See!" Sam screeched. "That's why I didn't want to say anything. For goodness sake, Jake, an arrow of pure light just came out of nowhere and landed right in the middle of that thing's chest, and all you want to know is what games I've played!" She gestured at the dummy, still rocking back and forth from the force of the hit.

Jake put his hands up defensively, and took a step back. "All right, all right," he said, "so it was bad timing."

Sam took a deep breath. "I want to go back home, Jake. I want to play my saxophone and I want to go back to school. Who knows, maybe I'll even go bowling with Grandma. If I *am* going to do any of that, we have to get out of Fermicia alive. Video games don't really fit into this picture right now. Maybe someday we can talk about them, but for now we have to learn about Fermicia and how to fight. Okay?"

Jake huffed out a breath of his own, but then gave up. "Fine, but some time you are going to tell me all about it."

Sam flashed him a little smile. "I'll decide."

By the end of two weeks, Jake felt a lot more prepared for the world that waited outside the vault. He was not sure what the Changelings had planned for him and Sam, but he felt reasonably sure that he would be able to contribute to the group, instead of just being a liability. Jake had learned a lot about Fermicia, and more than he wanted to know about Brael and his minions.

One of the things Jake and Sam had worked on during the latter part of the second week was how to fight alongside the Changelings. It had been Sam's idea, after expressing a fear that she might accidentally shoot one of them in the midst of battle, having found that she couldn't always shoot while in the cocoon of *Ragesong*. Sam had also learned that if she was not wrapped in the power, every arrow released from the bow seemed to weaken her physically.

So they practiced fierce mock battles in which Joraus and Swyf took their lives into their hands, darting in and out of Sam's line of sight as she fired arrow upon arrow at a row of dummies on the far wall. All the while, Jake would spar with one or both of the Changelings in the middle of the floor.

Late one afternoon, while Jake practiced with Swyf, Joraus rushed into the vault. "I found something in the woods to the south," he said, excitedly. "I think it will help us to determine what to do next." He looked around at the vault, distastefully. "At any rate, it is past the time that we left this place."

"What did you find?" Swyf asked, shimmering back into her natural form.

"The remains of an old fort," he replied. "It looks as if it were destroyed years ago, but there is something there that you *have* to see."

Jake heard the excitement in the Changeling's voice and it piqued his curiosity.

"Well, are you going to tell us?" Swyf demanded, but Joraus shook his head.

"No, trust me; it is something you will want to see for yourself."

The group spent the rest of the evening packing the things they would need once they left the vault. Jake found a bag with padded leather straps, which fitted him similarly to his backpack at home. The only major difference was that this one opened at the top, over which a flap folded, and it was secured by a drawstring. He stuffed his dirty clothes in the bottom and worked his way up from there.

Earlier in the week, Jake and Sam had discovered some clothes in the vault that fitted them. At first glance, the styles had appeared strange, but the Changelings were quick to assure them that they would be right at home in Fermicia. After more than a week of wearing the tighter-fitting garb, Jake was still trying to get used to it. He stuffed some spare pants and shirts into his bag, and then loaded it with some other things that might come in useful.

When he was done, Joraus hefted the bag before telling Jake to lessen the weight. Jake, realizing the Changeling was right, sighed and began to unpack it. He pulled out various items, trying to decide on the most necessary ones. *Where is a sack with infinite space when you need one?* It was not until the fourth try that Joraus cleared the pack for traveling.

When they were all finished, he urged them to sleep, adding, "This could be the last time you'll enjoy even the limited comforts of a sleeping mat for a while."

Remembering that first night on the sand, Jake made sure the cloak he'd chosen was still laid out next to his pack before settling on his mat.

The group woke the following morning, and strapped on their packs and weapons. In addition to their primary arms, Jake and Sam each had a dagger strapped to their waist, while Sam had another hidden within her boot.

Jake sighed in relief as he gazed around the room for what he hoped was the last time. Excited to see Joraus' discovery, he almost missed the sight of the torches extinguishing themselves as he exited the vault, as though the room somehow knew they would not be returning.

CHAPTER 16:
THE FORT

J ake squinted in the bright morning sun and cupped his
hand over his eyes as he looked around. He was glad they
were moving into the woods instead of roaming back
through the grasslands. Although he felt more secure with the
sword strapped to his back, he was still nervous about actually
having to fight with it, and he didn't want his first battle to be
with a patrol of Brael's soldiers. At least in the woods, it would
be harder for a bunch of men to come at him at once.

Joraus shimmered into the now familiar shape of a
mountain lion and led the way through the trees. The two girls
followed and Jake fell in behind them. Swyf had taught the
children how to guard the rear, and he made frequent backward
checks; they would not be surprised on his watch.

Jake grinned as he walked. With his pack, weapons and
Fermician clothes, he felt more at ease then at any time since
arriving in this land. This is how a real adventurer must feel, he
thought, excitedly. He started to practice unsheathing and

sheathing his sword, being careful not to cut the straps of his pack, until Swyf turned and gave him a disapproving hiss.

He felt a little bad for Sam, who was constantly readjusting the bow on her back. His sword was strapped down tight, and though the sheath still felt a little uncomfortable, running diagonally up his back, at least there was no weight to the blade itself. Sam had to deal with the pack and the bow, which looked pretty awkward to him.

After a while, the woods began to thicken and the bright sunlight dimmed. The huge, leafy trees made Jake feel small and insignificant as he walked beneath them. He was beginning to feel a little claustrophobic when he thought he heard a rustling ahead. Joraus stiffened, his ears leaning back on his head as he let out a quiet growl.

Swyf shimmered quickly into a tiny bird and darted towards the sky, while Jake and Sam ducked behind the closest tree and readied their weapons. Joraus shimmered out of sight and for a moment there was not a sound. The rustling grew louder and soon Jake heard the sound of someone approaching.

"There ain't nuffin' here, Raf," a nasally voice complained.

"I told ya, I saw 'em from them trees up there," slurred a second man. "They's in here."

"You been drinkin'," retorted the first voice.

"That ain't got nuffin' to do with nuffin'," snapped the man referred to as Raf. "They's in here and that's where we's gonna find 'em. Brael's been payin' good coin fer kids lately, I hear, and I mean ta git me some."

Two men walked out into the open where Joraus had stood only a moment before. They were big, but looked to be very out of shape. Their clothes were stained with food and greasy looking, and they were waving rusty swords in front of them.

"C'mon out, you kids!" shouted the larger of the two. "Don' make no trouble." He chortled. "You won' like no trouble."

As the men approached the tree where Sam was hiding, Jake took a deep breath and stepped out, holding his sword before him. The first thing he noticed was that his blade was not nearly as long as theirs. To his surprise, however, he found that this did not worry him. The two men turned to face him, and Jake could tell they were brothers. Their fat faces, bulbous noses and huge bellies made him think of two pigs standing on their hind legs. They grinned as they stepped forwards.

"Now yer gonna wanna put that down, boy," Raf said. "You tell us where the other 'un is and you won' get hurt, otherwise…" He ran his thumb and forefinger along the edge of his sword, and smiled unpleasantly.

"What do you want?" Jake asked, continuing to hold his blade at the ready.

Raf gave a high-pitched, snorting laugh, and the sound did nothing to dispel the image of pigs that Jake had in his head. "Wat we wan? You hear him, Tap?"

The bigger man guffawed stupidly. "I heard 'im, Raf. He talks big."

The guy turned to Jake. "It's like this, boy. Brael, well, 'e pays good coin fer kids. And we likes coin."

Raf approached with his sword raised. "He's jus' a stupid kid, Tap. Grab him!"

Tap stepped forward, but Jake whipped his sword around and held it in front of him. The man grinned and gave a clumsy swing, trying to knock Jake's weapon out of his way, but Jake easily parried the blow and landed a quick counter on Tap's arm using the flat of the blade. Tap howled in pain and retreated a little.

Raf charged, but Jake simply ducked and sidestepped, and the man's sword whistled harmlessly overhead as he ran past. Jake caught him on the rump with a stinging slap. The man dropped his sword, and hopped up and down, grabbing at his backside.

Jake was not sure why, but for some reason he was hesitant to really hurt these men. Tap charged again, a determined look on his piggish face, but Jake easily met each swing of the big man's rusty sword. He saw multiple openings for a killing blow, but instead he hit Tap with the same stinging, non-lethal slaps.

The big man wailed with pain at each strike, but he continued to hack at Jake. Then Raf was there too, and Jake felt hard pressed to keep both blades from reaching him. Their sword strokes were clumsy, but they kept coming. For whatever reason, Jake still could not bring himself to seriously hurt them. He was retreating slowly, only able to defend now as the angry men continued to rain down their blows.

A moment later, Raf buckled, dropping his sword and clutching at something silver protruding from the small of his back. Tap screamed in terror as Joraus darted in from the side. The big mountain cat leapt on the big man and bit deeply into his throat. Jake closed his eyes, but he couldn't block out the sound of Tap's scream fading into a gurgling moan or Raf's frantic whimpers as he groped at his back, attempting in vain to dislodge the arrow.

After what seemed like forever, the two men quieted and Jake opened his eyes. Raf lay face down on the forest floor, his body still twitching. Tap's lifeless eyes were staring into the green canopy of trees, his limbs contorted and his throat ripped out. After a quick glance, Jake ran for the nearest thicket and threw up. Once his stomach was empty, he continued to dry heave.

Sam approached him cautiously. "Jake," she said, placing a hand on his back, "are you okay?"

He turned to stare at her in horror with the back of his hand scrubbing at his mouth. "How could you do it?"

Sam's hand dropped as she gazed directly into his eyes. "They were trying to kill you, Jake." She dropped her head and stared at the ground. "I was afraid they were going to kill you," she whispered.

"Jake!" Joraus's deep voice rumbled angrily. "What were you thinking? Why were you toying with them? They could have killed you. I know you saw the openings, so why didn't you strike?"

Jake looked at the Changeling, but he couldn't say anything.

"I have spent too much time on you to watch you to die at the hands of a couple of inbred bounty hunters. Or worse, captured and turned over to Brael. Do you have any idea what that man would do to you? Do you!?"

Swyf put a calming hand on Joraus. He looked as though he wanted to say something else, before angrily turning away and marching back to the path they had been following. "Let's go," he growled, "before the forest scavengers find the bodies."

The group walked for the rest of the day in silence. Jake felt embarrassed and then angry for feeling that way. I shouldn't have to feel guilty about not wanting to kill anyone, he thought bitterly. He kept shooting angry glares at the mountain lion, which did not even turn to acknowledge him.

As dusk started to fall, Joraus stopped and shimmered back into his natural form. "The fort is in a clearing just up ahead," he said. "It was abandoned when I came here last night, but that doesn't mean there couldn't be someone there." He looked at Jake. "Think you can handle yourself this time?"

Jake did not answer and only gave the Changeling an angry glare.

"He'll be fine, Joraus," Swyf said, soothingly. "Go on."

Joraus shrugged before stepping out into the clearing.

As soon as Jake moved through the last of the trees, he could see the fort clearly, and he studied it as they approached. From the outside, it was exactly as he had pictured in his mind. Tall, sharpened stakes formed a wall around a bunch of log buildings. It wasn't particularly well built and he was not surprised that it was abandoned. It might be able to hold off a small army for a couple of days, but beyond that...

They walked through the open front gate and Jake saw there was more to the enclosure than he had originally thought. A crude platform had been built to run along the inside of the wall, allowing archers to shoot at the enemy from the cover of wooden stakes. Barriers made of stout logs were strategically placed in the area between the front gate and the first of the log huts. Jake figured those were the last resort for defending the fort once the gate had been breached.

Joraus led the way towards the back of the fort, moving around the walls and through the small log houses, which looked to have been built very quickly without much attention to detail. Jake thought back to when he used to play with his dad's log blocks; the cabins he had built then were a lot neater. Those he was studying now were just a bunch of small logs, stacked on top of one another, without regard to size or fit. Near one, Jake noticed the cold remains of what could only have been a smithy. A big fire pit, and scattered pots and pans in front of another hut marked the kitchen.

Joraus took the group into the tallest building at the rear of the fort. It was a large single room with a desk in the middle, sitting on a filthy rug. Crude weapons hung from the walls with faded wall hangings that attempted to bring a little life to the drab interior. A sleeping mat lay in one corner and there were a couple of bookshelves on the opposite wall, holding rotten, weather-beaten books.

Joraus stepped behind the desk and nudged something out of the way with his foot. Jake followed Swyf and Sam before giving a revolted look. The thing that Joraus had so casually swept aside was a skeleton. Jake was about to say something when he saw what Joraus was pointing at. Something was written on the floor under the desk. The message was faded, but with a quick glance at the bones, Jake could guess what it had been written in.

Sam asked the question that was on the tip of his tongue. "What does it mean, 'Klyle Lives'?"

CHAPTER 17:

BRAEL'S RULES

Jake sat on the thin sleeping mat with his back resting against the wall of one of the log huts. He stared, unseeing in the dark cabin as he thought about what Joraus had discovered. At last it felt like there was some direction to this uphill battle; something tangible they could accomplish.

Joraus and Swyf had torn the rest of the fort apart, searching for more information that might lead them to Klyle, but they had found nothing. It did not matter. For now, the slim hope that their friend could still be alive was enough to boost their spirits. The decision to stay within the relative safety of the fort for the night and leave in the morning had been unanimous.

Now, lying in the dark and as tired as Jake was, sleep would not come to him. Flashes of his fight with the two bounty hunters kept him awake. He had spent most of the day feeling angry and resentful, but sitting here alone in the darkness, something kept nagging at him to talk to his friend. With a loud sigh, he realized that he wouldn't be getting any sleep until he resolved things with Joraus.

With a quiet grunt, Jake pushed himself to his feet and wrapped the cloak he'd been using as a blanket around his shoulders. He knew where Joraus would be as he stepped out of the hut and into the chilly night air. It was colder here in the forest than it had been out on the plains, and he pulled the cloak more tightly around himself as he hurried through the darkness.

Jake found the Changeling huddled against one of the wooden barriers, his arms wrapped around his powerful legs as he stared into the night. Jake stopped for a moment as the sudden realization came to him that he could see Joraus clearly against the wooden planks. He was as transparent as before, yet somehow Jake was able to perceive every minute movement, from the quick shift as he repositioned himself to the tap of his fingers on his opposite leg.

He dimly recalled how hard it had been to see the Changelings when he first arrived in Fermicia, but gradually it had become easier to mark their exact locations. Filing the information away for later, Jake approached the barrier and sat down quietly next to Joraus. For a while neither of them spoke and only the strange forest sounds filled their ears.

Finally Jake cleared his throat, breaking the silence. "I'm sorry that I couldn't kill those men today, Joraus."

For a long time the Changeling didn't say anything, but only stared out into the night. "I wasn't angry that you couldn't kill them, Jake," he said at last.

"But, after the fight…"

"I wasn't angry Jake, I was afraid. When both of those men came at you together, I was afraid that one of them was going to kill you. When I saw you deliberately pass up the openings they gave you, it terrified me." He took a deep breath. "The last time I was that scared was when I was forced to leave Klyle on his own to face Brael and his Elites."

Looking down into Jake's face, Joraus sighed. "Jake, I know that this kind of adventuring is new and exciting to you, but no matter what you think, this isn't a game or a movie. If you die here, you will not wake up back at home. You learned very quickly how to fight, as you proved today, but the fact of the matter is that you've been training for two weeks. You were lucky your first fight just happened to be against unskilled opponents. The thing you did with the bounty hunters, if you had attempted that with Brael's soldiers, you'd be dead."

Jake looked down and studied the dirt beneath him. "I couldn't do it," he whispered. "I knew what I was supposed to do. I saw the openings, but for some reason I just couldn't take them." He traced his finger in the dirt. "I've never hurt anything before."

The youth realized how foolish it sounded, even as he said it, but it did not change the way he felt. It had been ingrained in him ever since he could remember.

Joraus reached out a hand and put it on his shoulder. "I know, Jake," he said gently. "I can only imagine how difficult this must be for you. And, believe me, if there was anything I could do so that you could retain that innocence, I would. But, here in Fermicia, things are not the same as in your world. Where you live you have a strong government set in place to protect the innocent. Klyle worked hard to set up a similar system here, but Brael tore it down.

"All those years ago, Jake, that jewel led me to you. I don't understand the magic of the stone. I don't know how it was tied to you, or how it determined that you would be the one to help restore Fermicia, but the point remains that you were chosen — you and Sam. Klyle had enough faith in those two gems that he was willing to sacrifice himself, so that you could be brought here when you were ready."

Joraus picked a small rock out of the dirt and hurled it out into the darkness. "I know him, and I know that he wouldn't have done that if he'd had any doubts. But if you are to have any chance of saving Fermicia, you are going to have to be able to kill. Brael has set the rules that define this kingdom now, and you either play by them or you die."

Jake swallowed the lump forming in his throat and nodded, not quite trusting himself to answer.

They sat there for a minute; Jake trying to get himself back under control, and Joraus giving him the time to do so.

"What was Klyle like?" Jake finally asked. "I mean, I get that he was a powerful king and everything, but what was he really like?"

Joraus thought for a minute. "If I were to choose one word to describe him, it would be kind. He was the type of man who would stop in the midst of a journey to care for a wounded deer, or give his last coin to feed a hungry child. One of his biggest reasons for unifying Kardonin was because he was disgusted by the way some of the tribes treated their poor and infirm. He hired healers from outside the territory to come in and train anyone who would learn. While he was king, there was no art nobler than that of healing.

"It was one of the major disagreements he had with Brael, who believed in the old tribal customs; something similar to your saying, 'Survival of the fittest.' Brael considered Klyle's compassion a weakness and would constantly mock him for it. Klyle never faltered though, and by the time Brael invaded, people came from near and far to be treated by Kardonin healers."

Jake listened in fascination. The more he learned about the king, the more he wanted to know.

"What else was he like?"

Joraus smiled into the darkness. "He was adventurous and playful. He was happiest while on the road with pack and sword. Klyle would jump at any excuse to leave on an adventure. He set up the ruling body so that the territory could be governed without him for extended periods of time without collapsing. I am pretty sure that fairness of rule wasn't his only concern when he developed it.

"He also enjoyed a good joke or prank, as much as anyone, and laughter was common in the throne room." Joraus chuckled, wistfully. "He could come up with the most elaborate pranks I've ever seen. This one time…" He paused.

"Yes?" Jake prompted.

"Well, there was this ornery town official who used to bring forward complaint after complaint against a neighboring village. The offending village just happened to be led by a young widow that was just as eager to condemn the aggrieved town. Klyle used to listen to a huge list of grievances every time they came to court. The two would bicker back and forth for hours in the throne room, and bore everyone to tears.

"Klyle had a suspicion that they had gotten to the point where they argued just for the spite of it. The grievances were always recycled versions of previous complaints. We were pretty sure they did not pay much attention to what they were reading once they started, and they definitely didn't listen to one another.

"Anyway, after a particularly dull afternoon, Klyle decided to test his theory. He had me sneak into the town official's room that night and slip something into the following morning's list. At the same time, he sent Swyf to alter the widow's list in a similar fashion. When they entered the next morning, Klyle had the official begin, much to the outrage of the widow.

"Well, the man read straight through, completely unaware of the wedding betrothal request I'd added to his document. He didn't even slow as he proposed to the woman, but went right on reading. Apparently, the widow hadn't been paying much attention either, because as soon as he finished, she started right in. She was a little more attentive to her own reading though and caught on to Swyf's alteration – right after announcing her acceptance of the official's proposal!

"I still remember the laughter dancing in Klyle's eyes as he told them, 'Who am I to deny such love? Let the two of you be married this instant. I'll do it myself.'"

Jake's eyes widened. "But he didn't really, did he? Make them get married, I mean?"

"Are you kidding?" Joraus asked, trying to stifle his deep laugh. "He married them on the spot and told them they couldn't have the arrangement annulled for at least a year."

"I bet they didn't like that much."

"That was the beauty of it, Jake. The two of them were so angry with Klyle that it gave them a common ground on which to start their union. Whenever they argued, they could always fall back on blaming the whole thing on the king. By the end of the year, the towns were trading freely and the villagers were as happy as could be. When Klyle called them back a year later, they were expecting their first child. The Kardonin nobles laugh about it to this day."

Still chuckling, Joraus looked down at Jake. "To be honest, Jake, this is one of the reasons I like you, because you remind me a lot of him." He cleared his throat gruffly. "Now go get some sleep. It will be your turn for watch soon enough."

The morning dawned cold and damp. Dew darkened the dirt floor of the fort and droplets glistened from the log cabin walls. The group shivered over a small cooking fire as they waited for the sun's warmth to break through the thick branches above. Over breakfast, they discussed what to do with the message Joraus had discovered. With this being the first real direction since arriving in Fermicia, everyone opted to see if they could find any more information on Klyle.

Swyf suggested they start by investigating Kithalo. The city was big enough to allow the children to blend in without too much trouble, and it had a large enough population for the Changelings to be able to glean some information. No one had a better idea, so after breakfast they put out the fire and set out on the forest path.

Most of the early morning was spent in silence. Swyf shimmered into a hawk and disappeared as soon as the small trail they had been following emptied into a wide dirt road. Joraus led the way in the form of a wolf. He was a little different from the wolves that Jake had seen pictures of at home, being bigger, and his fur was a dirty brown instead of gray.

Back in the vault, Swyf had referred to such animals as forest wolves, teaching the children that the people of southern Kardonin would sometimes raise them as pets. It had been Sam's idea for Joraus to guide them in this form; he had been none too thrilled about it. Even now, Jake smiled at the irritable twitch of the Changeling's tail as he stalked down the road in front of them.

As he walked, Jake thought about his talk with Joraus. He wondered if Klyle really was still alive and what it could mean if he were. Thoughts of the mysterious king transitioned into the things that Joraus had told him about Brael's savage rules. Jake was coming to see that things really were black and white in Fermicia. Kill or die, it was as simple as that. Still dwelling on this unpleasant concept, he decided to slow and wait for Sam.

When she caught up, they walked together quietly for a moment as Jake considered what to say. Finally, he opened his mouth. "I'm sorry I got after you yesterday. About shooting that guy, I mean. It just that I—"

With the same grace as she'd shown throughout their time in Fermicia, Sam spoke quickly to save him from further embarrassment. "I'm just glad you were okay. That would've scared me to death to have two guys attack me at the same time. It was pretty awesome the way you fought them both. I could barely even see your sword; it was moving so fast. I couldn't have done it."

Jake gave a self-conscious smile. "Yeah, I doubt that, but still, thanks." He looked at their guide and thought about the observation he'd made the previous night. "So, is it just me or has it gotten pretty easy to see Joraus and Swyf, even though they're supposed to be invisible?" he asked.

"It isn't just you," Sam replied. "I started noticing it a little while ago too. I asked Swyf about it one night while we were in the vault. She was kinda surprised at first, but then she said it probably had something to do with *Ragesong*."

Jake huffed. "That's convenient. Have you noticed how often they shrug stuff off by saying *Ragesong*?"

Apparently, he hadn't said it quietly enough. Joraus suddenly shimmered back into himself.

"Have you ever noticed that wolves have exceptionally good hearing?" he asked.

"And exceptionally big noses too, apparently," Jake muttered as Sam laughed.

Joraus turned to peer over his shoulder at the girl. Ignoring Jake, he asked her, "So how long ago did this start happening?"

"I'm not really sure. It seems like it happened a little bit at a time." Sam looked questioningly at Jake, who nodded his agreement.

"At first, I figured I was just getting used to you," Jake said. "But last night I was able to see you clearly in the dark from a long way away. It was kinda weird, like you were still see-through, but at the same time you weren't."

"Hmm," Joraus mused. "Swyf may be right, you know. Klyle did say it was possible for you to have *Ragesong* with you at all times. Maybe this is one of its latent abilities, and now the power is starting to awaken inside of you. To be honest, Jake, that's as good a guess as anything else right now."

As the day wore on, Jake began to have fond memories of his bike back home. Walking is seriously overrated, he thought, sourly. Looking down at his feet, he wished that Joraus had let him keep his tennis shoes, because the boots he wore now were stiff and unforgiving. Joraus had said it would take a few days of walking in order to break them in properly. While Jake understood the Changeling's arguments about his old shoes leaving distinctive tracks, they had been so comfortable. Sighing discontentedly, he trudged on.

"How much further until we get out of the forest?" he asked Joraus during one of their quick rest periods.

Joraus squinted down the path. "A couple more hours, I think. We should be coming out of it soon, but we may want to camp in the trees tonight. Kithalo's gates will close at sunset, so we'll need a—"

He was cut off by the frantic beating of wings and the cries of birds. Swyf darted through the air overhead. Right behind her was a large pack of huge black birds. Jake watched as Swyf changed quickly from a hawk to a falcon.

"Rugals!" Joraus shouted. "Sam, you've got to help her!"

The girl quickly unslung her bow and aimed at the black cloud. Jake pulled his sword, wishing there was something he could do to help Swyf, but the birds were far out of his range. Over the flapping wings, Jake could hear the sound of heavy footsteps.

"Soldiers," Joraus warned as a group of Brael's men appeared on the path ahead of them. "They must have heard the noise. Jake, we need to rush them. We have to keep them away from Sam, so she can help Swyf." He raised his voice, "Sam, if any of the Rugals get away, they will report our location to Brael. That *can't* happen!"

The soldiers were in clear view now, and Jake counted ten. As the Changeling started to run at them, he followed right behind.

"Brael's rules, Jake," Joraus called out, before shimmering into the forest wolf.

As one, the soldiers unsheathed their blades and prepared to receive them. This is mad, Jake thought as he ran at the armed men. *We don't stand a chance!* He guessed that Joraus must have had the same thought because the wolf instantly changed into a huge, charging rhino.

Jake heard one of the soldiers gasp, "Changeling," before the creature barreled into them, horn lowered. He gored one of the men and mowed through the rest. Many were knocked over and most of the others dove out of the way.

Jake rushed the only soldier who was still on his feet, swinging his sword. The big man easily parried the attack and flicked a fast counter at Jake's side. Jake pulled his sword back and deflected the curved blade before taking a quick step back. He struck out probingly, testing the soldier's reaction time and reflexes. The man continued to block and counter as they circled one another, trading blows.

All around, the evening air was alive with the sound of battle. Birds squawked and shrieked in pain as Sam fired arrow after arrow into their midst, while Swyf burst in and out of the flock to peck and rake with her fierce talons. The other soldiers had quickly recovered from the charge of the rhinoceros and were attacking the Changeling, which flickered from shape to shape faster than the eye could follow. He harried the soldiers, keeping them focused on him and away from Sam.

A quick glance was all it took for Jake to see that Sam was in trouble. While the ground was littered with dead Rugals, she was starting to waver as she aimed her bow. The arrows she was shooting were beginning to flicker, with some disappearing altogether before reaching their target. She can't touch *Ragesong*, he realized with a sickening fear.

Though the glimpse had been brief, Jake's inattention nearly cost him his life. The soldier, noticing his momentary lapse, rushed him with a quick flurry of blows. Jake blocked frantically, but the attacks kept coming. It was an exposed tree root that saved him. As he stumbled backwards, desperately trying to keep the curved sword away, his foot caught in the root and he fell to the ground. A vicious slash whistled through the air, directly where his head had been a moment earlier.

Gritting his teeth, Jake rolled, dodging the soldier's downward cut, and jumped back to his feet. With speed born of desperation, he rushed the man. His blade flashed and the soldier parried once, and then twice, but Jake's third swing bit deep into the man's side. The warrior gasped in pain and clutched at his body with his free hand. Jake did not wait this time. He ripped his sword free and thrust it into the man's exposed chest. The soldier instantly buckled and Jake frantically wrenched the weapon out before the man's body fell on top of it.

I can't believe it! I killed him! I just killed a man! Tears stinging his eyes, Jake forced the painful thoughts down as he sprinted towards the remaining soldiers. They had surrounded the Changeling and were slowly tightening the circle. Joraus was a mountain lion again and three soldiers lay dead at his feet, but there were still five more. The cat's eyes flicked up and saw Jake running towards two of his opponents. He let out a wild scream that filled the air as Jake swung at the back of the closest warrior.

Not waiting for the man to fall, Jake whipped the blade around and attacked a second soldier. The warriors spun in confusion, which was all Joraus needed as he tore into the remaining guards. Cat and boy danced through the soldiers, cutting, biting, slashing and clawing, until the last of the warriors screamed in pain as Joraus clamped on to his leg, before falling to the ground with Jake's sword buried deep in his stomach.

Joraus did not waste any time. He shimmered into a large eagle and streaked towards the remaining Rugals, his talons tucked under him and his beak extended. Swyf was tangled with one of the birds while another clawed at her exposed back. Joraus rammed the offending creature and it instantly dropped. Swyf gave a quick twist of her beak and the bird she was engaged with fell to the earth.

There were only three Rugals left, but they each fled in a different direction. Joraus followed one while Swyf darted after another. Sam, sweat beading on her brow, trained her bow on the third.

The shaft of light resting between her fingers was flickering so rapidly that it hurt Jake's eyes. "You've got this, Sam," he whispered as she released the string.

The arrow shot forward and buried itself in the Rugal's eye. In a spray of feathers, the black bird dropped like a stone. Jake tore his eyes away from it to watch in horror as Sam's bow tumbled limply from her grip. He rushed to catch her as she crumpled to the forest floor.

CHAPTER 18:

SWYF'S TALE

"Jake, she will be fine!" Joraus called urgently. "Swyf will tend to her, but now I need your help!" Swyf limped over to Jake and briefly touched his arm as he laid Sam down carefully on the hard ground. He looked up to see that Joraus had a dead soldier draped over his shoulder.

"We have to get these bodies cleaned up and clear out of here before another patrol comes searching for this one." He patted the back of the soldier. "I'll take care of the men, but you have to get the Rugals."

For a moment Jake stared transfixed at the feet of the dead warrior as they dangled in front of the Changeling. He realized with dismay that it was the first man he'd battled; the one he'd killed. I killed someone, he thought in numb disbelief. Grief washed over him and his eyes clouded with tears. *How many of them did I kill?? I've never hurt anyone in my life and now I've killed people.*

"Jake, there isn't time," warned Joraus. Walking over, he shook him sharply with his free hand. "We can talk about what happened later, but we have to hurry now."

Jake nodded woodenly and wiped at his eyes before picking up a few of the dead birds by their feet. He followed Joraus as he led the way off the path and into a dense thicket of smaller trees. Joraus heaved the body inside and sprinted back the way he had come. Jake followed his example with the handful of dead Rugals. He moved stiffly, but forced himself to continue with the repetitive chore. By the time they had managed to clean up all of the bodies, weapons, birds and feathers, Swyf had revived Sam.

The girl's eyes were still glazed over, but, thought Jake with relief, at least they were open.

"Swyf, we can't wait for her," Joraus said in a serious tone. "Can you walk? I'll take Sam, but we have to get out of here."

She nodded wearily and rose. Joraus picked up Sam, and started off down the path, with Jake and Swyf falling into step behind him. Before long, he stopped with a curse, his face wincing in pain.

Jake noticed for the first time that there was a shallow cut running down his side. A light silver substance dripped into the dirt. "Joraus, you've been hurt," he said stupidly.

"Startling observation, Dr. Obvious," he retorted.

Jake felt embarrassed until he saw the Changeling grin, though the pain was still evident on his face. "Sorry, but to be honest, I've wanted to use that expression for years. I heard your dad say it once." He grunted wearily. "I guess there is no help for it," he said, carefully handing Sam to Swyf. "You better not tell anyone, ever!"

He shimmered into the form of a mule, and with a light laugh, Swyf placed Sam on his back. Joraus gave an annoyed

"Hee-haw" before continuing onward, his hooves kicking up dust as he walked. Swyf gave Jake a sidelong wink as she fell into step behind the portly animal.

When the group arrived at the edge of the forest, the sun had already disappeared, leaving behind a deep orange afterglow in its wake. Instead of walking out into the open air, Joraus turned off the path, but stayed within the protecting cover of the trees. When they were safely away from the trail, he stopped. Jake helped Sam to scramble down, but her knees nearly buckled when they took her full weight and she leaned heavily on him to keep from falling.

Joraus shimmered and looked around. "This will work for now," he said, studying his weary friends. "Unfortunately, we are too close to the city for a fire tonight. It will be cold, but if we all huddle up, we should be okay until morning. In the meantime I think we need to worry about cleaning ourselves up."

He pointed at Jake's bag. "Jake, I slipped a few medicine bottles into your pack before we left. They are in the side pocket."

Jake reached inside and pulled out four small, sealed containers. "There isn't a lot here," he said, passing them over.

Joraus tossed two of the bottles to Swyf before breaking the seals on another. He dabbed a little of whatever was in the container on his fingers and began to gently massage it into the cut on his side. Swyf was doing the same thing with multiple cuts and abrasions all over her arms, legs and neck. Joraus blushed when she asked him to take care of a number of wounds on her back, but he obediently stepped over to help.

Jake took a seat next to Sam on the ground and leaned against the tree as he let out a small groan. He felt as though he could sleep through anything. Next to him, the girl let out a huge yawn as she stretched both arms into the air.

"Stop that," Jake said as he began to yawn himself.

"Sorry," Sam giggled. "I am just so tired right now. I feel like I haven't slept in weeks."

"I think I know what you mean."

"Believe me, Jake, you don't."

He studied her with concern in his eyes. "So are you okay, really? I mean, I've seen you get tired from shooting the bow, but you completely blacked out."

Sam looked down at the ground. "I'm not sure. I could feel *Ragesong* there, but it seemed to be just out of reach. It was strange. At first I was so full of adrenaline that I didn't notice anything, but a lot of my arrows weren't landing where I meant them to. By the time I realized that I was shooting on my own without *Ragesong*, it was too late. I couldn't leave Swyf up there all by herself with all those birds, so I just kept telling myself 'one more, one more' over and over again. I don't even remember what happened in the end. Did any of them get away?"

Jake shook his head. "No. After me and Joraus finished with the soldiers, he turned into an eagle and went up to fight with Swyf. The last three Rugals split apart, but Joraus and Swyf each went after one and you shot the third. Then you fainted."

"I must have pushed myself too hard," she mused to herself. "I better figure out how to use *Ragesong* fast or learn how to shoot better."

Sam looked over at him. "How are you doing? I saw some of the soldiers on the ground and they weren't all killed by animals."

"I know," said Jake softly. "I've been trying not to think about it."

"I'm sorry," Sam began. "I didn't mean–"

"No, no." Jake's eyes grew wet. "It's okay. I should probably talk about it. I know that I didn't have any choice, but–" His voice broke and he hung his head. "I killed some of those men. I actually swung my sword into them and they died. I've never hurt anyone before."

Sam reached out and wrapped her arms around Jake as he sobbed quietly into her shoulder. After a couple of minutes he pulled away and wiped at his puffy eyes. "Sorry," he said, embarrassed. "I guess I've been holding that in for a little while."

"You don't have anything to be sorry about," she said quietly. "I'm glad that killing those men wasn't easy for you to do."

They sat against the tree, chatting as the night fell around them. They talked about home and school, and their friends. Jake kept hoping that Sam might mention video games, but they never came up. He sighed inwardly. *She is probably doing it on purpose.*

As the night sounds of the forest came alive around them, Jake volunteered for first watch, knowing that he was the only one not injured or physically drained. The others agreed, and quickly set up the rest of the schedule for the night before dropping off into an exhausted sleep.

As Jake prepared for a long watch, he glanced down at the ground and spotted a small branch. It was about the size of his flute. Reaching down to pick it up, a pang of homesickness

179

flooded through him. He shut his eyes tight as he waited for it to pass, like all the other times, but it lingered. Jake finally let go and opened himself to the memories: wrestling with his dad after work; his mom's gentle instructions as they practiced; his first day of band, and playing basketball with his friends.

He missed his parents, his house and his room, but for some reason, tonight Jake missed his flute most of all. Slowly, he lifted the branch to his lips and blew, fingering one of his favorite songs on the cold, dead wood. It was strange, but in the cool night air he could have sworn he heard the soft, sweet melody of his flute echoing through the trees.

Jake jerked awake and sat up, rubbing his eyes. His cloak fell off, and he reached down to wrap it back around him, shivering. When he saw Sam lying next to him on the ground, he changed his mind and gently laid it over her. Rubbing his arms briskly, he looked around, feeling sure that a noise had woken him, but all he could hear were chirping crickets.

Jake squinted in the dim, pre-dawn light and saw Joraus asleep on the other side of Sam. Swyf was leaning on a tree not far away. She put a finger to her lips and motioned for him to join her.

"Did you hear something?" he whispered as he approached.

Swyf nodded and pointed towards Kithalo. "It was music of some kind," she said softly. "Something is happening in the city. I'm not sure what day it is, but I don't remember any holidays that are celebrated like that."

Jake sat down next to Swyf, a little nervous to talk to her one on one. Despite the length of time he had spent with her over the last couple of weeks, he still didn't feel like he knew her very well. "So, you and Joraus grew up in the same village?" he asked as a way to break the ice.

Swyf nodded, but didn't say anything. Jake waited, wondering if he should have just asked about the weather, but after a minute she finally spoke. "There was only one village of Changelings. We were not a big race."

"I'm really sorry Swyf," Jake said, catching the past tense of her answer.

She raised an eyebrow in surprise. "So, Joraus told you about us?"

"Only a little. He did tell me that you guys were kinda ignored when you were young though."

Swyf gave a small sigh, "We were feared, Jake. We were the most powerful Changelings to have ever been born and the others feared us." She pulled her legs up beneath her. "For as much good as our powers did anyone," she added bitterly.

Jake was not sure what to say, so he just waited. The sun peaked out over the distant mountaintops and he felt the air warm slightly.

Swyf picked up a stick and began to twirl it in her hands as she gazed out into the hazy morning light. "Not long after Brael fled from Klyle and the guard, he visited my village. Joraus and I were out training on our own."

She paused for a brief moment, and then continued in a flat, emotionless tone that bespoke her anger and frustration more than any words could. "Though we were still young, we had already far outstripped the other Changelings in both physical and mental ability. My people thought to limit our power by keeping us ignorant. They could be remarkably blind, wrapped in their delusions of security and protection. It was that shortsightedness that pushed me and Joraus out into the woods when we could have been there to help.

"When I realized that our people had no plans to train us, I made up a game. Looking back now, I realize how reckless and dangerous it was. The slightest mistake could have killed us, but we were still young; we thought we were invincible. We spent days in the libraries, researching the anatomy of different animals, and then we would go into the woods and try to best each other. We quickly discovered that Joraus had an affinity to ground animals while I was most at home in the air. We would battle for hours."

Jake smiled a little. "Was this the same game that you played when we came out of the mountains?"

Swyf laughed lightly in soft, musical tones. "The very same. Once we had learned everything we could from the village books, we would go out every day. It kept our reflexes sharp and our minds sharper. It was also the most fun I've ever had."

Abruptly, Swyf stopped laughing and used the stick she held to push her hair out of her eyes. "It was during one of those contests that *he* came. Though we thought we lived in secret, somehow Brael found out about us. He went to the village elders seeking an alliance. No doubt he thought that Changelings would fit quite nicely into the new army he was creating to overthrow Klyle.

"When the elders refused, he–"

Gritting her teeth, Swyf snapped the stick in half. "He slaughtered everyone. The males, females, even the babies." She hurled one of the pieces of wood at an unoffending tree. "When Joraus and I returned, Brael was gone, and everyone was dead. I could only think of revenge. I wanted to go after the man that had destroyed my people. They may not have accepted me, but other than Joraus, they were the only family I had ever known."

Swyf threw the other half of the stick and it hit the tree in the exact same place as the first. "At the time, I didn't even know who had done it. Joraus had to hold me down until he could talk sense into me. He said, 'If someone could do that to our whole village, what chance do we have of defeating him?'"

She gave Jake a little smile. "He always was a quick thinker, and after he brought me back to my senses, we decided to investigate. For weeks we followed Brael's trail. We were young and inexperienced, but he wasn't trying to hide. Wherever he went, we heard his name whispered in fear. Eventually, we began to hear another name in the whispering, Klyle. Only this name was spoken with awe and reverence.

"Once we discovered who Klyle was, Joraus insisted we journey to Kardonin to find him," Swyf continued. "I was skeptical, but I didn't want to separate from Joraus, so we journeyed to Faldona and presented ourselves at Klyle's castle. The soldiers guarding the place looked formidable, and at first they were leery of our intentions. I learned later that they were his personal guard and the most respected soldiers in the land. When they encircled us and drew their swords, I was going to attack, but again, Joraus cautioned prudence.

"I still remember when Klyle entered the room. He was dressed simply, but majesty was in every step he took. He motioned for his soldiers to lower their weapons and gazed at us inquiringly. Joraus explained our story and I saw compassion in his eyes as he listened. He immediately invited us to stay and we've served him ever since."

"Wow," was all Jake could think of to say. He'd had no idea that Joraus and Swyf had suffered so much. Coming from a loving family himself, he could not imagine being an outcast for his whole childhood, and then coming home one day to find that everyone he had ever known was dead. He hoped he'd never have to know the amount of pain and sorrow the Changelings had suffered.

From the way they both talked of Klyle, Jake knew that the kind-hearted king had done more than take them in; he had become a father figure to them, or at least an older brother. Jake hoped, for their sake, that they would find him. *Not knowing must be driving them crazy.*

Swyf and Jake sat in silence for a while, watching the sunrise together. He felt a little awkward, wanting to say something, but at the same time Swyf did not appear to want to talk any more. As he sat there considering what he should do, he was startled by the sound of music drifting into the forest. At first it sounded like the military fanfares from back home, but as Jake listened he was surprised by the minor inflections in it.

"Is that standard in Fermician music?" he asked.

Swyf cocked her head. "Not for celebrations or holiday music. It sounds a little ominous." She stood up and dusted herself off. "I think it is time we woke the sleeping beauties. I want to get into Kithalo and find out what is going on."

After Sam and Joraus were roused, the group packed up and prepared to leave. As they were walking out of the grove, Swyf had a suggestion that made Jake's blood run cold. "Joraus," she said, "don't you think we should keep their weapons away from the city? I think they might draw a lot of attention."

He turned and looked at Jake and Sam speculatively. "Hmm, you may be right. I'll be right back." Changing quickly into a wolf, Joraus darted off through the forest.

Jake was not sure that he liked the idea, but he could see Swyf's point. Perhaps a couple of kids walking around the streets with a bow and sword would be a little conspicuous. The sword had been a kind of security blanket for him and, judging by Sam's mixed expression, he was pretty sure that she felt the same way about her bow.

Joraus soon returned with some dark pieces of cloth clamped in his jaws. He padded over and dropped the material on the ground. Jake recognized the black cloaks that Brael's soldiers had been wearing. Joraus shimmered back into himself and picked them up.

"We can wrap the weapons in these," he suggested. "There should be plenty of spots where we can hide the bundles. We can come back and get them when we exit the city."

Jake knew it was a good idea, but he removed the sword and scabbard reluctantly. He hesitated before wrapping them in the black cloth and Joraus saw the concern in his eyes. "Don't worry, Jake. We will hide them well, and the weapons know how to protect themselves. You'll both have them back before you even realize they are gone."

Jake sighed and wrapped the sword tightly in the thick cloth. He reached out to hand it to Joraus, but the Changeling quickly pulled his hands back. "No, thanks, I'm not touching it. I have no desire to be a guinea pig when that sword decides it's in the wrong hands."

"That would've been a lot funnier if you had changed into a guinea pig to emphasize your point," Sam observed offhandedly.

Joraus ignored her as he led them all through the trees to search for possible hiding places. Most suggestions were quickly dismissed, but in a heavy thicket far from the road they found a fallen tree surrounded by deep underbrush. Sam and Jake tucked their weapons beneath the log and stepped back. The bundles were completely hidden; not even the black of the cloaks was visible. Joraus nodded in satisfaction before leading the group back towards the road.

CHAPTER 19:

TRAITOR'S WALK

The forest road joined the main highway not far beyond the confines of the forest. Throngs of people were traveling to and from the city. Joraus stayed close to Jake and Sam, and although they received some strange looks, the threat of the Changeling in his forest wolf form caused other travelers to keep their distance. Over the past few weeks, Jake had grown used to the company of his own small group, and being around so many people all at once made him nervous. He took the time to study these strangers and he was increasingly glad that Joraus was with them.

Most of the travelers wore shabby and filthy clothes, and their faces were unwashed and haggard. The apparent suspiciousness of the Fermician natives made Jake uneasy, but he soon realized it was not only directed at him. It was as if no one trusted anyone else here. He wondered how the people could stand to live that way.

Jake wished Swyf or Joraus were in a position to be able to talk. The sight of these downtrodden Fermicians presented him with a lot of questions that he'd never really had to think about. He wondered if this was the normal way of life for them, or whether Brael had something to do with their distrusting glances and unhappy demeanor.

As the group crested the top of a large hill, all thoughts of the natives were driven from Jake's mind as he stared down at the city of Kithalo. As if it were specifically designed to greet them, another fanfare blasted through the air. Sam stood next to him as he paused to listen. The noise was thunderous. He tried to imagine how many instruments it would take to create that level of sound.

Sam tilted her head as she listened to the strange fanfare. "It's kinda creepy, isn't it?"

Jake nodded. "That's what Swyf said this morning. It's a lot different than the normal marches you hear back home."

"That's for sure."

Jake examined Kithalo. It wasn't exactly what he had pictured. He had imagined a small town with a few squat, ugly buildings, but this place appeared to be very well established. He looked past the large, open wooden gates and into the city itself. Great buildings lined both sides of the main road, in front of which were display stands covered by large canopies. Jake could hear the cries of shopkeepers attempting to draw customers.

There was a line of people in front of the gate. Jake and Sam turned to join the queue, but instead of following, Joraus slunk off quickly. High overhead, Swyf circled once before flying off towards the surrounding forest.

"That's quite a formidable animal you've got there," came a voice from behind them.

Jake turned to see the face of an older man with short, graying hair. His deep blue eyes fit his weathered face and a silver goatee accented his strong chin. He was dressed in black pants, a black shirt and a deep blue vest. Though not an overly large man, he exuded a confidence that was a little disconcerting. Jake opened his mouth, not quite sure what he was going to say.

"He was a gift from our father," Sam said quickly. "We've had him since he was a pup. Father trained him to escort us into the gates of a city and then wait for us from afar."

Jake stared at her in amazement. She elbowed him in the ribs and he gave a late, and very unconvincing, nod of agreement. Sam rolled her eyes and smiled at the older man.

"Your father is a wise man," he said with a kind smile. "But are you not a trifle young to be visiting the city without a proper escort?"

Again Sam had an answer ready. She put on a tragic expression. "Father is currently caring for our mother. She was injured during a journey to Foldona and has not yet recovered. He would not have let us come had there been another choice. She is in need of medicine and we do not live all that far from the city. We assured him that we would be safe, but he insisted we take the wolf for protection."

"I see," he replied with concern. "Well, I wish for the speedy recovery of your mother."

Jake sensed an opportunity. "Sir, we heard music a moment ago," he started to ask, but he trailed off uncertainly as the man raised a questioning eyebrow.

"'The Traitor's Anthem?' Surely you've heard it before?"

Sam stepped on Jake's foot, hard. "Of course we have, sir. You'll have to excuse my brother. He has always been a bit slow. It is another reason why father insisted on the wolf."

The older man was still studying Jake. "I see," he said slowly.

They arrived at the front of the line and Jake was saved from further embarrassment by a soldier who waved them forward. Two of Brael's guards were standing before the gate with their spears crossed while a third was questioning everyone who wanted to enter.

"Are you carrying any weapons?" the soldier asked in a resigned tone of voice as the children approached.

"Um, just these," said Sam nervously as she lifted her shirt just enough to show the blade belted at her waist.

"No weapons are permitted within the city today. You'll have to leave them over there," the guard instructed, pointed with his spear to a row of tables. "They will be tagged and you will be given a receipt. You may retrieve them upon leaving the gates."

The older man standing behind them raised his voice. "They are children, here to acquire medicine for their sick mother. Permit them their weapons."

"Sir, the law clearly states that—" the soldier began with an annoyed expression, but when he glanced at the man, a shocked look crossed his face and he stiffened. His boots clicked together audibly and he jerked himself to attention. "A-as you say, my l-lord," he stammered as he motioned them all through the gates.

My lord? Nervously, Jake glanced up at the stranger who had helped them.

"Thank you, sir," Sam said, gratefully.

"No thanks are necessary, young lady. My name is Liakut, and if you have any further need of assistance, you have only to ask," he replied with a gentle smile.

Sam appeared to be won over by the man's graciousness, but the way he studied them made Jake a little uneasy. He could not pinpoint anything in particular; he just didn't trust Liakut.

Suddenly, the man straightened. "I must go," he said quickly. "It is a busy day and I have much to do before the Traitor's Walk. I hope you find what you need."

Sam and Jake watched as he faded into the crowd of people gathering in the streets. The cobblestones were rough and uneven, and men with brooms were frantically sweeping the main road in preparation for something. Jake gazed around in wonder. The buildings were a combination of wood and white stone. At first the contrast seemed strange, but the more Jake studied it, the more he found that he liked the combination. It felt as if the building designers had wanted to remind the people of Kithalo that the city had originated from the forest.

"What is the Traitor's Walk, do you think?" Jake asked quietly, so as not to be overheard by the many passersby.

"I don't know," Sam retorted. "Why don't you run up and ask Liakut, you blockhead? Did you see the way he stared at us after you asked him about the music? Can't you be any more discreet than that?"

"Geez, sorry, so I'm not as quick as you are."

"I'll say," Sam huffed, but then she let the matter drop. "Anyway, I bet the Traitor's Walk has something to do with that music. He called it 'The Traitor's Anthem.' Doesn't it seem like there are a lot of people out in the street? I mean, I don't know if this is how it usually is, but it looks like everyone is lining up for a parade or something."

Jake realized that Sam was right. Though there were some individuals attempting to shop, the majority appeared to be standing around, waiting. Looking down the street, he saw that people were filing in from both sides of the road for as far as he could see. The uneasy feeling he'd had since talking with Liakut at the gate intensified. He saw that many in the crowd held rotten fruit or vegetables.

"Sam, there has to be a way that we can find out what is going on," he whispered.

"I know, but it feels like we've walked into something important. If we try to ask questions right now, we could raise the wrong kind of attention."

Sam looked around at the crowd. The road was getting even busier and people were starting to push so they could get a better view.

"I think we should stay quiet and find a place where we can watch," she suggested. "Maybe this parade or Traitor's Walk, or whatever, will give us some idea of what is going to happen."

"All right, but let's be careful," Jake cautioned. "I have a bad feeling about this."

They wormed their way through the crowd until they found a spot near the front that gave a clear view of the street. Jake wrinkled his nose at the smell of sour sweat and unwashed bodies around him. "It smells like a locker room," he whispered.

"Shush," Sam hissed, but she giggled softly.

After waiting for nearly thirty minutes, they heard a loud blast and a giant cheer went up from the crowd. Over the celebration, Jake discerned the same fanfare that he'd heard earlier. Some of the smaller children began to cry while others slapped their hands against their ears in a vain attempt to block out the sound. When 'The Traitor's Anthem' ended, the last thunderous blast lingered, echoing off the surrounding buildings. Jake heard some cheers from further up the street, towards the gate they had come through, and he craned his neck to get a view of what was coming, but the throngs of people blocked his view.

As he waited, Jake looked around at the people closest to him. Most wore expressions of anticipation and excitement on their faces, their hands clutching rotten produce eagerly. But he also noticed a scattered few who did not share the crowd's enthusiasm. They were wearing robes of a dark, nondescript brown material with large hoods that cast their faces in shadow. Unusual bulges in their cloaks told Jake that he was not the only one who was currently armed. He watched curiously as the figures shot quick, nervous glances at one another and fingered the objects under their robes.

He was just about to point them out to Sam when the people around him began to cheer. Jake looked up the street to see about twenty of Brael's soldiers marching into view, dressed in black furs and gripping weapons in their fists. One of the men yelled something and then all of them twirled their swords elaborately as the crowd encouraged them on.

Jake could tell at once that these guards were much different than the bumbling foot soldiers he'd seen out on the Skidippy plain. They were polished and clean cut, and each was as big as a bull. They handled their weapons with a deadly grace and precision that worried him. How would he fare if he came upon a group of these men in battle?

Behind the soldiers, Jake saw some large animals that vaguely resembled horses. There were a few distinct differences, however. Their mouths were full of sharp teeth and they had yellow, catlike eyes. When Jake peered closer, he saw that they were covered in scales instead of hair.

The creatures were ridden by wild-looking men dressed in leather breeches and vests. Their massive arms were bare and their long hair was tied back with leather cords. There were also small white things tied in with their hair, but Jake couldn't tell what they were. The riders gripped the beasts with their legs while in their hands they held drawn bows, which seemed to be made of polished bone. Many of the women in the crowd screamed in delight when the riders looked in their direction. Jake had to admit that he was a little relieved when Sam huffed out an annoyed breath.

Massive cages full of black-feathered Rugals followed the strange riders. Seeing the birds beating their wings behind bars was a vivid reminder for Jake of the battle from the night before. Sam's inaudible gasp told him that he wasn't the only one thinking about it. He reached down to give her hand a reassuring squeeze and she grabbed it in a vice-like grip.

The Rugals were only the beginning of a menagerie of fantastical beasts. Jake watched the procession in awe. There were other birds too, and tanks full of strange water creatures. It was frightening to think that he was expected to fight against a man who had such animals and warriors at his disposal.

All of the sudden, all of the people around Jake began to boo and hiss. He looked past the last of the creatures and saw a man with chains binding his arms and legs, surrounded by four soldiers. The first thing that Jake noticed was that his body appeared to be wasting away. The man was tall, but his skin was stretched so taut over his bones that Jake could see his ribcage through his tattered shirt.

The prisoner shuffled down the middle of the road with his head down. He had a shaggy, blond beard and filthy, matted hair that covered his eyes and hung down his back. The crowd pelted him with rotten produce, but he did not acknowledge the stinking fruit, except to occasionally reach up to wipe it from his face. When the prisoner gazed at the crowd, Jake was surprised to see not anger, but sadness in his eyes. Even from that brief glance, he saw compassion and intelligence radiating from the man. He wondered what he could have done to elicit this much hatred from the people.

A part of Jake wanted to rush out and try to help the man, however he could, but the images of the rest of this horrible parade were too vivid in his mind. He was about to turn his attention to the chariot bearing a single rider, which followed behind the prisoner, when a brown-cloaked figure close to him raised a single arm up in the air. It was a signal of some kind and Jake watched as the man shed his robe. Dressed in silver and red, he pulled a sword from its sheath. The other brown-cloaked men followed suit and Jake heard them roar in one voice, "Long live the true king of Kardonin!"

Ten men clad in the same colors rushed towards the prisoner with their swords raised. At first Jake thought they were going to kill him, but instead they attacked and quickly overwhelmed the surprised guards. When the last soldier fell, the men encircled the prisoner and held their blades out, facing the crowd. Just as they were preparing to force their way through, the man in the chariot casually flicked the reins and approached. Jake blinked in amazement when he recognized the rider. He still wore the dark clothes and blue vest, only now he had spiked bracelets around his biceps and had two large, curved knives strapped to his back.

"Jake, it's Liakut!" Sam gasped.

"I know, I know," he said quietly. "Keep your voice down."

The kindly face that Liakut had worn at the city gate was gone. Instead he wore a wicked grin that made the hair on the back of Jake's neck rise.

"What did you fools hope to accomplish?" asked Liakut with a laugh. "Did you honestly think you'd be able to escape with your lives?"

He dismounted from his chariot, and stood facing the men in silver and red. Reaching under his shoulders, with a quick jerk he dislodged his weapons. The knives spun in his hands as he continued to laugh. Liakut handled them with no more concern than a drum major might his baton. The sunlight flashed off the metallic blades, and Jake saw the fear rise in the men surrounding the prisoner.

Unexpectedly, one of them charged Liakut, swinging his sword. Liakut sidestepped and flicked a knife out in a precise cut. It was a simple motion and he made it look effortless, but the swordsman immediately dropped his weapon, clutching his side. Liakut flipped the knife and thrust it behind his back without even bothering to watch where it landed, and the man with the sword fell face first into the dusty road.

When they saw one of their own dead, the other men surrounding the prisoner exploded into action, all of them rushing Liakut. As new as Jake was to sword fighting, he could see by the way these men gripped their weapons that they were experienced warriors. But Liakut moved faster than anyone Jake had ever seen. He weaved through the attackers with a grace Jake could not hope to imitate, his knives cutting through the air so quickly that they were only a blur.

After five more of their number had been killed, the remaining men halted their attack and stood facing him, warily. Only then did Jake notice that Brael's soldiers had stepped into place behind them. At a quick nod from the knife-wielder, two soldiers took hold of each swordsman and quickly disarmed them. Jake glanced quickly at the prisoner to see an expression of utter helplessness cross the man's face.

Brael's soldiers forced the men to kneel in the road in front of Liakut, who turned to glare at the prisoner. "Is this the best your followers can do, oh mighty king?" he scoffed. "If so, it is no wonder that you were so easily defeated."

Jake felt his blood rise as he saw the obvious cruelty and malice in Liakut's expression. *How could I have missed that?* The prisoner did not pull his gaze away from the men kneeling in the dirt as their heads were forced down towards the ground, their necks exposed.

"You now see the futility of opposing the Dread King's kingdom!" Liakut roared at the crowd. "We will crush any who would come against us. Let their fate be an example to any of you!" He motioned to the kneeling men. "This is the fate that awaits any who attempt to hold to the old ways!"

A massive soldier with a large executioner's axe stepped forward, and Jake could only watch in horror as he stepped up to each kneeling man and, with a quick downward cut, sent their heads rolling into the street. One of the other soldiers prodded the prisoner in the back with the butt of his spear, forcing him to walk as the parade slowly restarted.

"Idiots," murmured a man standing next to Jake. "What did they expect, trying to fight an Elite?"

Liakut is an Elite?! Jake stared at the small man as he ran his fingers along the blades of his knives to clean the blood from them. When Liakut was satisfied, he clipped them back in place behind his back. He was still grinning slightly as he climbed back into the chariot and shook the reins. As it jostled forward, Jake's stomach lurched when Liakut looked directly at him and slowly winked.

CHAPTER 20:

AWAKENING

Jake stood there, staring after Liakut. "He was *so* fast," he said softly. "I wouldn't have lasted two seconds in a fight against him."

"Jake," Sam whispered urgently. "Be quiet, you can't say stuff like that here. C'mon," she said, tugging on his arm, "we need to get out of here."

"I wonder who that prisoner was," Jake mused to himself, as she dragged him away from the mass of people that were still screaming and flinging rotten produce.

Sam stamped her foot, but continued to drag him up the street towards the gate. When they were away from most of the frenzied crowd, she turned to stare at him incredulously. "Isn't it *obvious?*"

His head reeling from the casual brutality of the Elite, Jake looked at her distractedly. "Is what obvious?"

She sighed, "Sometimes I wonder about you, Jake. It was Klyle!"

"How do you know that?" he demanded.

"C'mon, didn't you hear what those guys yelled when they ran out to him? Long live the *true* king of Kardonin. Well, except for Brael, the only other king of Kardonin was Klyle. Put it together, Jake!"

He paused to consider. "The guy didn't seem like a normal prisoner. He was, I don't know, different somehow. He acted like he felt bad for all the people watching and throwing stuff at him. I would've been mad."

"Please, Jake," Sam pleaded, pulling at him again. "We really need to talk to Joraus and Swyf."

A part of Jake was disappointed. He had been excited to see what a Fermician city was like, and he definitely wanted to see the things they were selling further on down the street. Reluctantly, he followed Sam. The crowd was starting to break up, but the street was still packed. There was already a line of people wanting to go back through the gate, and Jake and Sam quickly joined them.

Jake peeked down a side street and saw four soldiers standing guard. One of them noticed him looking and scowled menacingly. He turned away quickly, afraid of drawing attention to himself. The queue to get out of the city moved much faster than the one to get in, and soon the children found themselves outside the big, wooden gates. The line to retrieve weapons was much longer, however, and Jake was glad that he and Sam still had their knives. As he studied the weapons lying on the table, he wondered briefly how the rebels had managed to get swords into the city.

"Do you think Joraus and Swyf will be able to find us?" Jake asked with a touch of concern in his voice.

Sam simply pointed up in the air to where a hawk was circling lazily overhead.

"Oh."

They started back down the main road and before they had gone very far, Joraus rejoined them, still in the form of the forest wolf.

"Joraus," Jake said softly. "We have to talk. Now!"

The Changeling gave a small shake of his head and kept walking.

"But, it's about Klyle."

The wolf growled in warning and Jake stopped talking. They worked their way back to the place where they had originally entered the highway. Joraus started to move faster, forcing the children to jog to keep up.

When they were alone at last, Joraus shimmered back into himself, and said, "Okay, I want to hear everything that happened since you went in the gate. I would have tried to go with you, but there was an Elite at the gate and he would've felt me change. That was why I left so quickly."

Jake and Sam began to stumble over themselves in a rush to tell him what had happened.

"There was a parade—"

"Tons of mean-looking soldiers—"

"An Elite—"

"Klyle was there—"

Joraus held up his hands. "Enough," he said, loudly enough to stem the flood. "Now, speak one at a time. What do you mean, Klyle was there? What does he have to do with any of this? Walk and talk. We need to get your weapons."

Sam took a deep breath and started to explain. She began with the encounter with Liakut at the gate, and with Jake's help, she explained the Traitor's Walk. They mentioned the prisoner at the end of the parade and the men who had tried to save him.

"Wait," Joraus interrupted, "what color did you say the men were wearing?"

"Red and silver," Jake answered quickly.

"Those were Klyle's colors," nodded Joraus.

When they finished talking, the Changeling did not speak. The only thing that gave any hint as to what he was feeling was a slight increase in his stride. When they reached the hiding spot, Joraus pulled back the thick brush and Jake breathed a sigh of relief. The black cloaks were still there. He had been half afraid that someone might have taken them during their absence.

Jake quickly pulled the robe-covered sword out from under the log and unwrapped it carefully. He slid off his pack and hung it on a nearby branch, before slipping the sheath over his head and tightening it into place. When it was comfortably snug, he put his pack back on and looked around.

An immediate feeling of security enveloped him and only now did Jake realize how nervous he had been without the weapon. Although he'd only had it for a couple of weeks, it already felt like it was a part of him. He glanced over at Sam and saw that with her bow back in place, she was standing a little taller as well. When she looked back at him, he grinned. She smiled back and the mood noticeably lightened. Jake had not forgotten the horrible executions, but he was able to push the memory down for now.

Joraus was searching around irritably. "Where is Sw–" he started to say when she unexpectedly shimmered into view in front of them.

"They are coming," she said, breathlessly. "They were organizing at the gates when I left. Joraus, they have a Snoplout with them."

"What is a...?" Jake started to ask, but one quick glare from Joraus caused him to bite down on his words.

"Long nose or flat?" he inquired, cryptically.

"Flat."

"Well, there is that, at least," said Joraus. "Did you happen to see anything else that can help us?"

"There is a large gathering of soldiers and riders at the other end of the city. They were surrounding a large cage and they looked like they were about to depart," Swyf replied.

"We have to make our way to the other side of the city. We can't lose that cage. What is the size of the group tracking us?"

"Between twenty-five and thirty," she answered. "Why do we need to follow the cage? What is going on?"

"It's Klyle, Swyf," Joraus said softly. "Apparently they paraded him through the city for the amusement of the people of Kithalo. It appears that Brael kept him alive to serve as a constant reminder to them. We can't leave him like that. We have to find a way to save him."

Joraus reached a hand up and wiped his cheeks. He is crying, Jake noticed in astonishment. He had never expected to see the tough shape-changer cry. Then to his further bewilderment, Swyf's eyes welled with tears too.

"Truly?" she asked.

Joraus only nodded and all at once Swyf was hugging him, tears glistening on her cheeks. He held her for a moment, but then he gently took her by the shoulders and pushed her back.

"There is no time, Swyf. We can't lose him. Listen, you have to follow them while we take care of the trackers and the Snoplout. You have to be careful. There will be an Elite with them. Jake and Sam watched him fight off a group of swordsmen without difficulty."

"I understand," Swyf responded as she laid a hand to Joraus' cheek tenderly. "You know I am careful. Take care of Sam and Jake. I will watch for you. Work your way around to the other side of the city and I will try to find you as soon as I can."

Joraus suddenly pulled her in and kissed her fiercely. At first she stood stiffly, as though surprised, but then she melted into his embrace. For a long moment they stood together, until Jake could not take it anymore. "Get a room," he called out a little rudely. Then he recoiled as Sam punched him hard in the arm.

The Changelings broke apart abruptly. Joraus looked embarrassed, but Swyf was wearing a small, secret smile. She shimmered into a hawk and took to the air, her wings beating as they lifted her higher and higher into the treetops.

"Nice, Joraus," Jake said in disgust.

"You are about as romantic as a slug," Sam scolded him.

Joraus looked around. "We've got work to do. We need to take down this search party quickly."

"What's a Snop-whatsit?" Jake asked.

"A Snoplout. They are used for tracking. They are small, furred creatures, and they have either long or small, flat noses. Once one gets your scent, you can't shake it off. It will come straight at us."

"What is the difference between the noses?" said Sam.

"The long-nosed Snoplouts have a stronger sense of smell and they are smarter. It is nearly impossible to trick one. However, it is possible to trick a flat-nosed Snoplout, at least for short periods of time, as they aren't quite as intelligent. We should be able to confuse it slightly. It won't stay that way for long, but it should buy us time.

"Our best chance will be to get a little bit of a lead. Then I will double back and start to pick off the soldiers. That will make them more cautious and thin their ranks a little. Eventually, we'll set up an ambush to take care of the rest."

Joraus looked at the two children. "What happened? How did they know to track us?"

Jake looked at Sam. "Well, we talked to the Elite at the gate when we first went into the city, and there were some soldiers who saw us leave after the parade. I don't know if that has anything to do with it, but that is all I can think of."

"Never mind. It doesn't really matter right now." Joraus turned to Sam. "Are you okay to shoot? You will be vital in slowing them, so that Jake and I aren't overrun."

She gave a quick nod and glanced at Jake uncertainly. He gave her a reassuring smile and patted her on the arm.

"I don't have to tell you that this is going to be extremely difficult," Joraus continued. "We could have really used Swyf, but at the same time we can't afford to lose Klyle."

Joraus started pushing through the brush, moving quickly. "Let's go. We have to hurry."

Jake pulled the straps on his pack tight and followed the Changeling. After a quick moment's thought, he slowed enough for Sam to walk in front of him. When they found another trail, Joraus started to run and they jogged after him. When they left the trail, so they could keep the city in sight through the foliage, Joraus had them split up. He sent one of them straight through the brush while the other went about fifty feet further into the forest. When they all met at the next path, he started sprinting again. This pattern continued as they worked their way around the city. Every time a path ended, they split up, and when they found another trail, they ran.

After a while, Joraus slowed down. "Okay," he said. "I am going to double back now. Keep doing this same thing. Make sure you keep the city in sight, so you don't get lost. I will come back when they get too close and we will set up an ambush."

The Changeling shimmered into a mountain lion and took off through the trees, while the children kept going.

"I am just about sick of forests," Jake panted as he jogged behind Sam on one of the trails.

"At least it is slowing them down too," Sam called back.

Before long, Jake heard a scream of pain. It was distant, but distinct. He peered over his shoulder, but the trees blocked him from seeing anything. They continued on while more screams echoed around the forest. It was hard for Jake to concentrate on what he was doing, and more than once he stumbled as he kept trying to push ahead. They had just reached another trail when Joraus raced up from behind them. He shimmered back into his natural form.

"Hurry, they are coming," he said. "We have to find a place to set up. I killed about five of them, but there are still a lot left."

They sprinted along the path, desperately seeking somewhere they could defend. The trail ended at an open clearing, which Joraus raced across, stopping at the other side.

"This will have to do," he said. "Sam, you have to thin them out. We can't take that many."

Jake put his hands on his knees and took deep gasps, trying desperately to get his breathing back under control. Sam pulled her bow from behind her back and aimed at the other side of the clearing. It was not long before they heard yelling, and then soldiers poured out into the clearing.

Sam did not hesitate, and six men dropped before they realized what was happening. She continued to fire as Jake drew his sword. Hoping against hope that his friend was feeling *Ragesong*, he raised his sword and charged the soldiers. Joraus, again in his lion form, was right at his side.

Jake crashed into the men, swinging his sword. It took a few seconds for him to realize something; he was not at all frightened. Even though curved blades were slashing through the air all around him, he was not afraid. He quickly began to notice other things too. For one, the fatigue he'd felt a moment earlier was gone. Another, the soldiers' swords were moving ridiculously slow.

It was almost as if he were playing one of those video games where he could function at full speed while everyone else was in slow motion. Even Joraus moved as though he were underwater. Jake easily countered the strikes aimed at him, consciously having to redirect his own blade so that it would not arrive too early. Every one of his counters landed true; the guards having no chance to block.

Arrows crawled through the air, and more than once Jake simply cut a soldier down rather than wait for the bolt to reach its mark. In no time at all he had run out of enemies, and he looked around eagerly, hoping there might be more. When all he saw was the mountain lion and the archer, a part of him wanted to rush them. Another part of his mind tried to resist, and for a moment a silent war raged within as he fought to push back the desire to continue fighting.

Finally, reason won out and the world lurched back into normal speed. Gripped by a feeling of vertigo, Jake sank to his knees amidst the unmoving bodies around him. Joraus changed back to himself, and he and Sam slowly approached Jake.

"Are you okay?" Joraus asked, hesitantly, gripping the girl's arm to keep her from getting too close.

"I-I don't know," Jake answered weakly. "I'm a little dizzy."

"A little dizzy we can deal with. Are you feeling anything else?"

"Joraus," Sam said in a quiet voice, "that golden light is gone from his eyes. I think he is okay now."

Jake gave them a little smile. "I think I finally felt *Ragesong.*"

"You think?" Joraus asked, dubiously. "You just killed more than fifteen men. I've never seen anyone move that fast, including Klyle."

"Seriously, Jake," said Sam, "you were a blur. I was feeling *Ragesong* too, but you killed those guards faster than I could shoot. It was amazing."

Jake looked down at all of the bodies littering the floor of the clearing. "Let's go. I am going to be sick if we stay here much longer."

"You two go ahead," Joraus said. "I need to take care of the Snoplout and then I'll catch up. Remember, keep the city in sight."

Jake strode quickly through the grove, trying not to see all the death around him. Now that he had come out of *Ragesong,* the feeling of overpowering confidence was gone. All he could think about now was getting away from the carnage. Sam fell in behind him, but she did not say anything, and Jake was grateful that she wasn't pressing him for details yet. His thoughts were a little jumbled and he was having some trouble sorting them out.

Although he was still sickened by the fact that he'd had to kill, he did not experience the guilt he had felt the last time. He now saw that he was acting in self-defense and that he hadn't sought out this battle. Jake was a little nervous about the last thing he felt, right before he was able to push *Ragesong* away. When he had looked at Joraus and Sam, he hadn't seen them as friends, but only as potential threats; threats that he had wanted to put down. That scared him more than anything else.

"Are you okay, Jake?" Sam finally asked.

"I'm a little scared, to be honest," Jake answered, truthfully.

"Because of the soldiers?"

"Not really."

They walked in silence for a few minutes.

"Was it what happened after?" she pushed gently.

Jake glanced at her. "How do you know about that?"

"I saw something in your eyes when you turned and saw me. It was like it was you, but it wasn't you. I mean, I could see your eyes, but at the same time... I don't know; they were all golden for a minute and when you looked at us..." She paused, staring at him helplessly, before adding, "It seemed like you didn't know who we were for a minute."

"I didn't," he whispered. "That's what scares me. I saw you and Joraus, and for just a second I wanted to attack. If that is what *Ragesong* means, I don't want it."

"Whether you want it or not, it is a part of you."

Jake and Sam spun around to see Joraus walking behind them. He had approached unnoticed as they were talking.

Jake's voice trembled. "I almost attacked you. I still remember how it felt. I didn't see *you*. All I saw was a mountain lion and an archer. Another part of me was able to figure it out, but is that what happened to Brael?"

"Jake," Joraus said quietly, "I wish I knew what to tell you. The only person who could possibly know is Klyle. As soon as we rescue him, he may be able to answer your questions."

The Changeling stepped in front of them. "Try to think of something else for a while."

Jake watched sourly as Joraus shimmered back into a mountain lion and led the way. "Easy for you to say," he muttered.

"So," Sam began with the hint of a smile in her voice, "my favorite games are first-person shooters."

CHAPTER 21:

NOAUM MOUNTAINS

It took them the rest of the day, but Joraus finally led Jake and Sam out onto the main road on the far side of Kithalo just after sunset. Without any sign of Swyf, they started walking down it, with Joraus back in the form of the forest wolf. Jake was glad for the road. His hands and face were scratched and stinging from all of the roughage in the forest, and there were burrs stuck to his socks inside his boots.

Hearing a loud groan behind him, Jake turned to look back at the distant city. The large gates were slowly closing and he caught a glimpse of lights winking from the buildings within. He wondered if he would ever visit Kithalo again, hoping that if he did there would be a little more time for exploring. Jake studied his surroundings and realized that all of the land had probably once been forest. He wondered if the city had started out as one of those woodland villages, with people living among the trees.

The road cut through large fields, and Jake wondered how long it had taken for the people of Kithalo to clear this portion of land for cultivating crops. It was interesting to speculate about what grew from the plants and stalks growing around him. Some were vaguely familiar, but he had never had a garden of his own, so he lacked any real farming experience.

Joraus would occasionally leave the road and Jake assumed it was to search for a place where they could rest for the night. It was not until the stars were winking brightly overhead that the Changeling trotted out of the forest and shimmered into his natural form.

"Please say you found some water," Sam said when he rejoined them.

Jake nodded in agreement. Their water skins had run dry hours ago, and the dusty road was making him thirstier than ever.

Joraus motioned them to follow him. "There is a small stream a little ways in."

"I want a shower," Jake complained. "What good is a stream going to do?"

"You need more than a shower," Sam teased, wrinkling her nose.

Although numerous retorts entered his mind, Jake simply answered with a dry "Thanks" before following Joraus back into the woods.

"Hey, Joraus, how come we haven't seen more people?" he asked. "Don't they travel very much in Fermicia?"

"They used to," Joraus replied over his shoulder as he walked. "I am not sure. Those people we saw on the road yesterday didn't look like they wanted to be out at all. I wonder if it has something to do with being this close to Brael's stronghold. I have tried to keep you off the main roads for as much as possible, but we should have seen more people then we have. It really is too bad that this is your first view of Kardonin. It used to be a wonderful place. The people were happy and well cared for. Maybe with your help, it can regain that former glory."

The Changeling pointed ahead. "The spring is just up there. It is going to get too dark to see soon, so we need to fill our water skins and prepare for the night."

"Joraus," Sam said tentatively, "I hate to bring this up, but I am starving. We haven't eaten very well for the last couple of days and nothing at all since early this morning. Could you find us something to eat?"

"Yes, of course, Sam," he answered. "Jake, I think we can risk a small fire. If you can get that started, I will bring back something for us to eat. Make sure to clear out the area and dig a small pit, like I showed you. We can't take a chance on setting the woods ablaze."

By the time the Changeling returned, Jake had a good campfire burning, and he and Sam were huddled around it, holding their hands out for warmth. They looked up to see him holding a pair of fat rabbits by the ears.

Joraus quickly prepared them and set them to roasting over the small flames. The group ate quickly and when they were done they sat back, enjoying the warmth emanating from the fire.

"Do you think that Swyf is–" Jake began, but he cut off abruptly at a warning glance from Sam.

"I'm sure she is fine," the girl said, consolingly. "She is tough and knows how to take care of herself."

"I'll take first watch," Joraus rumbled and stood up. "Put the fire out before you go to sleep."

"You are such an idiot," Sam whispered to Jake.

"What?" he protested. "It isn't like this is the first time she's been gone."

"Can't you see how worried he is?"

"What are you talking about? He looks the same as always."

"Boys are so stupid," Sam muttered. "Listen, just don't bring up Swyf for a little while."

"Fine," Jake said, pouting. He threw the bone he'd been picking at back into the fire. "Do you want second watch or third?"

The group followed the road all of the next day and camped again in the forest at night. There were few travelers and, thankfully, no soldiers. Jake wondered how far ahead Klyle really was. He started scanning the skies for Swyf, and every time a bird came into view his excitement rose, but the creatures never slowed or stopped; they just continued on to wherever they were going.

Jake found himself missing home the most during these long, uneventful days of walking. When he had first arrived in Fermicia, the thrill of being in a new land was enough, but that had long since faded. Now it was just hour after hour of tedious wandering in the trees. Even the cleared fields of Kithalo had given way to the ever-present forest ages ago.

As he brooded about all the things he was missing at home, Jake finally stumbled on a way to entertain himself. He was thinking of one of his favorite games, wishing he could play it again when he unexpectedly thought, well, why can't I? As he began to picture the beginning of the story, and all of the things he needed to do to advance, he forgot about the tedium and his weariness. He had just arrived at a good part in the game when Joraus stopped. The wolf walked over to the side of the road and studied something.

"Are you okay, Jake?" Sam questioned. "You were a little out of it for a while there."

"Um, yeah, where are we?" asked Jake, a little annoyed to be pulled out of his thoughts. It reminded him of when his mom used to call into his room for one thing or another while he was in the middle of something.

"Joraus saw something, I think." Sam looked at Jake curiously. "What were you thinking about?"

"Ah, well..." He hesitated, a little embarrassed to admit what he had been doing.

The girl crossed her arms. "Does it have something to do with video games?"

"Maybe. So what?" Jake replied, defensively. "I didn't ask you to talk about them and I got bored."

"Get a life, Jake," she snapped.

"Children," Joraus warned with a low rumble. He had changed back into his natural form and was examining the roadside.

"What is it?" Sam asked, walking over to join him.

"A message from Swyf."

Jake stepped up behind them and looked down at what appeared to be some oddly scattered stones. Apparently they meant something to Joraus, because he suddenly straightened. "Up ahead a small road will branch off. The road we are currently following will eventually merge with the Kardonin Highway. Her message says that Klyle's captors took the small, branching road," he explained.

"Where does that road lead to?" Jake questioned.

"I am not sure. It goes up through the Noajim Mountains, but I've never had cause to follow it."

"Kardonin has it all, doesn't it?" Jake said, wryly. "Mountains, plains, forests, coasts – how in the world did Klyle conquer all of this?"

"It wasn't as hard as you might think, Jake," Joraus responded. "Most people are inherently good, and when they are presented with a noble idea they embrace it. Klyle met with the various faction leaders and won most of them over. It didn't hurt that his warriors were known to be the finest throughout the land. After Brael and he had cemented their reputation, force was rarely needed. The people believed in him – at least they used to." The Changeling started walking, and motioned to Jake and Sam. "Let's go. I can feel them getting further away each time we stop."

It did not take them long to reach the diverging road. Jake wondered when the woodland would finally open up enough to allow a view of the mountains. He guessed that Joraus must have decided they would not see anyone else, because he had changed back into a mountain lion. Jake checked his sword to make sure it was loose in the scabbard before following the girl and the big cat.

After a few minutes, Sam slowed to walk beside him. "Sorry I got mad at you," she apologized.

"It's okay," Jake answered. "I probably should start paying more attention."

"It wasn't that. It wasn't even you. This forest has been making me edgy. I want to be able to see the sky, and I guess I took a little of my frustration out on you."

"It's really all right," Jake said. "I get what you mean. All this walking isn't as much fun as it was when we first got here. That's why I was thinking about one of my games. It helped to pass the time, instead of just watching the trees go by."

"Yeah," Sam replied quietly. "I've been trying to remember all of my favorite jazz songs, but it is getting harder and harder. I wish I had brought my saxophone."

Jake reached behind him and pulled out the short stick that he'd stashed in his pack. He showed it to her. "I found this one night when I was standing watch. I know it's stupid, but when I put it up to my mouth and blow, I can almost hear the sound of my flute."

"That's really kinda cute, Jake," Sam said with a smile.

Jake blushed and hurriedly tried to tuck the stick away again.

"Here," offered Sam. Still smiling, she took the stick from him and slipped it into his backpack. "It does seem to be about the right size."

"Yeah," said Jake, still embarrassed, though not exactly sure why.

They continued to talk about music, humming bits of their favorite songs, until Joraus finally flicked an irritated glance at them and growled. They smiled at one another, but lowered their voices.

The mountains eventually came into view, and before long Jake started to notice the increasingly steep incline as they started to climb. Each night when they set up camp, Joraus grew a little more withdrawn and surly. Jake and Sam did their best to keep his spirits up, but even to Jake it was obvious that the Changeling was worried about his friend's absence.

It was not until mid-morning on the third day that Swyf's familiar form circled overhead. Jake noticed her first and pointed her out to the others. Joraus immediately changed back to normal as she glided down to the earth and shimmered into her natural form.

"Swyf!" Sam cried, running up to hug her.

"Hey, Sam," the Changeling replied, patting her hair, but it was Joraus she was looking at. Jake hoped they wouldn't get all lovey-dovey again.

"It took you long enough," Joraus growled.

Swyf laughed. "I missed you, too," she said, letting go of Sam.

Instead of answering, Joraus changed into a grizzly bear and rushed her. Sam scrambled out of the way as Swyf changed into a massive snake. She wrapped herself around the bear and started to squeeze. The grizzly was gone and a small rodent-like animal jumped from the coils before they could fully tighten, and the chase was on.

Jake and Sam watched from the mountainside as the two Changelings flickered from animal to animal before rolling over the side of a switchback, through the trees and out of sight.

"That's likely to take a little while," Jake commented. "Should we sit down?"

Sam looked to where the others had disappeared through the trees. "Let's keep walking. They know how to find us."

When the two Changelings finally came back, they were both laughing and Swyf had her arm slipped through Joraus'.

"Oh, boy," Jake moaned.

"Shut up, Jake," Sam hushed him. "I think it is sweet."

"You would."

"Okay," Swyf said when they approached. "We need to find a place to camp for the night. We have some decisions to make."

She led them to a small stream, where Joraus put the children in charge of gathering firewood while he and Swyf went hunting for dinner.

"Keep the fire small," Swyf warned. "We are in a very dangerous part of the mountains. I'll explain when we get back."

While Jake tried to start a fire, Sam went to search for firewood. When she came back, Jake saw that she didn't have any wood at all. Instead she held the bottom of her shirt up and inside she was carrying a bunch of wild strawberries.

"Nice!" Jake congratulated her when she bent down to show him.

She smiled proudly. "I figured they would make a nice change."

Sam rinsed the fruit in the stream and piled them on a small piece of cloth. Then she went back out to find the wood she had originally intended to collect.

Soon everyone was back and dinner was cooking over the small flames. Jake and Sam were seated on small logs on one side of the fire while Joraus perched on a log across from them. Swyf sat on the ground in front of him, leaning against his legs.

"So what is it that makes this place so dangerous?" Jake asked, looking at Swyf over the dancing firelight.

He was suddenly struck by how pretty the Changeling was. Her long hair fell down over part of her translucent face, but it only accented the beauty hidden beneath. Jake thought of her as pretty in the same way that his mom and Mrs. Gladwell were. Joraus had one massive arm dangling down in front of Swyf, and his hand was clasped in hers. They seemed right for each other, thought Jake, as if together, they were complete.

"A little impatient, aren't we?" asked Joraus, and Jake could hear relief in the Changeling's voice.

"Yeah, sure, take your girlfriend's side."

"Sorry, Jake," said Swyf, laughing, "but I'm cuter than you."

"She smells better, too," Joraus muttered.

"Man, you guys are weird," Jake complained. "Anyway, would you please tell us what's going on up there?"

Swyf straightened a little. "About ten miles up the road there is a large path that switchbacks up the mountain. This morning the soldiers who have Klyle took that road. I followed the path to the end and there was a prison there, built into the mountainside. It's really old. I imagine that Brael found it during his exile. It would make sense that they are keeping Klyle there."

She turned and looked up at Joraus. "This isn't going to be easy. I flew around to see if there was any other way in, but it is very secure. You and I might be able to sneak in, but not Jake and Sam. They will have to go through the main gate."

"Have they settled in?" Joraus asked intently.

"They will arrive any time now."

"How many are there?"

Swyf considered, before replying, "Twenty riders and well over one hundred soldiers, not to mention the Elite and whoever is already inside the prison. It is well fortified and easily defendable."

"Hmm," thought Joraus. "We are also going to have to consider that the Elite will probably sense if we change anywhere near him, so we are going to have to incorporate that into whatever plans we make."

"How can the Elite do that?" Jake asked. "Sense when you change, I mean."

"It has something to do with the way they touch *Ragesong*," Joraus answered.

"You mean that they can touch *Ragesong* too?"

"As I understand it, yes they can. Their abilities are limited, but they learned from Brael directly."

"That's just great," Jake said darkly.

"Don't let it bother you yet, Jake," Swyf soothed. "The more you worry about something, the more you fear it. The more you fear something, the more power you allow it to have over you."

"Can either of you kill an Elite?" Jake demanded.

Both Swyf and Joraus hesitated, neither of them able to meet his eyes. Finally Joraus rumbled in a low voice, "No, we can't."

"Why not?"

"They can sense us, Jake. Their abilities allow them to see us, in the same way you can. They can sense when we change," Joraus explained. "I don't know how, but if they are close by they know as soon as we change. Even as a mountain lion, I could not get close enough to an Elite to kill one."

"But you expect me to be able to do it?" Jake asked, incredulously.

"Jake," Sam urged softly, "don't forget what happened with those soldiers following us."

"I don't know how I did that," he argued. "And I almost couldn't turn it off!"

Swyf looked at him inquiringly. "What happened?"

"I don't want to talk about it," Jake growled. He stood up abruptly. "I'm going to go and get some firewood."

Jake stomped into the trees. *How can they expect me to take on an Elite?* Furious, he picked up a thick branch and swung it viciously at a tall weed. The tip disconnected and whistled through the air. He raged silently for a few more minutes and several more weeds were viciously decapitated. In the end he blew through his bad temper and began to think a little more rationally. Finally, he tucked the stick he had been using under his arm and quickly gathered an armful of potential firewood.

When his arms were nearly full, he heard a scream, high and girlish. Sam! He dropped his load of wood and sprinted back in the direction he had come. With a speed born of panic, he crashed through the brush. *How could I have left them? How did I get this far away from camp?*

By the time he closed in on his friends, he saw about ten riders surrounding Sam, while Swyf and Joraus stood by helplessly. *Why don't they change and fight?* But it took him only a moment to discover the reason: all of the riders had their bows trained on Sam. If either of the Changelings made a move, they would most certainly kill her.

Jake watched in horror as one of the soldiers screamed at them. "Where is the other one? Liakut said there were two children. Where is the boy?"

When he didn't get an answer, he backhanded Sam. She cried out in pain as she fell to the ground.

"You fools! Did you not think Liakut would realize he was being tracked? He is an Elite! What could you possibly hope to accomplish?"

Jake's heart ached with guilt as the evil man continued to interrogate his friends. Finally, the soldier threw up his hands in disgust. "Bind them so that we can be on our way," he said. "It is only a boy. It was the Changeling that Liakut was worried about. If the kid shows his face, we can capture him easily enough."

Jake wanted to call out and reassure his friends that he would think of something, but fear of what the soldier might do held his tongue. He watched as first Sam, and then the Changelings, were bound and thrown on the backs of some of the horse-like creatures. One of the riders laughed when Sam cried out in pain as the ropes cut into her arms. Even from this distance, he could see her tear-streaked face. Watching helplessly as the animals trotted back up the road with his friends was one of the hardest things Jake had ever done in his life.

CHAPTER 22:
INFILTRATION

At first Jake tried to keep up with the riders, but he quickly discovered that it was not going to be possible. He had to stay off the road to avoid detection and the heavy brush slowed him down. Trudging through the rough, he began to berate himself. *How could I have been so stupid? I left my friends alone, so that I could do what, throw a fit, feel bad for myself? And now they are gone, captured and about to endure who knows what.*

This went on for several miles, but eventually other nagging thoughts began to work their way through his depression. *How is this going to help anyone? Would I really have been able to make a difference right then? Don't they at least stand a chance with me still free?*

At first Jake pushed the reasonable voice back, but eventually he found himself answering the questions it presented. He realized that had he not wandered off, in all likelihood they would have all been captured. There had not been any sign of a fight, so his group must have been completely surprised. *With me so new to* Ragesong, *there was no guarantee that I would have felt it, and what good would I have been without it?* At least with him being free, there was still some hope, however small.

When Jake tried to think of a plan, dark thoughts about Liakut, the riders and all the soldiers kept creeping in. He tried to list his advantages, but the list seemed to be pitifully small compared to the obstacles he was facing. The only three positive things Jake could think of were that he had his sword, he might be able to touch *Ragesong*, and that the soldiers did not consider him a threat, which meant they wouldn't be searching for him and would most likely underestimate him.

Jake continued up the road until he eventually found the branching path. It was rough and uneven, with rocks strewn everywhere. *This could not have been easy for Klyle.* He looked up the route and saw that Swyf was right, the road simply switchbacked all the way to the top of the mountain.

Instead of following the road, Jake opted to head straight up through the trees, so that he could remain hidden. It was a hard climb and he rested often in order to conserve his strength. He was not sure whether it was saving him any time, and certainly not energy, but it gave the illusion of being the shorter route, so he continued. At first when he rested, he would try to judge how far he had come, but the foliage was too thick. He could see one or maybe two switchbacks below, but not enough to make an educated guess.

Jake continued climbing, completely losing track of time. He reached the point where he was simply placing one foot in front of the other and forcing his weary legs to move. Jake had noticed clouds gathering early on in the day, but it was not until afternoon that they truly threatened rain. He hoped it would hold off for a little longer, so that he would not have to finish his hike in the mud.

Finally, after what felt like hours of climbing, Jake reached the top, where he found himself standing on what he could now see was one of the smaller peaks. The view that the woodland and mountain had been hiding now opened up to show a beautiful valley. A large lake lay in the middle, fed by dozens of small mountain streams.

It's like one of the screen savers on my computer back at home, Jake thought as he studied the valley. He searched for the prison and saw a faint outline of it, off to his right. The mountain that it melded into seemed to be mostly bare rock, while the others had trees growing on them. It looked odd when Jake compared it to the surrounding peaks, like a bald head among a sea of green-haired giants.

Realizing that he was standing in plain sight, he quickly scanned the valley for anything he could use as a landmark, so he would not get lost during his descent. Jake noticed that one of the streams emptying into the lake seemed to originate from the prison. When he was sure he would be able to find it once he arrived at the lake, Jake started to descend. Although his progress downhill was faster than his uphill climb, he had to be much more careful where he placed his feet. Roots and other protuberances were eager to catch the unwary. More than once, he stepped carelessly and fell to the ground.

The sun was hanging low in the sky when Jake saw the lake again. It was a lot bigger now, and some of those tiny streams he'd seen from up above were much larger than he had originally thought. Afraid to step out into the open field that led to the lake, Jake circled it from within the tree line, careful not to make too much noise. He was not sure if any patrols would have been sent down here, and not wanting to take any chances he silently drew his sword, grateful for its apparent weightlessness. It made threading through the trees more awkward, but he felt more comfortable with it at the ready.

Once Jake found the stream he was hunting for, he began to follow it up towards the treeless mountain. It was not long before he heard soldiers. Apparently they did not take their patrolling too seriously, he thought, because they spoke loud enough to warn anyone in the vicinity of their presence.

Jake hid behind a tree as they passed, wondering whether to attack or not. Leaving them alive meant the possibility of more enemies later, but he decided against killing them. The risk of someone coming to search for them or of one of the soldiers crying out was too great. He had already decided that his best chance of success lay in the fact that the enemy did not know he was here, and he didn't want to warn them.

When the voices of the soldiers faded, Jake abandoned the stream and started walking the way they had come. Looking at the ground, he realized it was not going to be that difficult to find his way. The guards appeared to be creatures of habit and had created their own trails by stamping down the soft forest grasses. Jake followed the makeshift path, avoiding soldiers whenever he heard them by ducking into neighboring trees.

The forest eventually opened up and he caught his first real view of the prison walls. Jake could see in the dim twilight that they were not made of stone blocks, as he had expected. Instead, the section he was studying seemed to be a single piece of rock, jutting out from the mountainside. It was as if it had been molded by a giant hand and carefully smoothed. Swyf was right; it would be impossible to scale, even had there not been archers at the top, waiting to pick off anyone who came into view.

The trail curved towards the front gate, but Jake knew that if he continued to follow it, he would be discovered, so he needed to find another way inside. However, Swyf had said there were no other entrances and that the walls were unassailable. Jake did not need to see the entire prison to know that she was right.

As he continued to study the scene, he realized something. The soldiers did not seem to be standing on the wall itself. He knew that due to his position at the base, there was a chance that he could be mistaken, but it was as if they were standing on something else. *They must be standing on buildings or something else inside the walls.*

Jake glanced at the mountainside next to the wall and wondered if he dared to climb it. It would be very difficult as it was almost a sheer face, but it did look possible, unlike the actual walls of the prison. If he somehow managed to get to the top, he would at least be able to see inside. The only other option was to try and break in through the open front gate.

"What are you doing here?" growled a voice behind him.

Jake spun around to see two large soldiers standing there. I am such an idiot, he thought savagely. All he'd had to do was step off the path while he studied the prison, but instead he had just stood there. Instead of answering, Jake rushed them. He wished there could have been another way, but leaving the guards alive would immediately alert the soldiers in the fort to his presence.

The men were not expecting an attack and had barely gotten their hands on their weapon hilts before Jake was upon them. With two quick thrusts, the soldiers let go of their swords and grabbed at their chests. Almost in unison, they sank to their knees. Hoping they would not scream out, Jake turned away and took one last hurried glance at the prison.

He had to decide now, as he wouldn't be able to hide the soldiers or the fact that something had happened here. Jake did not know how long he had before other guards arrived, but he figured it would be sooner rather than later. Making up his mind, he jogged towards the mountain, trying to keep to the trees as much as possible, so the archers would not see him.

There was a huge flash of light, which blinded him momentarily, followed by a clap of thunder. Knowing that he didn't have much time before the rain started, Jake sprinted the rest of the distance to the base of the mountain. He needed to get to the ledge that overlooked the prison before the rocks became slick with rainwater.

Quickly sheathing his sword, Jake scanned the wall for the easiest way to the top. He gripped the rough stone and started to climb. After only a few feet, he felt his bag weighing him down. Peering up at the mountain, he realized that he wouldn't be able to make the climb with the pack on his back. The sheath already made gripping the mountain awkward enough. With a regretful sigh, Jake dropped back to the ground and took off his pack, and on second thoughts he unbelted the knife around his waist as well.

Feeling a good deal lighter, he started to scale the mountain again. He knew there would be a couple of spots during his climb where he would be visible to the soldiers if they were watching, and all he could do was hope they were as lax in their duties as the men patrolling the forest below. As he climbed, the hard stone felt rough on his hands, and soon they were raw and sore. Ignoring the pain, he continued.

The thunder and lightning were more consistent now, but Jake disregarded them and focused on gripping the mountain so that he would not fall. The encroaching storm might at least keep the soldiers distracted, preventing them from hearing any loose stones that he might dislodge. Above, the sky was now nearly dark, so the lightning helped to light the way. You are seriously crazy, Jake, he thought as he ascended.

When he was about halfway up, the rain started to fall, not even having the courtesy to begin with a gentle drizzle. The clouds just burst apart, releasing a torrent. The side of the mountain immediately became slippery, and Jake forced his exhausted fingers to hold on all the harder. About ten minutes later, his cloak had absorbed so much rainwater that it felt as though it was strangling him. Regretfully, Jake unfastened it from around his neck with one hand while clinging desperately to the stone with the other. Hopefully, he'd be able to retrieve it, along with his pack, after leaving the prison.

"Hand, hand, foot, foot," he chanted softly to himself, over and over, as he forced his hands into the unyielding rock crevices. He moved agonizingly slow, but he was terrified of losing his grip.

Jake yelled out when one of his feet slid from a shelf of slippery rock. Digging in with his hands, he clung to the wall as he scrambled for a foothold. He looked down and when he couldn't see the ground, his head began to spin. When he was at last able to find a place to put his foot, he gripped the rock wall with both hands and feet, shivering from cold and fear.

Muscles he had never noticed until now ached fiercely. For an endless moment Jake clung there, not daring to move or loosen his hold. As the rain dripped from his hair into his eyes, he shook his head to try to remove it, not daring to wipe it away with his hands. Knowing he could not remain on the mountainside, Jake willed himself to let go. It took several agonizing seconds, but he finally pried his hand away from the wall and reached for another handhold.

Long after Jake had given up all hope of ever reaching the top, his hand reached up to grab the next handhold and felt only air. For a second he panicked and searched frantically for something to hold onto. Then his forearm banged painfully into the mountain ledge and he nearly cried out in relief that he had made it. Grabbing the tip of the overhang, he began to pull. His arms quavered dangerously, but he mustered enough strength to pull himself up and over the lip before collapsing on the rocky ledge.

For a long moment Jake lay there, panting in exhaustion as the rain continued to pelt down. His entire body ached from the strain of the climb and, combined with the long day's hike, it tempted a part of him to just stay there on the cold stone forever. But the thought of what might be happening to his friends had him clenching and unclenching his fingers, trying to work the stiffness out. Slowly, feeling began to return to his digits, and he was able to sit up and rub his aching legs and arms. When Jake could stand, he looked around and noticed a soft flickering light. Cautiously, he worked his way towards it.

As Jake approached, he saw that underneath the top of the overhang was a shallow crevice. A narrow crack in the rock allowed him to see right inside, where there was a single soldier huddled, wrapped in his cloak. Sitting with his back against the wall, he had a large wooden torch propped against a large boulder, the flame flickering softly in the darkness. Jake held his breath as he considered what to do next when he heard the man let out a large snore.

"Finally," Jake whispered with a grim smile. "Something is going my way."

He walked to the edge of the ledge and carefully lowered himself inside. The man snorted and muttered something unintelligible, but did not wake. Jake started to draw his sword, but then he studied the thick, wooden torch thoughtfully. Picking it up, he hefted it a couple of times before swinging it at the soldier's head.

The snoring man grunted before sliding limply to the floor. Jake replaced the torch in its original position, glad that it hadn't gone out or caught the guy's hair on fire. He peeled back one of the man's eyelids and when he saw only white, he dropped it back in place.

Jake walked back over to the edge and looked down. He was directly above the prison now, and he saw that his earlier guess had been right. Soldiers stood on the rooftops of buildings that hugged the inside of the construction. The roofs extended all the way to the walls, but Jake could see enough room on the ground for a small back alley.

The setup around the prison was simple. To either side of it were about ten large buildings. They appeared to have been made the same way as the wall, resembling single pieces of stone. There was a long, wide road running through the middle of the prison, starting at the gate and disappearing underneath the ledge he was currently standing on. As Jake had suspected, the entrance was heavily guarded. Five of those horse-like creatures with red eyes and sharp teeth were picketed near the building closest to the gate, which was open. Four soldiers stood in front of it, holding long spears, while behind them two riders fingered their bows.

Jake was sure there were more men within the building, only a shout away from bursting through the door with their weapons drawn. At either side of the gate was a large sentry tower, from which archers sat watching out over the valley.

Near the back of the prison was a large stable. Jake guessed that the rest of the riders' mounts were huddled inside. The stable looked as though it had been added much later than the other buildings. It was built of wood, instead of stone, and it was the only structure with a metal roof. Jake listened to the pinging sound of the rain hitting it. It was bothersome, but it should cover any sounds he made. Atop each building there stood at least two archers and he could also see soldiers marching between the prison buildings, holding a variety of weapons.

Then Jake saw something that heated his blood. On the far side of the prison was a set of stocks, completely surrounded by soldiers. Even through the darkness he could see Sam's small body bent over awkwardly with her hands and head clamped in the horrible device. To her right and left were the strangely transparent, yet completely visible forms of the Changelings.

Jake saw Swyf's head jerk to the side as one of the guards slapped her. Without realizing it, he had drawn his sword. When a quick glance showed him that there was no easy way down, Jake stepped to the edge of the cliff and jumped out into the night. Something inside him noted clinically that this should not be possible, that the huge drop alone should kill him, but it was a dim and hazy sound, as if it were detached from the rest of him.

Jake landed softer than any cat, one knee grazing the stone roof lightly. The archers must be killed first, he thought grimly, as he rushed the first set of soldiers. The guards were watching out over the wall and did not have a chance to react before Jake's sword whistled through the air, felling one and then the other. He then leapt to the next building; a jump he would have never have attempted under normal circumstances, let alone at night in the pouring rain. Tonight, however, the idea of falling seemed laughable. Jake's feet gripped the water-slicked stone roof easily and every step was sure. He quickly cut down every guard on his side of the wall and then stopped to check his location.

He was near the front of the prison, but there was a large gap between the last inner building and the guards' station. The soldiers at the gate and those on top of the guard tower had their attention focused on the front entrance. Jake realized that the closest building on the other side of the prison was too far away to jump, even for him. Instead, he lowered himself over the side of the roof, facing away from the guard tower, and shimmied down.

When Jake reached the street, he glanced around quickly. Through the darkness, his *Ragesong*-enhanced eyesight spotted a guard turn a corner and start walking toward him. Jake decided it would be easiest to backtrack and cross the open, central area from the rear of the prison. Then he could climb back up to the roof and take out the remaining archers. He knew the soldiers in the front guard towers and the two riders would still have bows, but he wouldn't be able to get to them without alerting the rest of the guards. This was the best way of removing as much of the long-distance threat as possible, before moving in close to melee with the other soldiers.

Jake edged along the walls of the building, moving slowly so that the guard would not detect any movement. He waited in the shadows of one of the buildings for him to close the last of the distance. It seemed to take forever for the man to get there, but when he did, Jake struck as quickly as a cobra. He did not wait for the guard to crumple, but sprinted away.

Hesitating behind the last building, Jake could hear moaning from within. He realized these were prison cells, or at least some of them. Suddenly, he was having trouble concentrating; his mind was pulling him in opposite directions. One part wanted to rush in and rescue the prisoners, while another desired to rush out and kill anyone and everything. A third part reminded him that his main objective was to rescue Swyf, Joraus and Sam.

For an agonizing second, Jake hesitated, unable to decide what to do. Then the need to rescue his friends and Klyle forced its way to the top, and he cautiously peered around the corner, only to see the one thing he had not anticipated – two soldiers stood guard at a gate into the mountain itself. Jake wondered how he had missed it, until he looked up and saw that the ledge he'd jumped from earlier hung out just enough to hide the cave entrance underneath.

The soldiers were out in the open, and he knew that once he killed them, it wouldn't take long for him to be discovered. Deciding that he had no choice, he dug deeper into himself, deeper into *Ragesong*. Just before he attacked, something flickered in his vision: a golden flash. Without stopping to consider it, Jake rushed the soldiers. They didn't even have time to open their mouths before they were both lying dead at his feet.

There was a guard marching toward him from the front gate, but it would take him a few precious minutes to get here. Fighting a sudden, mad desire to rush the man and then attack the soldiers at the front gate, Jake reached the cells on the opposite side and clambered up the side. Once he reached the top, he repeated what he'd done on the other side; noiselessly stalking the rooftop soldiers and silently eliminating them.

When he reached the last building, Jake did not pause. A part of him was afraid that if he hesitated, the desire to kill the rest of the soldiers would win out. He launched himself off of the building and right into the middle of the circle of guards. In three quick cuts, he shattered the locks holding the stocks closed and turned to face the soldiers.

Not waiting to see what they would do, Jake attacked the guards, trying to position himself between their blades and his friends. He killed three of them before the others recovered from the shock of his rooftop entrance. The soldiers drew their blades quickly and lunged. Jake danced in a circle, fending off the attacks, but he was unable to counter properly through fear of an enemy blade slipping through his guard.

A wild scream from his side told him that Joraus had changed into a mountain lion. That does it, Jake thought wryly. *The cat is out of the bag!* He smiled at how fitting that particular phrase was under the circumstances.

Jake waited to hear a similar cry from Swyf, but instead he heard a screech as a familiar-looking falcon darted up into the night. She must be going after the archers. With Joraus beside him, he started countering and the soldiers began to fall. *Get up, Sam, I need your help.* As if she had heard his desperate thought, the girl struggled weakly to her feet.

The more soldiers that fell, the faster Jake was able to kill those who remained. He did not wait to counter now, but attacked, with every cut striking a target. The last of the soldiers stepped back, but he pushed forward and struck them down in a flurry of swings. When he ran out of men in front of him, he turned around to see a big gorilla swipe out with a huge arm to smash a soldier to the ground.

Others rushed in, but Joraus spun in a circle, beating the ground with his massive fists, and the charge faltered. Jake took advantage of their hesitation and swung his sword. It connected with the curved blade of one of the soldiers, but the man dropped his weapon in surprise, crying out in pain. Jake's next strike took him deep in the chest.

Jake searched for Sam, but he could not see her. Not daring to worry, he prepared to charge the soldiers at the gate, but Joraus, now in his natural form, grabbed his arm. Snarling, Jake whirled on the Changeling, his sword raised.

"Jake," he yelled frantically, gesturing towards the rear of the prison. "You can't! You are the only one that can face the Elite!"

Jake looked to see what Joraus was pointing at. Liakut stepped out from the cave, still dressed in his black clothes and blue vest. Jake grimaced as he turned to face him.

CHAPTER 23:
THE ELITE

Liakut's stride was calm and unhurried. He did not seem in the least bit bothered by the rain falling around him, and when he grinned at Jake, it was that same warm smile he'd given at the gates of Kithalo.

Jake stepped out of the corner from where he was battling, and turned to face what appeared to be nothing more than an average-sized man, except for a flash in his eyes. It was similar to the silver flicker he had seen in Sam's when she touched *Ragesong*, only this time it was black, even darker than the night around them.

Liakut stopped in the middle of the compound. "How... unexpected." He studied what was left of his guard, and then turned back to Jake. "Young man, this is remarkable. Do you have any idea what Brael offers to those who display this level of skill? How old are you, twelve or thirteen? Yet you singlehandedly entered this prison and butchered so many of my men."

Jake shook his head at the word butcher.

"Afraid to call it what it is, *boy?*" The warm smile was gone now as Liakut swept a hand around him. "Look at the fruits of your labor. Look!"

Jake tried not to. He tried to keep his eyes trained on Liakut instead, but he could not stop himself from looking at the carnage around him. Bodies were sprawled on the ground in grotesque positions, their limbs splayed out at awkward angles.

"Don't listen to him, Jake," Joraus said urgently. "He is trying to play with your mind, make you doubt yourself. You can't let him if you want to have any hope of winning."

"I play no tricks!" Liakut retorted harshly. "Have I twisted what you have done in any way? Does this mayhem not speak for itself?"

He laughed, seeing Jake frozen in the mud, unable to take any action as his emotions warred within him.

"I know what you feel. I see the flashes of it in your eyes, even now. I know what *Ragesong* offers, boy, and I am willing to help," said Liakut. "Tell me was the temptation to simply kill not seductive? Why resist it when I can offer you ways to fulfill it that are beyond your wildest dreams?"

The man's voice dropped, but Jake could still hear every word clearly. *Ragesong* thundered within him, demanding release, if only he could decide on a target: the soldiers, the Elite, the Changeling? All of them?

"Boy, I can take you to the feet of the Dread King himself. Only he has mastered *Ragesong* and only he can help you unlock it within yourself. I offer you this in respect of what you have already learned. Only a select few in this world have been offered this gift once; none twice. Don't be a slave to *Ragesong* on the fool advice of those who cannot even wield it. The Dread King can show you how to make it your slave."

Jake's arm started to drop.

"Jake," Joraus whispered. "What are you...?"

For a long moment the world seemed to stop as Jake fought with the desire to give into *Ragesong* completely. It would be so easy. The war raging in his mind could finally end and there could be peace; no, not peace, but ecstasy. *All I have to do is let go.*

All at once, as though something inside was giving a final desperate push, images jumped into Jake's mind: Joraus and Swyf; Klyle marching down the street in his chains; Sam holding a bow in one hand and her saxophone in the other; and, finally, he with his sword and flute. As soon as Jake focused on his flute, he began to hear its sweet, high-pitched notes singing out over the deafening roar of confusion. It grew louder and louder until it drowned out everything else.

When the final note faded away, the war in his mind was over. Where he had previously been roiling in turmoil, he was now flooded with clarity. A decision had been reached. He bowed his head and Liakut began to laugh coldly, the sound echoing off the buildings around them.

"Joraus," Jake said softly out of the side of his mouth. "You and Swyf get Sam to her bow, and then find Klyle. I will drag this fight out for as long as I can, but I don't know how much longer I will last."

Joraus reached out and put a hand on Jake's arm, replying in a voice only Jake could hear, "May your end be wrapped in the embrace of *Ragesong*."

It was spoken reverently, almost like a prayer. Jake nodded once and then looked up at Liakut. It was not an expression filled with anger, rage or fear, only acceptance. He did not bother to say anything; his raised sword was the only answer he needed to give.

Liakut's demeanor changed, and the wickedness that Jake had seen when the Elite had butchered Klyle's supporters returned. "I am so glad this is your decision, boy; so much easier to just end things now. Normally, I would take little satisfaction in killing a child, but..." He drawled out the last word obscenely before reaching behind him for his blades.

Soldiers emptied out of the cave behind the Elite and circled around them. Out of the corner of his eye, Jake saw Swyf, Joraus and Sam slip carefully into one of the buildings.

"Don't worry about your friends," Liakut remarked, not missing Jake's flickering eyes. "I'll take care of the Changelings, and I'm sure the girl will prove useful in one way or another. The weapon she came in with was most intriguing. It nearly killed two of my men when they tried to remove it from her."

He saw Jake eyeing the long, curved knives in his hands. "Do you like them?" he asked, giving them a flick that sent them spinning. "They were a gift from the Dread King. I wielded them in his honor during the siege of Foldona. It was with these blades that I killed Morab, first captain of Klyle's personal guard. You should feel honored that I would allow you to die by them also."

Jake said nothing and simply waited for the man to finish. *Every second he talks is another second for Joraus to free Klyle.*

"You say nothing, boy, just stand there with your sword. Do you truly have no last words?" Liakut looked into Jake's eyes, but he simply gazed back. "Very well," the Elite growled. "If silence is what you want, I shall grant it – eternally!"

Lightning crashed, bathing the prison in light, as Liakut rushed forwards, his blades swinging. Jake raised his sword to block them and the metallic clang was drowned out by the cacophonous blast of thunder. At first he could only defend as the Elite hammered at him. Even through *Ragesong*, the man's knives were moving blindingly fast, and it was all Jake could do to get his sword between them and himself.

238

After several tense minutes of desperately defending the Elite's merciless assault, Jake saw Liakut step back. Jake looked into the man's face, hoping to see him breathing heavily, but he was merely grinning.

"You are good, boy," he said conversationally, as they circled one another. "Since we defeated Klyle and routed his armies, there has been no one to fight. Sure, little rebellions have cropped up here and there, but nothing that really gets the blood pumping."

Liakut flicked a lightning quick strike at Jake's middle, which he blocked and countered, but was in turn blocked by the Elite's second knife. The pace of the battle changed as Liakut probed, making quick strikes instead of tireless blows. They felt each other out and tested for weaknesses. Weariness beat on the outside of Jake's awareness, but he savagely pushed it back, reaching deeper into the strange power of *Ragesong*. Gold began to flicker at the corners of his vision and Jake shook his head, trying to clear it.

In that instant, Liakut struck. Jake blocked the first knife, but the second came too quickly and it caught his shirt. The Elite dragged his knife downwards, ripping the material open and exposing Jake's bare chest. Golden light blazed from the strange symbols curving along his collarbone. Liakut's third strike cut into Jake's exposed flesh just under his neck. Jake screamed in agony and fell back into the mud, grabbing at his wound as his sword tumbled from his hands. Liakut stood above him, knives held easily in his fists.

"Jake!" someone screamed, but through the haze of pain he could not think of who it was.

"And so it ends, boy," Liakut said softly. "You would have made an interesting Elite, but alas, the casualties of war."

Jake closed his eyes, awaiting the final strike, when his chest began to burn. Looking down he saw that the blood from his cut had run over the symbols, and their color changed from gold to a deep red. The golden flashes at the corners of his vision turned the same violent crimson, and ignoring the pain, Jake rolled through the mud, grasping the hilt of his blade. Liakut apparently saw something too, because rather than attempt the killing blow, he stepped back warily and raised his weapons.

With his sword in his fist, Jake pushed himself to his feet. The blood ran unnoticed down his chest, where it mingled with the rain and mud. He ripped off the remains of his tattered shirt and lifted his sword to face Liakut in a half crouch, with his other hand extended in front of him. A brief look behind the Elite showed him that his friends had rescued Klyle. They stood behind Liakut's troops at the entrance to the cave. Joraus cradled the dethroned king in his arms as they watched helplessly.

The Elite gave a bestial snarl and rushed at Jake with both knives out. Just as Liakut brought his arms together, trying to catch his opponent between the sharp blades, Jake ducked, stabbing his sword into the ground as he evaded the killing stroke. Coming up inside Liakut's guard, he reached out for each of the Elite's wrists. Jake gripped them tightly and pushed down on the center, hard enough that Liakut's hands popped open and the knives fell from his grip.

Jake released the wrists and, extending his arms, he clapped Liakut painfully on the ears. As the man stumbled backwards, Jake kicked the knives out of reach, even as he pulled his own blade out of the muddy earth. Advancing, he watched the blackness of *Ragesong* flicker and die from Liakut's eyes.

The arrogance and superiority once dominating the Elite's face gave way to fear and panic. "What are you waiting for?" Liakut roared at his men. "Kill him!"

Most of the soldiers surrounding Jake hesitated, but three riders bore down on him, their bows raised. Then all three limply fell from their mounts with silver arrows buried deep in their chests. As other soldiers began to rush forward, the Changelings were suddenly at Jake's side, Joraus as a mountain lion and Swyf as a great bear, as they held the soldiers at bay. Liakut staggered backwards, tripping over his own feet.

"And so it ends," Jake whispered, repeating the Elite's earlier words; the blood-red flickering of *Ragesong* still at the corners of his vision.

Jake sprinted at Liakut, his sword extended, and this time he did not stop the blade's journey as it thrust up through the man's stomach before exiting between his shoulder blades. Liakut grasped at the sword sticking out of him, shredding his fingers on its sharpness. When he opened his mouth to say something, all that came out was a bloody bubble. The Elite gave a long sigh as his body collapsed inward.

CHAPTER 24:
THE SENTRY GROVE

J ake let Liakut's weight bring the blade down, and then he deftly turned the body so that the Elite would land on his back. Wrenching his sword back out, he looked around. Swyf and Joraus were desperately fighting off soldiers behind him, even as Sam shot arrow after arrow into their ranks. Jake rushed back to help them, but in doing so he felt his legs wobble. "Only a little longer, Jake," he told himself through clenched teeth. "You've got this!"

He waded into the soldiers, swinging his sword, but his movements were beginning to feel sluggish, while their blades seemed to be speeding up. "Joraus, get Klyle," he yelled at the battling Changeling. "Swyf, Sam, we have to go, now!"

Jake pushed his way deeper into the soldiers, cutting a path to the prison entrance. The men flinched from him as he advanced, and it was their fear as much as his own abilities that kept him moving forward. Swords were coming closer to his bare skin, and his neck was stinging in the place where he had been cut. Trying to ignore the pain, Jake gritted his teeth and pushed deeper. He saw his friends up ahead, waiting at the gate. They must have gone around the buildings while the soldiers were focused on him.

The Changelings had changed into horses. Klyle was bent over Swyf's smaller form while Sam clutched Joraus' thick mane. Joraus whinnied urgently, and with the last of his strength, Jake broke through the remaining the guards. He tried to sprint forwards, but only managed a weak stumble. Reaching the large black stallion, he sheathed his sword and started to clamber on behind Sam.

"No, Jake, in front," she said, scooting back and gripping Joraus with her legs. "I need to be able to shoot."

Unable to say anything, Jake nodded weakly, and worked his way along the horse's flanks. He grabbed the thick mane and tried to jump up, but his legs refused to cooperate.

"Hurry, Jake," Sam cried out. "They are coming!"

It took him two more tries before he was able to scramble onto Joraus' back. The red flickers of *Ragesong* intensified briefly before fading completely as the Changelings stretched into a gallop, and sped through the open prison gate. Face down in the coarse mane, Jake tried to shake his head to clear out the cobwebs of exhaustion, but it did no good. Sam was yelling something at him, but he could not understand what she was saying. The world seemed to be going in and out of focus for some reason.

Then things slammed back into place and he could hear Sam clearly. "Jake, you have to help me! My legs aren't strong enough to grip and shoot at the same time!"

Jake winced as his body screamed out in protest, but he sat up and twisted around. He grabbed Sam by the waist with one arm while his other hand gripped Joraus' mane. Even with his blurry vision, he could see the riders chasing them through the valley. The thick trees prevented them from fanning out, but they were not far behind.

The riders were firing at them with their bone bows, and Joraus could only admire Sam's accuracy as she knocked the heavy arrows out of the air with bolts from her own weapon. Occasionally, a rider would be thrown from his mount, but Sam could not spare the time to shoot at them as she continued to try and block the shots at Swyf and Joraus. It was an amazing display of marksmanship, and Jake did not need to see the silver flashes in her eyes to know that she was deep in *Ragesong*. When they made it to the far side of the valley, Jake could hear Joraus' labored breathing.

"Sam," he yelled in her ear. "You have to hurry. Joraus is getting tired."

Sam growled and turned her bow sideways. In amazement, Jake watched three bolts of light extend from it at different angles. With a scream of rage, she released them into the night. One of the bolts deflected off an incoming arrow, but the other two slammed into two riders. Not waiting to see the results of her shot, Sam pulled back the string again and three more shafts appeared. This time each bolt took a rider down, and the rest of their pursuers reigned in sharply.

"Joraus," Jake shouted. "Now is your chance. They are stopping!"

With a burst of speed, Joraus shot forward, and Jake watched as the riders faded into the dark forest.

Joraus and Swyf carried the children for the remainder of the night. Once they were out of immediate danger, the two

Changelings slowed their pace to a trot. Jake turned around and wrapped his hands in Joraus' thick mane. Sam's bow was now slung across her back, and she was holding him around the waist with both hands, so that she wouldn't fall.

The stinging in Jake's neck had turned into a deep burn now that the adrenaline rush was finally gone. He ran a finger lightly over the wound, wincing at the touch and noting with some concern that it was still bleeding.

Jake had also noticed how cold it was. Sam's tight grip was helping to keep his back warm, but the breeze was definitely icy on his shoulders and chest. He looked at Swyf and Klyle, trotting on the road in front of him. Noticing the man's threadbare clothes and bare feet, Jake decided to buck up and tough it out. At least he still had his boots on, even if they were soaked and covered in mud. He couldn't imagine how Klyle was feeling right now.

Jake could not wait to talk to the man. There were so many questions that he wanted to ask about *Ragesong*, Fermicia, his sword, and more. He entertained himself for a while by making a list of the things he was going to ask Klyle when he got the chance.

It was well past sunrise when Jake was able to rouse himself from the stupor he had been in for the last few hours. Although not sleeping, he had zoned out completely. He scrubbed at his heavy eyelids, trying to stay awake, so he wouldn't fall off the horse and drag Sam with him. The bouncing and constant repositioning had helped for some of the morning, but now even his numb legs and butt could not keep him awake. Jake had been feeling Sam's head softly bumping into his back for the last couple of hours, so he knew that he wasn't the only one fighting back sleep.

"Joraus," he said wearily, leaning down close to the horse's ear. "We have to stop soon. We are going to fall asleep."

Joraus nickered softly, but continued onward. Jake looked around at his surroundings. More trees, he thought, staring glumly at the vibrant green. They were on yet another forest path. At least they were far out of the valley and away from the mountain prison. The heavy clouds from the storm of the previous night were clearing out and sunlight was peeking out from behind them. *Strange, I didn't even notice that it had stopped raining.*

"Are we still in those mountains, the Noajim ones?" Jake asked.

Joraus whinnied and Jake gave up talking. He was not sure that he would be able to understand the answers anyway, even if he'd been wide awake.

An hour later, Joraus reined in, although Jake could still feel the horse's body quivering underneath him. He watched as Klyle gracefully dismounted from Swyf and then held Sam's hand so that she could slide down. When Jake tried to climb down himself, the weight was too much for his exhausted legs and he fell to the ground.

"Jake, are you okay?" Sam asked, limping over to him.

"The boy is strong," a rich baritone voice answered.

It was the first time that Jake had heard Klyle talk and he immediately liked the voice. It was warm and comforting, and it matched the warmth emanating from the man's brown-eyed gaze. Even through the emaciated frame and unkempt beard, Jake could see the noble bearing that marked this man a king.

"Sorry," Jake muttered, pushing himself up onto his knees. "Give me just a minute."

"Take all the time you need, Jake," Klyle said quietly. "There is no hurry here. This area is protected."

"What do you mean?" Jake questioned as he sat on the ground and tried to rub some feeling back into his legs.

"We are in a Sentry Grove. Not many know of their existence, and fewer still understand their importance."

"What's a Sentry Grove?" Sam asked.

"The trees here are sentient. They offer their protection to the first people who enter." He pointed at the trees. "Watch!"

Jake and Sam looked on in amazement as the trees squeezed together, forming a walled perimeter, which completely encircled them.

"That is totally awesome," Jake said in awe.

"Yes, it is a thing of wonder," Klyle agreed softly. "It is one of the many beauties of this land."

He pointed to a small pond in the middle of the grove, surrounded by bushes full of colored fruit. "There is food and water aplenty, so we may rest here for as long as we need."

Jake hugged himself. "Can we start a fire? I am freezing."

"Ah," said Klyle, smiling gently, "so quickly you bring up the only stipulation. Fires are not permitted within this particular grove. As I said, these trees are sentient, and if they sense flame in their midst they will withdraw their protection. Unfortunately, while here we shall have to make do without the comfort of a warm fire. Content yourself with the shelter they provide," he added, looking up into the clearing sky, "and that, at least for now, we need not endure the rain."

Sam pulled off her pack and set it on the still damp grass. Reaching inside, she pulled out a shirt and threw it at Jake. He made a grab for it, but missed, and watched it flutter limply to the ground.

"Not quite as fast as you were last night, are you, warrior boy?" she sniggered as she cinched the pack.

Scowling, Jake bent to pick up the shirt. Holding it out in front of him, he saw that it was going to be way too small, but it would still be better than nothing. "I wish I still had my own pack," he muttered, glaring at the item distastefully.

"What did you do with it, anyway?" Sam asked.

"Had to take it off when I climbed the mountain."

"What mount—?"

"Sam," Joraus called over to her. "There are many questions to be answered, but there will be time enough for that later. Let us eat, clean ourselves, and sleep. Then we may talk."

Jake looked at the Changeling with a quirked eyebrow as he sounded more formal than usual. Joraus returned his gaze steadily before pointing meaningfully at the pond. While water and sleep sounded wonderful, Jake thought he might throw up if he ate any food right now. He walked over to the pond and bent to drink.

"Jake, not yet," Sam hissed.

He spun around to see Joraus and Swyf staring at him.

"What?"

"I think we are supposed to wait for Klyle," Sam whispered.

Jake pulled back, all of the sudden embarrassed. "Sorry, Klyle, I mean, my Lord, I…"

With a twinkle of mirth in his eyes, Klyle chuckled. Jake found that he liked the king's laugh even more than his voice.

"Worry not, my friend," he said, still amused. "There is no need for proprieties here. Joraus, Swyf, dissuade him not for after all he has done for us, he has earned the right of the first drink."

Still unsure, Jake hesitated, but then Klyle winked at him, and relaxing slightly he bent to drink from the pond. The water tasted absolutely wonderful. Through the excitement of the night, he had not realized how thirsty he was. As soon as he had taken his first mouthful, everyone else circled the water and drank.

When he was finished, Jake gazed down into the water. His reflection wavered on the surface and he realized how filthy he was. Dried mud caked his face, and his chest was splattered with dirt and blood. He moved to a stream trickling from the pond and began to rinse himself off. Feeling a hand on his shoulder, he looked up into the kind eyes of Klyle.

"Allow me to examine your wound, my young friend," the man said politely. Jake nodded and Klyle bent down and ran his fingertips across the cut. "Not deep, but it is in need of cleaning and dressing. Though I have the skill, I lack the necessary implements." Glancing around, he spotted Sam's bag. "May I take the liberty of examining your pack, my dear?"

Sam blushed and nodded wordlessly, water dribbling off her chin. As Klyle walked over to the pack and began to remove some items, Jake grinned at her, impudently. Sam glanced around quickly to make sure no one else was watching before sticking her tongue out at him.

When everything was laid out in front of him, Klyle picked up a vial, a large bandage and a small piece of cloth. "Though crude at best, these should suffice for now." He walked back over to Jake and submerged the cloth in the water. "I would ask that you please lie down so that I may more easily access the wound."

Jake did as he was told, and only flinched a little when the cold water dribbled over the exposed flesh. Klyle rinsed the cloth, and repeated the process again and again until at last he grunted in satisfaction. Reaching for the vial, he opened it, sniffing its contents. "Prepare yourself, Jake, for this will sting, but it will also work to kill any infection."

At first, it was not so bad, Jake thought. There was a light burning sensation, which was bearable, but then it began to intensify. Before long, he was gripping the grass with both hands and clenching his teeth to keep from crying out. The pain did not last long, before fading back to a dull ache. He forced his teeth apart and let go of the grass.

Klyle then had Jake sit up, and carefully wrapped the large bandage around him. "That should do," he said, tucking in the last of the dressing and dusting off his hands. "Time and rest will take care of the rest."

"I am okay with that," Jake replied with a smile as he rose from the grass. "Thanks for your help."

"Likewise, Jake," Klyle said seriously, as he extended his arm to Jake. "Know this day that you have made a friend for life."

Jake stared at the arm for a second. It was strange. Klyle had thrust it too far in for a handshake. Shrugging inwardly, Jake took a step back and grasped the man's hand firmly. Klyle, in turn, looked at him oddly, as though he had expected something else, before slowly tightening his own grip and pumping his arm in time with Jake's.

Jake woke to the sound of his stomach growling. He blinked a few times, trying to dispel the blackness from his eyes. When the darkness remained, he realized it was night. Hearing a low rumbling of voices, he sat up and rubbed his eyes. Sam lay next to him, curled up tightly as she slept. Over by the pond he saw that Joraus, Swyf and Klyle were huddled close together, deep in conversation.

He tried to stand up quietly, but winced in pain when his stiff legs protested. Hesitantly, he approached the group until Klyle looked up at him and smiled.

"Oh, Jake, I hope you weren't disturbed by our conversation," he said.

"Actually, no," he answered. "I'm feeling pretty hungry."

The older man grinned. "Well, it would please me greatly if you were to join us."

Jake walked over to the bushes surrounding the pond and studied the various colored fruits. "Which ones taste the best?"

Klyle pointed to a bright crimson bush. "I would recommend a fistful of the red berries. They are most delectable."

"Thanks," said Jake as he approached the bush. Picking a handful of fruit, he tossed them into his mouth without a second thought. His eyes instantly squeezed shut as his mouth puckered tighter than if he'd just taken a swig of lemon juice straight from the bottle. Hearing muffled laughter, Jake squinted to see Klyle and Joraus biting down on their fists to keep from laughing too loudly.

"Klyle," Swyf scolded him softly, but she looked as if she were fighting back a smile of her own. "Come over here, Jake. Rinse your mouth out and I'll show you the best way to eat these particular berries."

It took a quite a few mouthfuls of water before the sour taste faded.

"I beg your forgiveness, my young friend," said Klyle with a chuckle. "Joraus told me that you were amenable to the occasional jest. It has been quite some time since I've last had cause for laughter. I must say that you did provide me with a most excellent opportunity for sport."

"Well, I'll be paying more attention next time," Jake replied. "I just woke up."

"A win is still a win," Joraus intoned, philosophically.

Swyf threw a piece of fruit at him, before turning to Jake. "It's easy, Jake. Those red fruits you just tried are sour, as you have no doubt discovered. The green ones are sweet and the yellow ones are bitter. You mix and match until you find the combination you like. Go on," she motioned to the bushes. "Give it a try."

Playing with different blends was fun and Jake filled up long before he found the perfect amounts of each berry. By the time he was done, Sam was awake. They waited for her to take a quick drink and collect some of the fruits before everyone sat down in the grass, facing one another.

"I am sure that we each have questions for the others," Klyle started. "Allow me to start by explaining what I can of all that has happened to me here in Fermicia since Swyf and Joraus escaped." He pulled his legs up under him and picked at one of the tall strands of grass. "As can already be surmised, I was defeated by Brael. I was sure that he would kill me, but he decided that my humiliation would amuse him more.

"I was taken prisoner and transported to that foul mountain prison. I wish I could say how long I remained a 'guest' of those fine facilities, but I lost track of the days long ago. At this time, I will not frighten you all with what was done within the darkness of that evil mountain. It would serve no purpose for you to know, and the memories are still too painful and fresh."

Klyle gazed out into the night as he rolled a piece of grass into a tight ball. "Many years ago, certain supporters of mine attempted a raid on the prison. Brael's guards named them rebels, but I am unsure who led them or how they found me. Brael paid me a personal visit, so as to convey the message that all of the rebels who had attempted the assault had been either captured or killed. My first breath of fresh air in many years was for the sole purpose of witnessing Brael flaying the skin from their bones while they yet lived.

"Once the secret of my capture was discovered, Brael saw no purpose in my continued exile. It was then that he started the yearly tradition known as the Traitor's Walk." He paused and bitterness crept into his voice as he continued, "Once a year, I was marched from city to city throughout Kardonin, so the people, my people, could see what had happened to their *mighty* king. At first it was pity that I saw on the faces of my loyal subjects, but as time went on it was replaced with revulsion and hate. This year marked my seventh walk. Every year a few of my more zealous supporters would attempt a rescue, but Liakut was always waiting, ready and eager."

"We saw that in Kithalo," Sam said softly. "It was horrible."

Klyle nodded. "There is not much more to tell. I expected nothing more than to return to my cell for another year of horror and exile. It was then that Joraus and Swyf appeared at the door of my prison with a young woman armed with a bow from ages past. From there my story melds with yours."

He turned to Joraus and Swyf. "What of you, my friends? Tell me of your travels and adventures. Surely they were more exciting than mine? A new world... Often, as I lay in the darkness of my cell, I dreamt of the strange world I had sent you to. Please tell me, I beg of you."

Jake watched the former king as he hung on the Changelings' every word. He had a hungry expression on his face, as though he might be able to experience their adventures for himself, if only he could listen hard enough. Although his face was sunken and filthy, Jake thought it contained more life and expression then any of the Fermicians he had seen in Kithalo.

Klyle's eyes still carried a haunted expression though. Jake could tell by looking at him that he didn't really want to hear what had happened to the exiled king during his time in captivity. But he also saw an eagerness in Klyle; a desire to put the things of the past behind him and prepare for a new future, free from the clutches of Brael and his minions.

The group sat talking for most of the night, each taking a turn to tell Klyle about the things he wanted to know, and it seemed like he asked about *everything*. He was intrigued by the children's choice of musical instrument, having seen the pictures on the weapons in the vault, and he was fascinated by Joraus' explanations of things that Jake considered perfectly normal. Cars, telephones, computers and radios were only a few of these. Sam huffed out an impatient sigh when Jake and Joraus launched into an explanation of video games.

Klyle also questioned them all closely about their journey, showing particular interest in Jake's and Sam's experiences with *Ragesong*. Jake was a little disheartened when Klyle acted surprised by the pillars, having hoped the wise king would be able to explain them.

When they all finished talking, Jake started to ask Klyle his own questions about *Ragesong*.

"Jake," Klyle said, holding his hands up. "I would like nothing more than to tell you all I know of *Ragesong*, but I am hesitant to limit your mind with anything that I have learned. I witnessed things last night that I would have never imagined possible. Combined with the other things I have been told, I am led to the conclusion that you need to discover *Ragesong* within yourself."

"But…"

"Jake," he said gently, "in less than three weeks you have discovered more about *Ragesong* than I was able to with years of dedicated study and training. You fight in a style that is unknown to me, unique and powerful, yet full of grace and fluidity, and that blade you wield is one of the oldest and most priceless relics in Fermicia. Did you not feel its power when first you picked it up?"

"Yes, Jake," Joraus grinned. "Didn't you feel it?"

Jake hesitated. "Umm, well…"

"He was bummed out," Sam said, smirking. "He didn't think it was cool enough. He wanted to throw it away and take a do-over."

"Well," Jake replied, defensively, "it is so ugly. There were some awesome-looking weapons in there, and then there was that!" He pointed over to the sheathed blade, lying in the grass.

Klyle laughed. "I am not yet so removed from boyhood that I cannot understand your sentiments, Jake. The vault was full of truly intimidating arms. Those, however, for all of their outward magnificence, are but dross when compared to the one you wield. It is a blade that men and kings would kill for."

"I guess…" Jake reached over and picked it up. "I mean, it's cool and all, and I especially like the way it doesn't feel like it weighs anything, but it doesn't seem to do much beyond that."

"Though you have learned much Jake, you have barely dipped below the surface of what you are truly capable of. I daresay that as you grow in strength, you will uncover the many secrets concealed in that blade," said Klyle. "I'm sorry I can't be of more assistance, my young friend, but I fear that I would do more harm than good if I were to try and pass on my particular understanding of *Ragesong* at this time. I must ask, however, is it true that you leapt from the top of the mountain to one of the buildings within the prison?"

"Yeah, I kinda surprised myself with that," Jake answered, a little sheepishly.

Klyle just shook his head. "Truly astounding…" Turning to address the rest of the group, he said, "Now, decisions need to be made. Although I am free, we are far from liberating Kardonin from the black fist of Brael. Opposition this close to the capital has been completely crushed. I fear that if we wish to stoke the fires of rebellion, we must move further to the south. I must also meet with the forgers of Garshone, as I find myself in need of a new blade. We begin as a small army, my friends. This resistance is not something that we can accomplish quickly. It will take several years of struggle and dedication."

"Years?" Jake asked in disbelief. "Why don't we just go and kill Brael? You could get a weapon out of the vault."

"Jake," Klyle said patiently while reaching out to place his hand on Jake's shoulder. "You are young. I admire your passion, but you give no thought to the magnitude of this war. Brael sits on my throne in Foldona, surrounded by Elites. Do not think me weak or powerless, my young friend. Before Brael overcame me, six of his Elites died on the end of my blade. They were warriors with the same skill and abilities as Liakut, yet Brael defeated me in a manner of minutes."

"Six?" Jake whispered. "Wow."

"As strong as you are, the truth is that you were nearly killed by a single Elite," said Klyle. "We all need to grow in strength before we attempt to attack Brael directly. As hard as you all worked to free me, this is but a hair in Brael's stew; an annoyance, nothing more. I assure you that had he considered me more of a threat, he would have killed me or placed a stronger guard over my prison."

He looked seriously at Jake and Sam. "However, I do not believe that you should remain in Fermicia at this time."

"What do you…?" Sam started to protest.

"Hear me out, my young friends. From listening to the accounts of Joraus and Swyf, I, too, believe that your grasp of *Ragesong* is dependent upon your musical abilities back in your own world. It is imperative that you return and continue to develop those talents. Make no mistake, I mean to summon you back, but I would have you return more formidable still. I seek to gain every advantage in this fight that I possibly can. It will take some time to rally the support of my people, but when that day comes, I will send for you."

"But that could take ages," Jake cried out.

"Doubt not my skill, my young friend. I know many powerful people, and the kings in the south hold no love for Brael. I swear to you, by my fallen kingdom, that I will have an army prepared for you on your return. Now I believe that we should rest. Brael will have, undoubtedly, received word of my escape and soon the territory will be flooded with his soldiers."

"I thought you said we aren't that important to him," Sam argued.

Klyle winked at her. "Brael's pride has always been his biggest flaw, and this escape will no doubt infuriate him to no end. Let us eat and rest, for though it pains me to say it, tonight we part. Swyf shall join me as I journey to the south and Joraus will guide you back to the portal."

CHAPTER 25:

HOME

Though Jake had only just met Klyle, saying goodbye to everyone had still been difficult. He knew that it was much harder for Sam, and more still for Joraus. Sam had grown very close to Swyf during the past three weeks and tears dampened both of their cheeks when they hugged. Joraus and Swyf parted from the group for a private goodbye. Klyle watched sadly as they embraced on the opposite side of the grove.

"It gladdens my heart to see them finally acting on the feelings they have harbored for so long," said Klyle, "but I find no joy in being the cause of their separation. Guard him well, my friend, for he is as dear to me as any son." Looking down at Jake, he winked. "It would also displease me to incur the wrath of what would seem to be his future mate."

Jake grinned. "We'll take care of him."

As the two Changelings slowly returned, their hands clasped and swinging between them, Klyle put his arms on the shoulders of Sam and Jake. "Be well, my new friends. It is my most humble pleasure to have met you. Words cannot accurately state how grateful I am that you were willing to offer your help when called upon."

Jake opened his mouth to say something sarcastic about how Joraus had not given him much of a choice, but Sam must have sensed it because she stepped on his foot. "It was our pleasure, your majesty," she said sweetly, even as she glared at Jake.

"Yeah, anytime," he added, wincing.

The journey back to the coast was long and uneventful. Joraus kept them off the main throughway, and they followed some little-used trails and small side roads until they reached the Skidippy. The plain was as endless as Jake remembered, but Joraus did not take the same route back. He simply cut straight for the coast. They stayed the night at the cove again, but did not talk much.

Jake and Sam were torn between their excitement at the prospect of returning home and worry for their new friends in this strange land they had come to love. Jake was pretty sure that Joraus' thoughts were on Swyf and Klyle. Jake smiled to himself when they reached the meadow where Joraus had been sent sailing through the air in the form of a pig.

The returning climb through the mountains was not nearly as difficult as the descent had been. Jake realized that the weeks of hiking and beating through woodland brush had done wonders for his endurance and strength. He was almost sad to see the outline of the small forest of trees that separated them from the portal. While Jake could not remember much about it, he hoped they wouldn't follow the same route back. He had no desire to see what was left of the soldiers who had been killed outside the portal.

As the group approached the forest, Jake gazed around in awe. No wonder Klyle had wanted to stop here and explore the area. The trees here seemed to be greener and more vibrant than any that Jake had ever seen. When he had left the Sentry Grove, he thought he'd be happy to never saw another tree, but this group was different; they were so much more alive. Walking beneath the high branches, Jake felt at peace, as though the forest were welcoming him in.

To his relief, the trail that Joraus chose to lead them through was devoid of dead soldiers. When they reached the mountain stairs, Jake hesitated. His adventure was finally over, and he felt the same letdown as he felt whenever he watched the final cut scene upon completing a game. Following Joraus and Sam, Jake climbed the steps slowly and gazed at the large pillars spread out before him. His gaze was immediately drawn to the column he thought of as his own. Walking forward, he reached out to touch it. The golden lettering immediately appeared and he stared at the strange symbols, wondering what they could possibly mean. Then he looked at the one word he could read: *Ragesong.*

Jake wondered if he would be able to understand more the next time he came to Fermicia. On a sudden whim, he loosened the sheath of his sword from his back and laid it at the foot of the column. Without knowing exactly why, he touched a couple of the still-glowing symbols and watched in amazement as tendrils of solid stone snaked out from the column and wrapped themselves around the blade, securing it in place. In excitement, Jake attempted to tug the blade loose, but it was as though the weapon had become one with the stone.

He turned to point it out to Joraus, but the Changeling was standing behind him with a faint smile on his face. "Very well done, my friend," he said softly.

Jake started to grin foolishly, but it soon faded. Here was the moment he had been trying to avoid since they all left the Sentry Grove. It had been hard enough to say goodbye to Swyf and Klyle, but this was Joraus; the one constant he'd had since entering Fermicia and his link to this world. He studied his friend's kind face and saw that he was not the only one that was struggling.

Joraus gruffly offered his arm, but, instead, Jake wrapped his arms around him. Joraus hesitated for only a second before returning the hug. A few seconds later, they separated, both looking embarrassed at the display of affection. Sam, however, was studying her pillar, or at least pretending to. Jake opened his mouth, but everything he wanted to say kept getting stuck in his throat.

"Thank you, Jake," Joraus began. "I am grateful for what you have done for my world."

"I didn't really…"

"You rescued my king. Not to mention me, Sam, and…"

Jake smiled slyly. "And your girlfriend?"

Joraus scowled. "All right, yes, for lack of a better word, my girlfriend."

"Well, you wouldn't have been in that mess if I hadn't stomped off."

"Because I have my own pride, I am going to agree with you, so thanks for saving us from your mistake."

They both broke out into laughter and the mood lightened.

Jake kicked at a loose stone on the ground. "So, it sounds like you are going to have your hands full."

"Hey, at least I don't have to go back to Junior High," said Joraus with a laugh. "I'll take my chances on raising a rebel army any day."

The two of them walked over to where Sam was securing her bow to the pillar.

"How do we get home?" she asked Joraus as they approached. "I bet it has something to do with music."

Joraus nodded. "Correct. I will teach you the song." He paused as though he had just thought of something. "Do you still have the stones?"

When the children stared at him blankly, he gave them a worried frown. "The jewels you used to come to Fermicia."

Jake thought about it. "I don't think I had it when I came through the portal."

"I didn't either," said Sam. "I remember searching for it. I wanted to ask Swyf, but there were all those guards outside. By the time we escaped, I had forgotten about it."

"That's strange," Joraus remarked. "I wish I had thought to ask Klyle about this earlier. If I were to hazard a guess, I would say they will act as return markers, but we'll find out soon enough." He looked at them seriously. "Are you ready?"

It didn't take long for Jake and Sam to learn the notes of the melody, but the words took a lot longer, as they were unfamiliar and difficult to pronounce.

"That should do it," Joraus said, nodding gravely after they concluded the song without any mistakes. He started toward the cave, motioning for them to follow him.

Jake's thoughts suddenly began to rush. What were his mom and dad going to think? He'd been gone for more than three weeks. Would they be terrified? What was going to happen when he got home? All of a sudden he felt very nervous.

It must have shown, because Sam slowed to walk beside him. "Are you thinking about it too, how long we've been gone?" she asked. "This stuff is going to be a little hard to explain, and I am not sure how I am going to tell my mom or my teachers."

"Yeah," agreed Jake. "I didn't really give them much info, just a quick note."

He pulled back the hanging moss covering the cave entrance for Sam before following her through.

"I didn't even leave a note," Sam admitted, sheepishly. "I didn't think of it."

Joraus waited for them in the middle of the cave. Jake looked around at the light shining down from little holes in the ceiling and the walls sparkling with jewels. It was breathtaking.

"Farewell, my friends," said the Changeling. "I will miss you both. Jake, pet Nala for me."

He held out his arm to Jake in the same strange way that Klyle had. Jake started to step back, but Joraus stopped him. "Jake, grip my forearm, like this." Joraus took his forearm in his own hand and fitted Jake's hand around his own muscular arm. "This is the Fermician equivalent of your handshake."

When he released Jake's arm, he did the same to Sam. "Be well, you two," he told them. "Learn fast. I am sure you will be needed soon."

"I hope you find Swyf and Klyle quickly," Jake said. "Take care of yourself, and beat Swyf in that animal game for me."

Joraus smiled and stepped back, while Jake and Sam entered the circle and turned to face him.

Jake took her hand. "I guess I'll see you in school, if we aren't both grounded for life."

Sam laughed nervously and he counted them off. Their song echoed around the cave, and when Jake looked down he saw the floor glowing. The stones on the walls were pulsing in rhythm with the melody. The light intensified until the children were forced to close their eyes or be blinded. All at once there was a brilliant flash that Jake could see, even through his closed eyelids, and then he could no longer feel Sam's hand in his.

Jake waited a few seconds for the blinding light to fade before opening his eyes. When he did so, he realized that he was in his own bedroom. Glancing down at the ground, he spotted a blinking, golden light – the marker. It must have landed there after sending Joraus and him to Fermicia. Jake reached down to pick up the jewel, but it faded away before he could touch it.

Glancing out the window, Jake saw that it was getting dark. The sun was nearly gone, and the lingering sunlight was pale and weak. He looked over at his clock. It read 8:45pm. The electronic lights blinking around his room seemed foreign and strange. Jake turned a slow circle, and was surprised to see that everything was still in place. *What's going on?*

Surely the police, or at least Mom and Dad, would have gone through his things? Jake looked for the note he had left for his parents and found it still resting at the foot of his bed, untouched. Then he glanced around for something that might have the day's date on it. Not seeing anything else, he flipped on the TV and his game console, and waited anxiously for the home screen to come to life.

When the date popped up, Jake hurried over to his backpack to pull out his binder. He flipped it open and his eyes flicked to the dates he'd marked at the top of his syllabi. *It's still the same day! How is that possible?* Mom and Dad were not going to be mad at all, because as far as they knew, he'd been here the whole time.

Shaking his head in wonder, Jake turned off the electronics and checked his reflection in the mirror. He was a disaster: his hair was a mess and he had dirt all over his face, and he was still wearing the shirt that Sam had given him back at the Sentry Grove. Jake pulled it off and looked at his chest. The symbols were still there, but they had faded a little. The cut he had received from Liakut was still there, too; a morbid souvenir of his time spent in Fermicia. He wasn't at all sure how he was going to explain the markings or the wound to his mom and dad.

Jake quietly tore up the farewell note and threw it into his small trashcan, thankful his parents had not needed to read it. He stuffed the binder back into his backpack, and then pulled off the rest of his filthy Fermician clothes, and stuffed them under his bed. Looking at his boots, he saw that they were a muddy mess; not wanting to worry about them now, he shoved them under the bed as well.

Glancing at his bed, Jake debated just jumping on it and falling asleep right now, but he decided that he should shower before getting in. He wanted to rush out and give his parents a hug, but he was afraid that might only worry them.

Cracking his bedroom door open, he hurried to the bathroom. Hoping his parents were engrossed in their TV show, he set the temperature of the shower. It was only when he was standing underneath the warm jets of water that he let the thought start to sink in – he was home. He could enjoy warm water, brush his teeth, and eat cooked food, and…

He heard a knock at the door.

"Jake?" asked the muffled voice of his mother. "Can I come in?"

"Uh, sure, Mom," he replied, secretly delighting in the melodic sound of her voice.

The door opened and his mom walked in. She sat down on the toilet before asking, "Didn't you already shower tonight?"

"Yeah, but um, I forgot to wash my hair."

"Oh, okay. Well, I forgot to tell you. I called the school earlier, and you need to stop by the office tomorrow morning to get your new schedule. You are signed up for advanced band."

It took Jake a second to remember what she was talking about. Then it came to him. *Ms. Gladwell and advanced band.* "Awesome, Mom!" he cried out. "Thanks."

"You're welcome, sweetheart. Now hurry up and finish. It's late and you have a full day tomorrow," she added, standing up and walking out.

Jake listened for the door to click. He enjoyed the heat of the shower for a few more minutes before climbing out and drying off. The shock of the mint-flavored toothpaste was another reminder that he was not in Fermicia anymore. When he finished, he walked back into his room and closed the door. Putting on a fresh pair of pajamas, Jake looked excitedly at his bed. He had dreamed of sleeping in it for weeks, and now he finally could.

He felt a little guilty as he lay down, however. Joraus, Swyf and Klyle were still out there in the wilds of Fermicia, while he was back at home, enjoying the comfortable life. Jake wondered what would happen when he returned to that strange world, but the invitation of his soft pillow was too hard to resist and with a dreamy smile he drifted off to sleep.

Jake jerked awake to an unusual beeping sound, nearly knocking the offending object to the ground before realizing that it was his alarm clock. He quickly silenced it and kicked away the covers. With a long stretch, he jumped out of bed, feeling more refreshed than he had in weeks.

Looking down at the floor, he remembered the glowing stone that had disappeared from that exact spot the night before.

Jake thought about it as he rooted around in his closet for some clothes. Joraus had said that Klyle called it a marker. The Changeling had not known why, but maybe it was because it had marked his place here in this world while he was in Fermicia, kind of like a bookmark. When he had come back out of the portal, it had returned him to the exact same place and time that he'd left. I'll have to ask Sam about it, he thought as he fastened the button on his pants.

The jeans and T-shirt felt loose and baggy to Jake, compared with his tight-fitting Fermician clothes, and he walked around the room for a minute, trying to get used to them. After pulling on his socks and an old pair of shoes, he glanced at himself in the mirror. He looked normal enough now, except for some faint scratches on his arms and face, but they were not too noticeable.

Grabbing his backpack, Jake headed for the kitchen. His mom was sitting in the same chair as always. She had a cup of juice in one hand and was rubbing at her face with the other. Jake quickly pulled out the first box of cereal in the cupboard and poured himself a bowl, before sitting down next to her.

"So are you going to play the same song again if Ms. Gladwell makes you perform for the advanced band?" she asked him.

Nala barked, and Jake, remembering his promise to Joraus, reached down and tousled her hair fondly. "I don't know, I'll think about it," he replied. "I'll let you know tonight."

As he spoke with his mom, Jake tried to act as though he had just woken up after an ordinary day of school, which he could not even remember clearly.

"Do you have all of your signed forms? I didn't miss any, did I?" his mom asked.

"Um, I'm not sure, maybe I should check." Jake pulled out his binder and quickly thumbed through it. "Yep, you signed them all," he said. "Quit worrying, Mom. I'm good."

Jake finished eating, and after rinsing out his bowl, he rushed into the bathroom to brush his teeth and comb his hair. As he stood, gazing at his reflection in the mirror, he couldn't help raising his shirt one more time to see the faint *Ragesong* markings and his wound. They are kinda cool, he thought, especially both together like that.

Hurrying back into the kitchen, he gave his mother a quick hug and a kiss. "See you after school, Mom."

"All right, sweetheart. Have fun."

She stood up and followed him as he reached for his backpack. "Didn't I take you to get your hair cut last week?" she asked, eyeing his hair.

"Umm…"

"Well, they didn't do a very good job. It's looking pretty shaggy already." His mom lightly ran her hand over his hair.

"Gotta go, Mom, I don't wanna be late." Jake slipped over to the door before she could notice anything else. *Good thing she isn't a morning person.*

"Well, be safe. I want to hear all about band when you get home. I love you, sweetheart!" his mom said, holding the door open for him as he ran out.

"I will, Mom!" Jake called over his shoulder.

He started to walk towards the bus stop, but suddenly he spun around and ran back, wrapping his arms around his mother in a big hug.

"What is this for?" she said, laughing as she hugged him back.

"Oh, nothing, just I love you too!"

Jake thought about the morning as he walked slowly down the hall towards the band room. It had definitely been different. Everything seemed to have him on edge. He tensed up whenever someone touched him and he had forgotten how loud people could be. After spending so long avoiding large crowds, the idea of mingling with the hundreds of students in the school unnerved him.

"You ready for this, warrior boy?" someone whispered from behind him.

Jake spun around quickly and only relaxed when he saw Sam's reassuring smile. Her red hair was pulled back in a tight braid and she was dressed in the same kind of faded clothes as he'd seen her in on their first day of band; only yesterday, yet weeks ago at the same time. The girl had her saxophone case in her hand, but it was strange to see her without a bow strapped to her back.

"Chill out, Jake, we aren't there anymore," she said.

"I know, but I can't seem to get used to this. It is so weird… and boring."

Sam laughed. "I know what you mean. I guess this isn't the same as taking on a small army all by yourself, huh?"

"Or shooting three guys at once," Jake shot back, playfully. "That was seriously awesome. I meant to tell you that, but I didn't get the chance."

"Not compared to the things you did," she replied. "So, do you have a song ready for if Ms. Gladwell asks us to play?"

"Yeah, I thought about what you said. I think I have the perfect song. I hope she lets us play again."

"Me, too," Sam agreed.

Jake stopped by his locker, and Sam waited while he dropped off his books and pulled out his flute. Together, they walked into the band room. It still looked the same, with pictures of instruments hanging from the ceiling and covering the walls. *Why shouldn't it? It has only been one day, after all.* Jake studied all of the older kids, already seated in their sections.

Ms. Gladwell gave the newcomers a smile and motioned them to find a seat.

"Good luck," Sam whispered as she walked over to where the other alto sax players were sitting. "You too," Jake replied, noticing that just as he was the only boy in the flute section, she was the only girl among the saxophone players.

He found a seat at the end of the flute players and glanced around. A few people were looking his way, but almost everyone else was either preparing their instruments or warming up. Following their lead, he quickly flicked open his case and fitted the pieces of his flute together. Putting it to his lips, he blew into it.

Finally, something familiar, Jake thought with relief. He had worried that he would be rusty after so long without practicing, but it came to him as easily as it ever had. After tuning the flute, he then started fingering the song he would play if Ms. Gladwell gave him the chance.

"Welcome, class!" the teacher called out over the noise. "If you would please quiet down, I have a couple of announcements. First of all, chair auditions will be held at the beginning of next week. You will each need to have a piece ready and be prepared to sight read. There will be no extensions or retries. If you are not prepared, you will sit at the back and work your way up through challenges.

"Now, we have a couple of new band members. Please join me in welcoming our newest flute player, Jake, and at the alto saxophone, Samantha."

There was a light smattering of applause, but Jake heard his share of derisive snickering as well. Remembering back to what Sam had told him on their first night in Fermicia, he ignored them and smiled.

"Jake and Sam," Ms. Gladwell said, as she smiled at each of them. "I know you played for the other class yesterday, but I'd like to give you the opportunity to play for this band, as I feel this is the best way for you to introduce yourselves in this particular class. Do either of you have a problem with that?"

Well, how could I say so now, even if I did? Jake shook his head.

"Wonderful! Why don't you start, Jake?" Ms. Gladwell suggested.

He rose and climbed up the dais that she had just vacated. Sam smiled at him encouragingly. Closing his eyes, Jake raised his flute to his lips and played through one of his favorite classical pieces. For a few minutes, he lost himself in the music. It surprised him when he heard applause as the final notes faded.

"Excellent, Jake, thank you. That is a wonderful piece and you played it beautifully," Ms. Gladwell said when the clapping died down.

Jake nodded and stepped back down to sit in his chair, privately pleased with the jealous stares he was receiving from the other flute players.

"Okay, Sam, your turn."

Sam stood, the alto sax still looking huge in her small hands as she took her place on the raised platform. Jake noticed a confidence in her that she had lacked the last time she had stood up on the dais to perform. Turning to face the band, she slowly raised her mouthpiece to her lips. When she glanced at him, Jake caught a twinkle of laughter in her eyes. Then his jaw dropped as he heard the opening run of notes that marked the theme song of his favorite video game.

To Be Continued...

Follow Jake and Sam on their next adventure in Fermicia with:

RAGESONG: UPRISING

Coming in 2014

ABOUT THE AUTHOR

J.R. Simmons lives in Northern Utah with his wife and 4 boys. He loves spending time with his family and coaching his kids in all of their different sports. He is an avid gamer and is very excited that his boys are picking up on his hobby. J.R. was recently introduced to triathlons and has since found that he loves the sport. Most nights he can be found either sitting down with a good game or hunched over his iPad writing.

Connect with J.R. Simmons
Facebook: http://www.facebook.com/RagesongBook
Blog: http://jrsimmons3.wordpress.com
Twitter: jrsimmons_3